. . . I expect they would tell us the soul can be as lost,
For loving-kindness as anything else.
Well, well, we must scramble for grace as best we can.

—Christopher Fry, *The Lady's Not for Burning*

the sky so big and black

❦ **At least I** don't have to pretend I'm a scientist. I can admit I'm an artist. And a cop. I do have to admit that I'm a cop.

I raise my glass to my own reflection in the mirror by my door; lately this is as close as I get to drinking with a colleague. There might be a couple of hundred of us shrinks, nowadays, in all the parts of the solar system where there's any reason for us to exist—here on Mars, over on the Moon, out on the twenty-some settled asteroids, hunkered down in the Jovian moon colonies. Right now, during the emergency, I doubt they can afford any of us on Titan or Mercury, but there's probably someone with the training, currently emptying bedpans, cooking soup, mining methane, or something, and if an occasion came up I guess they could shift them to cover.

There might be seventy shrinks on the Moon, many of them exactly the kind of expert that Teri's case needs, and if anyone upstairs had had any sense that's where we'd have sent the poor kid in the first place, a whole Mars year ago, once we knew what was going on. But they didn't; the district officers decided that it could all be dealt with right here, so that they wouldn't have to arrange transportation for Teri, so that nobody above them would have to look at the case seriously—oh, sure, reports went up the bureaucratic pyramid, but nothing alarming, nothing with the big red stamp of INVASION POSSIBLE or WE'VE GOT TROUBLE.

And now there's this new problem. Maybe I should keep it from the district officers, just deal with it here and send them a report later. That would teach them a lesson. Last time they insisted that I cope with Teri all by myself; maybe this time I just will.

I wonder if cases like Teri's are happening a lot. I wouldn't necessarily know. People don't tell me things. I run up against walls of secrecy all the time. Almost anything might be being kept from me. So maybe cases like Teri's current situation are happening three a week, or something, ever since the Sunburst, and all being kept quiet. It's possible. I don't know. I'm not a scientist and I don't pretend to be. I'm not even a very good cop. But at my art . . . well, now that's an interesting question. I think I'm good.

Conscious thoughts are indices of deeper internal states. So thinking I'm good at what I do is an index. Is this particular index an observation, a delusion, or symptom?

It would also be so very much easier if I didn't like Teri. I should have been able to manage objectivity, I think, or maybe even to get really cop-ish and detest the brat. But, no, I wince when I think the word "brat" about her.

She's anything but, really. Unless you say that all roundita girls are brats, and I've been working here too long to think that; what they are, is confident.

And what water is, is wet.

I laugh at that. It's a habit, laughing at my own feeble jokes. The kind of habit a man gets when he has drunk too much by himself too often for all his adult life. Teri is brash and rude and aggressively ignorant, but she's also tender-hearted and trusting and exuberantly young despite everything that's happened to her, so of course I like her.

Besides, liking her is part of the art. To get to where you have at least some dim understanding of what it's like to be the person sitting across from you, you really have to find a way for you to like the suspect, or the patient, or the rogee, or whatever the term that we're allowed to call them currently is. (Way down here in this frontier town, I only have to go through standards and practices review every few groundyears, and in between I don't bother to know the currently correct terminology. Hell, if

I wanted to I could probably title my weekly notes to the chief "Dangerous Nut Report" and I'd never get hassled.)

I have received a recorded message from Teri, which clearly calls for a reply.

That's what triggered all my maundering silly speculation and all my bullshit philosophy. It's not what triggered my drinking, tonight or any other night; that requires no trigger. Everyone else has gone home for the day, out through the big front doors down the hall, into the warm afternoon sunlight that always makes Red Sands City glow so beautifully. It's the middle of southern autumn, as it was a Mars year ago when it all started. We still measure our own ages in groundyears and celebrate our birthdays on the Martian day that includes the exact groundyear anniversary of our births, but we do everything else now in Martian days and seasons and years, because that's what the sun obstinately insists on doing.

I look at the clock. That's another index—"lose time and find trouble," as we say. If I had looked up and it had been hours later than I'd expected, I'd have to hit that red button on my desk, the one that locks me in and calls in cops and shrinks to deal with the mess. But my time sense is just fine, so apparently so am I.

So the clock is, so far, only the index of what it's like outside: the last hour of daylight. I love autumn sunshine. I could be down in the park, looking back this way, watching that yellow-orange sunshine glow on the rock wall that forms the older, east side of the city, above. I could watch the people out enjoying the evening, or look out through the dome, over the shantytown, at the sun setting over the Hellspouts. I could be down there on that bench in five minutes, and com for a pizza, and have a little picnic there in the park.

Instead I reach for the bottle again. There will still be plenty of sunlight in the future, and what I'm thinking about is suited to profound darkness.

I don't really like the other cops much—the real cops, I'm sure they'd call themselves. They'll be out there enjoying the sun with their families; I have no family, so we don't usually have much to make small talk about.

All of the other cops piled out of here right at quitting time, maybe ten minutes after I got Teri's note. Some of them rode the big escalators down to their levels—most of our city is set back in the crater walls here, like old-time cliff dwellers in Arizona or Arabia or wherever that was (sometimes I'm nearly as hazy about history and Earth and all that as Teri or any other kid of her generation). Some now live out on the crater floor inside the dome—there are more and more residences there—though ever since the Sunburst and its aftermath, I think most sitters will want to live and work with plenty of dirt over and around them. Probably in a generation or two the stereotypical sitter will live in a cave and the rounditachi and Marsforms will make fun of us for it.

Well, I was fifty-two groundyears old when the Sunburst hit, and that's really too old to acquire any new, deep-rooted fears; I'd be scared if I saw it get suddenly bright or if all the power went off, but I'd know what I was scared of, and we'd be talking about *scared,* not unreasoning panic.

The idiots running the schools are trying to *induce* unreasoning panic in the next generation, now. For a whole

Mars year they've subjected these kids to grief-counseling and anxiety-discussions and plain old fear-mongering intended to make the children permanently dependent on the self-misnamed "helping professions"—that is, make the children be permanently children. God, a tough roundita like Teri, if she heard all the counselors and human-servicers and educatoids talking and planning, would knock every one of them to the floor, and kick and spit on them while they begged for mercy.

The stupid things we're about to do to kids, just so the world will be a little more comfortable for grown-ups—it used to be the point was to get them out of school so they could go have lives, not keep them around as toys for their teachers and counselors to coddle and moon over. Hell, I got the certificate to be a shrink when I was eighteen, and by the time I was twenty, I'd lost count of the dying people I'd comforted, the crime scenes for which I'd answered the question "now what sort of person would do a thing like this?", the cops twice my age I'd lent an ear to when they had seen something horrible and needed to talk. Of course being a shrink was different, too—the main duty was still "tidings of comfort and pills," as my supervisor used to call counseling, and then after that came "putting all the nuts into one tree," which is what he called profiling. If you ask me, that work was harder, even if it wasn't quite as urgent as what we do now, and I miss that difficulty.

Before I was even twenty, I had had to improvise my way out of so many things that I had lost any fear of the new. We saw more, and we learned more, and it is the opinion of this experienced shrink that these kids don't really need counseling, they need a chance to get to work, to make and do and dream and think, to make adults out of themselves. And if you gave them half a chance they all would.

But so many in my damned generation say that they've had too much stress already and they want the world to calm down, just because it wasn't calm when they were kids. So we're going to build society in the form of a quiet garden for old people and let the kids rust away unused, soothing Grandma's nerves at the minor expense of making Junior narrow and dumb and lazy. The way every basically comfortable society turns out, given half a chance. The only thing we learn from history is convenient metaphors for our current follies.

God, I think. God.

He doesn't answer, and I'd be justifiably scared—but not in a panic!—if he did, since I would know it really was Resuna, or a tiny brain tumor, or some boo-boo in my mix of neurotransmitters.

But since he doesn't answer, I'm not afraid to talk to him, and I say, God, I am sounding more and more like Teri. Well, not like Teri right now, but like the scrappy, independent, rude bitch she's going to be when she's a grandmother—may her grandkids be numerous and just like her, if you're actually listening, God! Those are parts of my feelings and personality I usually keep under control, but there you have it, Teri always had a knack for bringing them out in me. There are many more ways than one for a human mind to be contagious, I suppose, and

Resuna is only the way that's so overt that we have the good sense to be frightened. The ancient, slower, subtler ways may still be the most profound.

I like that word, "profound," or rather I like thinking the word while looking at the glass of whiskey, my third since official quitting time. God probably likes the word "profound," too, but he's being as quiet about that as about every other issue, today, just like every day. Thank God.

I was going to go right home but Teri's message showed up. So I played it, and now I have all her files called up on my werp, and I'm reviewing them, from right back at the start of the case.

I'm on salary. And this is a closed case. They don't pay me any extra to do this. But I have a profound need—there's that word again. Smooth and deep and full of promise, I slide into "profound" the way the warm brown whiskey slides into me.

I watch her message all the way through—it's only a couple of minutes—and because I already know that she and I will have to talk, I send her a reply and tell her that I'm not doing anything tonight, to call if she wants, and we can talk all night if she needs to—and if I don't hear from her I'll get back to her with a written reply within a day or two.

She's about an hour and a half east of here. Ecospectors have to roo while the sun's up, they stop moving whenever the sun goes down, and they go to sleep early, so right now is about the exact center of the two-hour window in which Teri might call me. Very possibly any minute. I feel like just sitting and drinking and watching my blank screen, waiting for the chime so that it will be time to switch it over to com and talk to her. There really isn't anything else that feels important.

Meanwhile I can have at least one more whiskey, sipping it slow and making it last, for the road I suppose. And still have enough working brain cells to be profound.

I like the way that word makes me think of Freud and Jung, of all the old profilers, of all the deep linguists—of every systematic shaman and cunning priest and kindly bartender and wise coach and perspicacious prostitute—of all the people who practiced this weird art I practice, before it had a name.

They were profound.

I'm a small-city cop. With enough whiskey and an interesting case in front of me, I can sometimes be a profound small-city cop. Or feel like it.

I call up Teri's first recording, from a Mars year ago, and fast-forward through all the business stuff and all the little tricks and jinks you do to get the rogee to talk at all, until I get to the trick that worked.

One of the oldest, which you tell them about directly, is to ask them to think about whatever they think of as the start of the story, and talk about whatever they associate with it. In fast-forward I see my lips drumming out "Don't tell me about it yet. Tell me about what it makes you think of. Tell me what it was like. Tell me what it reminds you of."

And she did, and I got in there to see what was happening inside her.

Some of those old tricks are good.

Profoundly good.

◐ **The school session** when I'as seven (I remember when it was because it was right after Mummy died), there was this unit (schools are always having units like people have boils) about the early frontiers, the ones way back on Earth, while the Europeans were conquering everybody else, before the real frontiers out here even started. Studying this was supposed to Teach Us Something or Other. They called it "The Frontier Tradition," which was pretty silly because even if the roundings is a frontier, it isn't one bit like the outback, the West, the New East, or El Norte, or any of the others were. But we had this unit, "The Frontier Tradition," and in that unit we learned a song I posreal hated. Hated limward, you know? Is this far enough off the point, Doc?

The lyrics made no sense to us because the song's mostly about things we don't have here on Mars at all, and when you look up what the words mean, they don't make any sense to *anyone*, because the people who wrote that song had never actually been to the frontier and they just used whatever rhymed, so they talk about cows eating weeds that are actually poisonous to them and things like that.

CSL school was always like that: incomprehensible pointless information presented to make you smart, and stupid games and activities to teach you how to get along with sitters and other clowns. Not that every sitter is a clown, Doc, didn't mean to say that. As far as I know you're not, I mean I don't know you well yet. But I don't mean I'm looking for you to—you know what I mean, don't you? Why don't you talk a skosh more often, Doc?

Okay, whatever you say, it's your ball and your game, and I guess you'll learn more about me if I talk. I mean, it stands to reason.

So where was I? Talking about hating school. Only as far as I know the only kind of school I hate is CSL school, which is the only kind I've ever been to. And anyway I wasn't really telling you about hating CSL school even though there was plenty to hate. This part was about hating that song, because you wanted me to talk about something completely irrelevant that I associated with the beginning of everything that happened, right, Doc? Okay, now the thing I hated the most about that stupid song, even when I'as seven, was that it got stuck in your head so easily. You could catch yourself humming it over and over and over. It had this line about "you sleep out every night and the only law is right."

Well, I don't believe they ever got by with just one law, especially not one as vague as that one. Most especially not on a frontier. Getting the land and the people and the resources and everything all tied up and cataloged in the laws is what settling is *about.* As soon as there's people somewhere, there's laws, lots of 'em. And I just kind of bet that if there weren't very many laws then most of what was going on was wrong. It stands to reason.

But that line about "you sleep out every night" always made me feel kinda sorry for those people back on Earth. Because they don't, you know. Most of 'em spend their whole lives under roofs.

I always figure that's why, in their stories and films and so forth, it's so hard for 'em to get out of bed in the morning—because bed is the only place where they're ever really comfortable. I kinda get the impression that that's what sitters are like, too, but they don't seem to be as limward about it as Earth people were. But still I don't see how you can really like or trust people who don't even know how to get up in the morning and enjoy the day.

You're not asking me because *you* don't know how, are you, Doc? This is one of those clever shrink questions to get me to reveal something, isn't it?

Thought so. Hey, is having me catch on part of the trick? Thought so too, it stands to reason. But anyway, okay. Here's the way to get up in the morning. Just in case you're really interested or you really don't know. When me and Dad were out in the roundings, we always woke up the second the sun hit our faceplates; we'd just sit up on the ground where we'd been lying, and stretch, and start the day. Just switch off the extra padding and insulation on the back of the exosuit, excrete and eat and get on our feet. We'd be rooing off to wherever in zilty. So the way to get up in the morning is to wake up in the world, not all snuggled down in a little hidey-hole away from it. That's the way to start a day. Aren't you sorry you got me going?

Yeah, course it helps that the sun comes up on Mars the way it does, I suppose that might explain some things about Earth people. People who came here from Earth say that they really miss long lingering sunrises and sunsets. I guess they're pretty or something. Out here on Mars the sun's a smaller disk and even though we've been making air as fast as we can for decades, it's still limward thinner, and the horizon is less than half as far away as it is on Earth. Morning light comes on quick, you see the colors move, the whole eastern sky goes bright pink in less than a minute, then a blue egg forms on the horizon, then, like a very undersized orange yolk in the blue egg, bing! the sun bounces up over the horizon like it's going places and has things to get done.

It was like that the morning everything started. It was like that every really good morning there was.

I opened my eyes to see the rocks in front of me coming alive with the red light, and looked over to see Dad sitting up. Each of us rooed around behind the rocks. You can't really see what someone is doing when they're squatting down in an exosuit, but you know. So you want some privacy.

I got done, pushed the "clean" button, enjoyed the warm, comfy feeling, and removed the little bag of waste from my lisport pack. I rooed back to the dune we'd slept on.

I'as expecting to see Dad setting up the scale and collectors, like on an ordinary morning. Then we'd weigh the night's waste, record rubbies—

Rubbies? Thought you knew us ecospectors, Doc. Rubbies is RBVs, which stands for the released-biogenic-volatiles billable line of the Development Corporation, which is the word for "God" out on the roundings. In a year, you can get paid a fair chunk for having crapped into ecosystems that need it, so Dad'n'me'as always careful about that, because rubbies is the anchor revenue for an independent ecospector, and there's no reason to ever give any away free. It stands to reason, you know? Anyway, we kept our part of the bargain—a contract's a contract—as soon as we had weighed and billed it, we dumped the wastebags onto soft dirt.

Then we'd eat suit rations through the helmet ports, like always, sitting plugged in so that our exosuits got a top-off charge. All four of the suitration flavors are pretty good and they fill you up and you don't get fat on'em, and like Dad always said, they sure help you make your quotas of rubbies. Dad said if they helped him any more they'd start to violate the conservation of matter.

That's not too crude, or anything, is it, for your record? Okay. You let me know. Dad'n'me used to talk about everything, and I don't know exactly how but you remind me a skosh of him.

After eating, we'd fold up what there was of camp, put it back in its expected places in our carry packs, and roo.

That was what I'as expecting to do this morning. But when I came around the rock, Dad had set up our tajj, which we usually only did every ten days or so to bathe, clean out boils, and exfoliate. It was a plain old Bean Marshell with vis-orange walls, white front airlock, and triple-nested clear dome. When I saw that tajj standing there in the deep red Martian dawn, early sunlight dancing around inside the top dome and walls glowing with light reflected from the rocks behind it, already plugged into our full 200 × 200 array, I knew it was bad news. Anything good, he'd've told me over suit-to-suit or satcell, at breakfast, or during the day; if it was private, we could just fiberlink, much less trouble than setting up the tajj. So he wanted to be able to see my face while we talked, to see how he'as doing, because he'as looking for a way to not fight.

Course it might be he wanted to see how happy I'as about to be. That was often the reason. If "often" means birthdays, Christmas, or finding a scorehole.

Inside the Marshell, with our exosuits and wickies thrown into the protolyzer to get fresh and clean, it was plain as God's balls that what was coming was bad news. Dad got out the special ration packs, which were for celebration or consolation, and nothing to celebrate had happened lately. "Come on, Teri," he said, "at least smile a skosh for a chance to get a helmet-off breakfast, not to mention having your exosuit freshened."

Dad looked like any roundito: pale, soft, grayish ashy skin, except for the wrinkled deep-tanned strip that ran from temple to temple across the eyes and most of the nose, like a brown leather bandit's mask. After a few years out in the roundings, even people with a lot of afro in their ancestry ended up grayish with a brown mask, just different shades of gray and brown. At least one roundito could always spot another one in the city, if they both had the bad luck to be there.

Dad's eyes were sort of washed-out gray-blue and his hair and beard stubble was brownish-red going gray, when he bothered having any. Today he did, because he always grew some in for a Gather, and there was a big one in a few days—in fact we had just one more stop to make before it.

Usually hair's a nuisance and you just wipe it off every time you're in the tajj; it's one of the few good things about tajj time. If it weren't for having to get rid of hair, and bathing so you don't get skin infections, and how good it feels to get rid of dead skin and boils, I don't think most of us would ever take our exosuits off at all.

"Well," he said, "I'm sure you've figured out bad news is coming. Do you want the bad news now, and then the meal after, as a consolation, or do you wanna enjoy the meal and then get the bad news after?"

I shrugged. "What's the meal?"

"French toast, scrambled eggs, sausage, and hash browns. Still had some left from the last mail rocket that your mother's folks sent out; your aunt Callie is real nice about accidentally getting luxury goods to wander into our mail. If I didn't know it was impossible, I'd say she's a teeper with a heart."

"Callie's got a big heart and you know it. And all the teepers in the world are not as stingy as the Tharsisitos, Dad. I don't know where they got two nice girls like Mummy and Callie. Probably they repossessed them from some ecospector they'd pushed to the wall. So, anyway, you're fixing my favorite breakfast; you must really be fixing to have a fight."

Wisely ignoring that, he said, "Since we'll be at the Gather and able to restock my stash soon, I thought we'd have some from-scratch coffee."

"Great, I always like that."

"So back to the question—bad news and then breakfast, or breakfast and then bad news?"

"Well, normally, I'd rather have the breakfast and then the bad news, but like I said, if you're fixing my favorite breakfast, you must figure it's really bad. So you might as well give me the bad news first and then see if anything can be salvaged with the breakfast."

"Fair enough." He turned to set up the coffee maker; I could never quite believe he'as willing to take the extra 300-gram penalty to bring that gadget along, even though I hadda admit that he'as right, from-scratch coffee really did taste better. He measured beans into the little hopper at the top, added distilled water from the tajj's recovery system, and pushed the button. There was the faint whine of the ultrasound generator as it powdered the beans and heated the water. Dad settled back, resting his weight on his elbows, legs sprawled in front of him, pretty much the picture of comfort. So now that he'd put it off as long as he possibly could, and didn't know what else to do, he just plain old walloped me with it all at once. "Teri, I've been thinking about several ideas that you've brought up, or hinted about, or implied real hard—you're good at that, nearly as good as your mother was. I know it matters to you a lot. So just because I'm not giving you your way, please don't think I haven't listened and please don't think I'm doing things just to be mean, all right?"

I nodded, reluctantly, my heart already settling like a ball of CO_2-slush on top of the cold stone I could feel in my belly.

"Well, then, here's the story. I know you wanted to

talk about marrying Perry, and the Gather would be the logical time to get it done. And he's a fine young man, and I'll tell you right now, any objections I got ain't to Perry, and not to you getting married, either. Your mother'n'me got married when we were younger than you are now, after all. So just to begin with, I'm not, posreal not, not, not, saying no to your marriage."

I sighed. "That means you're gonna make me finish school." I didn't like the whiny tone already creeping into my voice; I had been planning this conversation for days—not what I'as gonna say, course, I wouldn't've known that, but to be dignified and reasonable. I kept repeating that to myself—*dignified and reasonable, dignified and reasonable, dignified and reasonable*—and maybe it helped because I'as at least smart enough, then, to shut up and wait for him to talk again, instead of giving him myself to focus his anger and argue against.

"Look it over, things are changing, Teri. When I started out as an ecospector, there were almost no rounditachi, resources were huge, the Development Corporation didn't pay well or fairly but they paid, and the number of possible scoreholes out there just seemed like there was no limit. The great scoreholes were still out there waiting. Now you know what kind of bragging rights I have—"

I did; doors opened for me all the time, among ecospectors or people who knew ecospecting, just because I'as Telemachus Murray's daughter. Back around the time I'as born, Dad and his partner, Kindness O'Hart, had drilled one spring that had started a huge surface river, up north in the Acidalia country, and brought the whole Alice

Valley into being. Dad was credited with planting three forests, and it was on the shores of Lake Telemachus Murray that Marsform pine trees first took root. I always told people I wanted to be an ecospector, but I couldn't say "like my Dad," cause I just couldn't imagine being able to accomplish as much as he had.

"Teri," he said, "you're getting that faraway look in your eyes. I oughta not've mentioned it. I know how much you love the ecospector's life and I know how many dreams you have bound up in it. The point is, in the early days, there was so much to be done that anyone who'as any good got a great scoresheet fast. If the payment system that the Development Corporation uses now would've been what they used then, there wouldn't be an ecospector who started before 2080 who wouldn't be a billionaire today."

That was a sore spot with Dad and pretty well all the old timers; most of'em were comfortable but not rich, but if, back then, they'd had the contracts and payment system they got with the General Strike in 2088, they would've been rich—posreal rich. A lot of'em thought they were allowed to win in '88 cause the Development Corporation knew the great scoreholes were all opened by then.

"Teri," Dad said, "you're still drifting off. Now just listen to me a skosh longer. Look, I know that plenty of people my age say that large parts of the surface haven't even been touched yet, and there's still plenty more to find and do. But even though there's still plenty of land out there and there could be many more scoreholes before it's played out, that's not what's gonna happen. Bet you anything, the government will be reassessing the value of releases downward pretty soon, and the value of seedings upward. And you can find a big scorehole for rubbies even now—we're gonna, tomorrow, you just wait till I show you the numbers—but there never was a big scorehole for seeding, all that is, is steady work. Well, when the government starts to pay the Development Corporation less, you think that's gonna mean lower profits for the Development Corporation? For a monopoly? Like hell. They'll pass it right on to us and it will come out of rubbies. They just ain't gonna need to release as much as they thought they would. The Marsforms are taking off limward more'n anyone dreamed, so nobody is gonna pay for taking this planet all the way to shirtsleeve conditions. Not when it can be populated with thousands or millions of species that will live here just fine for a fraction of the effort. Not when we've gotta get this place ready to support the Grand Fleet when it comes in—especially since that's the only reason to terraform it at all. If we can get redded up for the Grand Fleet, while leaving Mars dry and cold and without much to breathe, we will."

"That's another one. We're the ones here. The people on the old transfer ships are on their way backward in time to other star systems, and by the time that their descendants get here traveling in regular time, it's gonna be, what, ten generations separating us? Why are we doing all that for them, and nothing for our own grandchildren?"

Dad shrugged. "Teri, you like thinking your own thoughts, don't you? And you'd rather other people did, too, you know. And as long as One True holds Earth, that could change any bright morning. One day we all wake up to an emergency widecast and it says those four words we don't say, and we all start to run Resuna, and then there's a Mars One True and none of us ever thinks for ourselves again."

The four words we didn't say were "let override, let overwrite," the phrase that activated Resuna, which was the meme that people who lived under One True ran all the time. The meme that every single person on Earth, except maybe a very few cordilleristas or bedouins, was running. The meme that they always worried that someone here might acquire . . . because once you get memed, your only purpose in the world is to spread that meme. And not least, the meme that the Fourth Wave had come here fleeing, thirty-five years ago, and since the Fourth Wave had more than doubled our population, they were firmly in the saddle as voters.

Thing was, Doc, and I know you spend a lot of time thinking about memes and looking for them too, you all've done way too good a job for kids my age to be afraid of them, you know? I mean it stands to reason. We've never met them. We know people who were memed forty years ago, and who still act terrified of them, but for most of us—well, when I was a little kid and Mummy had just died, there was this Ecucatholic kid at school that taught me how to pray, which I did for a lot of that term, every night in bed talking to the ceiling in the dark. Cured of it, of course, soon as I was out in the roundings again; you look at the sky and the land and you know nothing could have created this, it's all too big and grand to be a creation. But back then I used to pray and it was always the same prayer—"Please take care of Mummy and make sure she's not lonely, please keep Dad safe out in the roundings, please don't let a vampire bite me, and please don't ever let me get memed." The vampire and the meme were both about equally real to me, Doc.

Dad sighed. "I know it's hard to remember that One True is always there, on Earth, wanting to get the rest of the solar system, but you know, every month Planetary Defense shoots down little Resuna carriers on solar sails approaching Mars. Every shipment we import from Earth, every bundle of mail, has a few copies of Resuna hidden somewhere. So I don't mind working to get the planet ready to support the invasion fleet. I wish the Grand Fleet was getting here tomorrow. I wish we'd at least gotten a message that said when they'll be coming, or that if the government already got one they'd let us all in on it. And I'm glad that they are coming, cause now that Earth doesn't need or want our help to rescue them from their catastrophes, if we didn't hafta get redded up for the Grand Fleet, there wouldn't be much to do. We'd all live in the cities and watch old movies all day, or something, and let the robots feed and care for the cities."

"There are people at school that say they wanna do just that—"

"Unh-hunh. What do you think of those people?"

"Oh, they're fools. Course."

"Well, there you have it, Teri. The trouble is, the needs of the Grand Fleet created ecospecting, and now those same needs are gonna bring it to a close sooner than anyone would've expected. The glory days of big scoreholes and chances to get rich are about over, that's what I'm saying. I'll show you some stuff I put together on that, when we're done talking.

"And then there's the fact that the ecospector population has exploded, so you have a lot more rounditachi developing a decreasing number of scoreholes. You know better than anyone that this is a great life for many, many people—and for the ones where it's not, they can move into the cities so easily that nobody has to feel trapped. So there's getting to be more and more of us out here, and the big scoreholes'll get found faster, and for the most part, the big wild areas are gonna be overrun in short periods of time, something like I imagine the old gold rushes were a long time back. Whatever is gonna be found and exploited will mostly get opened up and ecoactivated all at once, probably in the next ten Mars years or so, so you probably won't be forty yet when the last big scorehole, whatever it may be, pays off. And then there's all that stuff going freebies."

Freebies were the bane of ecospectors; they made us call 'em "second-order events" in school. This was supposed to Teach Us Something or Other. They were what happened when the surface of Mars, getting warmer and wetter and with denser air all the time, spontaneously activated a biopotential. They happened all the time now, as Dad had said, in a small way, as methane, CO_2, or water deposits would abruptly spontaneously release into the atmosphere, and the new Marsform life would colonize things before they could be seeded.

The first big freebie had happened just six Mars years before. The Chryse closed basin had turned out not to be so closed after all—an aquifer flowing under it, filling steadily in the decades since Lake Chryse had been re-created, had sapped under the ancient ejecta wall, so that it collapsed abruptly and sent a brand-new unplanned river, Mars's longest, crashing right through the Acidalia country and on down to the baby ocean around the North Pole. The Marsform kokanee from the basin had been swept down the New River (silly, bland name, but everyone called it that and it seemed likely to stick), and had discovered they liked the Boreal Ocean just fine, pulled a few adaptive rabbits out of the hats of their DNA in a way that demonstrated Bear's Conjecture beautifully, and reverted all the way to full-fledged salmon, swimming up the New River every Mars fall since.

If an ecospector had triggered it, that would have been the scorehole to make him or her the richest man on Mars. As it was, the Development Corporation hadn't paid a millicredit for the New River event.

Since then there had been big freebies every few months, and little ones happened so often that they weren't even reported in the news anymore. Every one of 'em had been a pure accident caused by the improving surface conditions. It was quite possible that most of the big scoreholes still out there would be released, not by ecospectors, but by Mars itself. "I've thought about that," I admitted.

"Well, then, so tick it off, Teri. It all comes down to they need ecospectors less and less every year, and every year there are more and more of us, and then the final blow is that we did create the nations and sign the treaty."

He didn't mean us; he meant the referendum that the stupid Legislature had held two Mars-years before, which the equally stupid voters, dominated by utterly brainless sitters, had voted in. Course the gentech people might have been the most brainless of all, for creating the froyks in the first place.

"Froyk" was one of those words you didn't use around adults because they got all weird and "don't talk like that" and stuff, and course you didn't use it in front of the froyks themselves. They were called that cause the goofy Dr. Perrault who created'em actually designed over 200 genotypes, classified them by the main Martian surface condition he designed'em to resist, and it happened that the cold-resistant strain, *froid K,* was the one onto which he could graft all the other genes he'd found in the Bear Regions of the human/mammal genome. So the first such babies he grew in his test tubes were "modified froid-K's," and that phrase turned into "froyks" out in the roundings, where the idea wasn't even a skosh popular.

We needed Marsform rabbits and pine trees and flowers and bees, sure. But we didn't need Marsform cobras, rats, or bears as far as I could see, because those species are dangerous and useless, and human beings are about as dangerous and useless as anything you'll find—that's why cities are such awful places—and making Marsform people made about as much sense as making Marsform cockroaches would have. Perrault was such a moron!

Anyway, the oldest froyks were about thirty groundyears old now. They had low per-weight oxygen demand, very high tolerance for carbon dioxide, chests the size of a stove, and flexible ribs and extra muscling so that they could pump air in and out at an incredible rate, holding and pressurizing every breath to push oxygen into their low-pressure bloodstreams. Their legs looked something like a camel's and ended in broad hairy feet. Thick red-brown body hair covered them all over, and on the front of their shaggy heads were a rounded snout, small eyes set deep, and big, tufted ears. They were about the ugliest critters anyone had ever seen. If you hadn't known they were human stock you'd have assumed that their genome was put together out of bears, bats, apes, and goats.

There wasn't yet enough air for them to breathe and move on the surface without respirators right now. But as Mars changed further, froyks would be able to live on the surface, unaided, probably within twenty Mars years. They could already live comfortably without an exosuit; on a nice day, a Marsform wore a pair of pants for modesty, a knit cap for warmth, and a gadget that looked sort of like what old-time scuba divers used to wear, attached to a pack that pressurized and warmed their air. Where in a crisis I could probably have run fifty meters across the surface, unprotected, before I collapsed, a froyk could probably survive for a couple of kim.

Right now there were about six hundred adult froyks out there, and maybe two thousand children, organized loosely into five "nations," and each of the nations had been given a gigantic tract of land and resources to populate. Of all the stupid things to do, instead of making Mars fit for humans, we were gonna create sideshow freaks to live on Mars. The madness was spreading, too, cause terraforming of Earth's moon was under way now, and already there were pictures on the drawing board for huge, ridiculous, winged Moonform humans that looked like a kid's nightmare of a devil.

"We did agree that they were nations, and we did sign the treaties with them," Dad repeated.

I shook my head. "I sure didn't agree. And neither did anyone I know. You voted against the referendum just like every other roundito, and dead right too. It passed on votes by sitters who never, never, never go out here; they voted to give away our land and resources, as far as I'm concerned. And for no good reason at all. We could have Mars all the way to shirtsleeve if we'd just stay on the plan. There was no need to create those *things*."

"People, Teri, people. At least while you're in my tajj, they're people, and I won't hear any other language from you on the subject." His eyes were suddenly cold and hard like they got when he'as in a bar, feeling drunk and mean and looking for the first available fight. "Besides, you know most likely our descendants will be Marsforms; they need the genetic diversity and they'll be taking samples from everyone they can, Marsforming them, and putting them out there with those families. The people that you call 'things' and 'freaks' and I don't know what all will be raising your great-grandchildren—who are gonna look like'em."

Dad said and did some disgusting things—I had given up even trying to get him to not fart in the tajj, and every now and then at a Gather, when he went to the rent-a-bitch, he'd bring back some posreal ugly nasty old grandma cause he liked'em skoshy cheap and dirty—but telling me that my descendants were gonna be froyks was about the most disgusting thing he'd ever done. I don't think he even noticed or realized that.

While I'as seething about that, he went right on like it was just something anybody might say. "Right now Mars is three million unmodified humans and twenty-five hundred Marsforms," he said. "Three hundred years from now, it'll be a billion Marsforms and fewer than ten thousand unmodifieds." He'as still giving me that cold glare, and even though I'as now close to his size, it scared me like I'as four years old and about to earn a spanking. "So no more of that kinda talk. Things are settled with the Marsforms; they have their share, we have ours, and we're going to treat'em with all the respect due to them, end of story, end of subject."

Frustrated and unhappy as I was, I wasn't crazy. I swallowed my temper and said what the old bastard wanted, hating him all the while. "I'm sorry, Dad. You're right. I mean, we gave our word, and now we hafta keep it. A contract's a contract and all that." (But you can't make a contract with an animal—everyone knows that, you learn it in school. I guess school is good for something.) And then 'cause I couldn't help it, I burst out with "But to throw away one third of the planet on so few . . . people! To create a world for them and not for ourselves! Dad, the Legislature was just plain crazy."

"All the same," Dad said, his frigid glare not changing yet, "It's not whether you *want* there to be water in the rock, and it's not whether it would be *good* for there to be water in the rock—"

" '—it's whether or not there *is* water in the rock,' " I finished for him. "You know I'm gonna be remembering that phrase on my dying day."

"But, I hope, *not* because you're thirsty," he said. "And believe it or not, long before that day, you'll have driven your own kids crazy with that little saying. Trust me, you won't be able to stop yourself."

I couldn't help laughing, skoshy. Dad was so hard to stay mad at. "I promise I'll give you a call the first time I say it to one of 'em. So I can ask you to take me out somewhere and cut my air hose. But how am I ever gonna have this litter of little Marsforms that you want me to drive crazy, if I can't get married and start a family—sheesh, Dad, I *am* fifteen, you know, and you and Mummy started younger than that."

"There will be plenty of time," he said. "A hundred years ago lots of people didn't start families till they were past thirty, and the human race still had a population explosion." He looked into my eyes, very seriously, like this really mattered or something. It was almost spooky. "Now, look, Teri, before I got around to trying to fix that god-awful bigoted attitude—don't try and pretend you don't have it—that you picked up from other kids—sometimes I swear it's the only thing you ever learned in school—I was trying to put all this stuff I've been talking about together into one big package. So here's what's up, I think, and why I've got the plan I've got, and why I want you to stay on it just a little longer even though it's squeezing blood out of your heart and I know that, Teri-Mel. So you listen close, now, and if you see something wrong with my thinking, you say so, but if you see I got the facts and the logic, and you hafta agree with me, then I want you to promise to use that clear head of yours and not that big tender heart—just for about a year. After that, if what I'm thinking is right, you can be just as big a fool as you wanna be, with my full blessings. Contract?"

"Full contract," I said, and stuck out my hand. He shook it, posreal serious, so I stayed serious too. Out in the roundings, "a contract is a contract" is not redundant; it's the way we all live, it's the basic reason we struck in '88, and it's the one thing sitters have learned not to step on or try to give away.

"Well, then. Put it together." He ticked it off on his fingers. "Terraformation is gonna go less than a third as far as was originally planned. The number of ecospectors working on it has been doubling every Mars year for the past six. There can't be many big scoreholes left, and what scoreholes there will be will mostly go freebie. Big parts of the planet are being reserved for Marsforms. Marsforms themselves will make much better ecospectors than we ever can, because they can eat Marsform plants and fish raw, without having to chemically treat them to get the antifreeze compounds out, and they don't need exosuits or half the gear we do."

"But they can starve to death in seventy-two hours, because of that loony metabolism they hadda give them," I pointed out. "They hafta burn so much fuel just to stay alive—and not efficiently, since they don't have enough oxygen."

"But once Mars is covered with all kinds of sugary plants," Dad said, impassively, "they'll be able to eat, and we still won't be able to breathe. No, you wait two generations and most ecospectors—except for a certain cranky old grandma, I guess—will be Marsforms. You know that. All true?"

"All true," I admitted, though almost every point he'as making was something that made me mad, cause I din-wanna get reminded, again, that "it's not whether you want the water to be in the rock . . ."

He nodded, pleased that I had just accepted it, and went on. "So come on, they make you take economics in school. What does all that add up to?"

I shrugged; it was staring me in the face and there was no way around it. "Some ecospectors're gonna get forced out," I said. "How bad do you think it'll be?"

The sun was further up now, hitting the triple clear fabric of the dome over our heads and reflecting down in; the inside of the tajj was glowing more yellow than pink. It was flattering light and it made Dad look younger than the thirty-five he really was, or at least it made him look city-thirty-five (almost like a kid) instead of roundings-thirty-five.

He pulled out his werp, an old-fashioned heavy one that must have weighed a hundred grams, which I'as always trying to get him to junk—everybody nowadays just used an always-on virtual werp that hooked in through a permanent satcell line and gave you no weight penalty at all, since the processor wasn't located anywhere near you. "Let me show you the graphs, you'll see what's coming," he said.

"Aw, it's schooly, and I don't like school."

"Nevertheless, it's also what's going on, and it's what you need to be thinking about, Teri. And remember, I don't like it any better than you do, but what I'm showing you is the water that's in the rock, whatever we wish or hope."

Well, just cause I don't like school, and I'm not much of a reader, doesn't mean I'm stupid, and after all ecospecting is mostly a matter of margins and ratios, tipovers and trends, and all that stuff, so much as I hated to do it, I could read his little pile of graphs and figures well enough—it was no harder than looking at the relative profit potential of two possible routes through an erg—and no matter how you hatched it, patched it, or matched it, it jumped right out at you—there were only so many slots for ecospectors in the Martian economy in any given year, and though slots would exceed ecospectors for about seven or eight more years to come, after that it would be the other way round, and for at least five or six years there would be a big shakeout in the industry. I asked "Any reason to think us small operators will do better or worse than franchies or salarymen?"

"Nothing I can see. We can't get fired and most of us aren't in bad debt, but we can be ground right down right away if the Development Corporation drops the prices they pay on rubbies. The others have a backer, course, and the Development Corporation ain't going broke anytime soon, but on the other side a backer can fire you. So I think it'll all just depend on what arrangements they make when the crunch hits. And they're not gonna make arrangements until right close to the crunch cause right now it still pays for them to get as many people into ecospecting as they can; it'll make the Development Corporation more money to hit the wall than to hit the brakes, whatever it might mean to all the little guys between them and the wall. That's what this little graph shows."

He'as right, it did. I felt slightly sick, thinking about all my friends out in the roundings—not just the ecospectors but the teepers and the roadthumpers and the contractors—for all my life it had always been growing and booming out here; the idea of free, independent-living rounditachi being forced back into the nasty crowded rodent-warrens of the cities was just far too much, and too horrible, to take in all at once. "Has this been on the news?" I asked Dad.

"Some, not much. They're downplaying it, I think. Maybe so they can keep on recruiting ecospectors, and as long as it looks like there's always work out here, they'll keep signing up. Lots of people love the idea, most that try it find they don't like the reality and go back, but there's still lots more who would be happy to try, and enough'll stick to help keep the pool expanding and put downward pressure on earnings. I don't think the Development Corporation wants the line at the window to go away till they slam that window down.

"But one way or another, the boom is about over and only the smart and the lucky are gonna come out on the other side." The coffeemaker pinged, and Dad used it as an excuse to take a zilty and pour us each a cup, dumping plenty of sugar into mine, the way I like it. We sipped coffee for a minute, maybe longer, just sitting with each other, and he let all that sink in. "Maybe I'm dumb, but, bad as the news is there, I still don't see what it's got to do with getting married and quitting school," I said, "and still less what all that has to do with this big thing for tomorrow that you've been so secretive about."

"Well, you know you'll pass the academic part of the Full Adult exam, easy, even if you take it tomorrow; you hate school but you don't hate learning and you've learned much more'n you think you have. And you also know that there's at least a big risk that you would flunk the emotional maturity interview, don't you?"

I could have argued, but that would probably have been more evidence that I'as immature. "Suppose I just say that it isn't a big surprise."

"Fair enough. Now, with another year at school, you'll pass easily. I know that there are people, my age and especially older ones, that think sixteen is awfully old to be qualifying for Full Adult, but the truth is nowadays *most* people wait that long—the crisis they had in the last few generations is finally getting to be over. When your grandpa was a kid and even when I was, they had to get everybody qualified as fast as possible and everyone was cut the maximum slack, so they looked for any way they could declare you adult so you could work full time right away. Nowadays they look for any reason to *not* give it to you, seems like."

"You're telling me," I said. "But they give you FA at seventeen; you don't hafta take the exam."

"That's FA with no voting rights, no jury duty, no government job, you go to the foot of the line for any additional schooling—"

"I don't care about any of *that!*"

"Not right now you don't, but it's hard to know what

you'll want later." He tapped his finger on the werp screen where the panel of graphs still spelled out the coming collapse.

"So you could get your Full Adult by doing one more year of CSL school, and have it a year earlier than you would without. And don't even think about trying to start off married life and a business partnership without the FA. Think about Perry. To marry you, he'd hafta sign a certificate that says that he's willing to be responsible for you. I don't know how to tell you this, but being responsible for you, Teri, is not a job I'd inflict on an eighteen-year-old who just got FA himself last year, especially somebody who only had enough ambition and maturity to wait till he'as seventeen and take the one that they just give to you."

The worst thing about being told something like that is how badly you wanna scream and cry and throw things, right when you really need to act mature.

So nothing stopped Dad from going on talking, and saying things that hurt even worse. "Now, Perry loves the ecospecting life. I can't say I blame him—I love it myself. But he's never even tried to learn a thing about anything else, and that might well be trouble. At least one of you needs to be able to take some other job when the bottom drops out of ecospecting. And since he *won't* learn any other occupation, you're the one that's gonna hafta retrain. And people who finish CSL school and get a real, earned Full Adult are way ahead in the line for retraining, in every industry. The FA you get that means you kept breathing for seventeen years is foot of the line. You can't afford to both be at the foot of the line."

It was like Dad'd already hit me in the stomach once and now he'as gonna do it over and over until I agreed that I needed to be hit, or something. Dad wasn't as bad as some old people that thought they oughta never have started giving the age-based FA, and usually he'as polite enough not to talk that way in front of Perry, but just the same I knew that Dad thought my guy'as stupid or lazy just cause he dinwanna waste time learning all that point-less stuff—reading books with crap in'em about people that are all dead, solving problems that aren't half as com-plicated or interesting as what you do every day out in the roundings, doing all this teamwork crap and being friends crap and you-and-your-society crap. Dad seemed to think that everyone oughta wanna wallow in that crap.

I took a deep breath and held my peace. This close to taking an FA exam, they monitor your communications limward, and a good tantrum would about nuke my small chances.

Dad said, more gently, "Ecospecting is great, it's a great life, and I wish—I truly do—that you could live the rest of your life, with Perry and some kids, the way that I lived with your mother'n'you. But there's only one Mars, it only has so much rubbies, and what's left to do is mostly the mopping up—and there's not enough of that to last out your lifetimes. You might get real lucky and be among the few that make it through the shakeout okay, but you saw the numbers—more won't'n will. So you gotta be ready to move on, and that means a diploma from the school, and getting Full Adult from the examiner, not by just waiting out the calendar."

I guess that was one more shot to help it hurt some more.

I wanted to cry. Why had I bothered to rein in my temper and plan what I was doing, to be responsible and courteous as much as I could, for all these months, when it hadn't gotten me anything? Perry'as eighteen, two and a half years older than me, very old for a bachelor out in the roundings. He'as a healthy normal man, and I knew he'd passed up plenty of chances at Gathers, just for me. We'd been together for just about exactly two years, which was about one year and ten months longer than most girls went between getting attached and getting married. And there was plenty in each of our starter-kicks; we'd be launching one of the best-capitalized start-ups anyone ever had.

The plan had always been that I would pass my FA at the Gather, a few days from now. Then I could marry Perry as an equal, and you only needed one earned FA in a couple to be able to own a business and have kids together. But Dad was right, just cause I sometimes hadda let my feelings out when things were really unfair, likely they'd decide I'as too immature anyway.

So before we could get married, it was gonna be another year, and Perry must be getting to feel like a posreal old bachelor, though every night when we talked on the com, he was limward nice about everything, didn't seem worried at all. Actually, lately he hadn't been worried *enough,* it seemed to me, but I figured that was 'cause he'as older and could stay a little calmer about it, and besides he had just never been much of a talker.

The more I spent time with free adults like Dad, the more I wanted my freedom *now*. And although they certainly did teach some things in school that were useful—math, reading, business practices, that kinda thing—most of it was just crap, like history and languages and music and everything else that was supposed to Teach Us Something or Other.

And then too I hated the idea that I would be tested on whether I was responsible enough to understand that I was not yet responsible enough. It just seemed grotesque and terribly unfair, and there was nothing to do for it. It would be another year. I would see Perry at the Gather, and he usually found ways to come by RSC and visit me at school—though all of last term he hadn't.

I was good and stuck. Dad had thought it through, and since part of the proof of my maturity was supposed to be making myself agree with hard-but-correct decisions, disagreeing with him would very literally only make things worse.

And since, when you were getting close to FA, they always turned on the monitors more often, for the next several days, including the Gather, I didn't dare get all peevy or snap at anyone or even sort a look like I could've been having trouble swallowing the whole unpleasant mess of my life.

"Well," I said. "You know I don't like it. You know it hurts."

Dad nodded.

"I guess that's all I have to say. Let's have the breakfast, and let's take it slow and easy so we can both really enjoy it, and then, what's this other thing that's left, that you've been so secretive about?"

He looked at me very intently. "You know, I'm only about three quarters sure I'm right. You're handling this pretty well. You wouldn't have last year."

My eyes started to water—bad news when you're trying to look mature—so I looked down and rubbed my face, to get my composure back. "Let's not push my luck."

"Sorry. Teri-Mel Murray, I really am sorry."

"Teri-Mel" was a little nickname he had for me when I'as very small; nowadays he used it mostly when he'as trying to be comforting and didn't know how. At least he never called me by my full name, Terpsichore Melpomene Murray—such an old-lady name; it would have been conservative in his generation and in mine it was ridiculous. It was somehow perfectly my luck that I'as saddled with the names of my mother's and my father's favorite aunts.

"Well, then," Dad said, as he dropped the food blocks into the reconstitutor, "yes, there's one more big thing we're gonna do before the Gather, and that's why I've routed us so far out, through the middle of nowhere, on our way to the Gather. In two days there's a deep driller making a near pass almost bang overhead, and I've put in a bid for it. Think I've got something interesting on the seismic."

A deep driller is expensive—you hafta pretty much push your credit over the top to afford to get one committed to your project—but on the other hand, nowadays since the remaining big deposits are mostly way down, a deep driller is often the only choice you've got for a posreal major scorehole. Physically it's a few-ton satellite in an extremely elliptical orbit, streamlined like an old-time cartoon rocket with a sharp, heat-shielded nose, intended to come through the atmosphere as fast as it can. Special gear inside it—don't look at me, I'm not a physicist—keeps a softball-sized sphere of neutronium and a microscopic dot of antineutronium sitting near each other, almost all the way up in the sharp nose.

When the deep driller is diverted to a target, it fires its jets to impact at a particular point; they promise you meter accuracy and usually deliver to the centimeter. It's coming in down from the tip-top spot on a limward elliptical orbit, so it's coming fast to begin with, and then on top of that it runs the jets flat out all the way in, trying to arrive just as the tank empties, getting every last bit of speed available.

As it's coming in, some other gadget in there whips the little dot of antineutronium around and around a little three-centimeter diameter "racetrack," getting it up to such a speed that, an instant before the deep driller impacts, the antineutronium gets thrown down a narrow tube right into the center of the neutronium sphere, where it hangs, for microzilty, suspended by a mutual electric charge.

Meanwhile, outside, the neutronium sphere goes through ordinary matter like a bowling ball through smoke. It smashes through the nose of the impacting deep driller and plunges kim deep through the rock, making a perfectly smooth hole as it packs all that rock up ahead of itself.

At the planned depth, the suspending charge is turned off, the MAM reaction happens, and the heat conducts throughout the neutronium sphere. At exactly the targeted depth, the neutronium boils off, converting into thousands of tons of ordinary matter at rock-vaporizing temperatures.

Some of the mighty blast goes back up the hole, reaming and fusing and creating a tube a few meters wide down into whatever material you've hit. Most of it stays down there, shattering and pulverizing the rock around it and heating the volatiles into white-hot plasma. A zilty later, the plasma rebounds from the walls of the underground chamber, and rushes back in and up the tube. It bursts onto the surface still white-hot, forming a plume many kim high.

Deep drilling is an expensive way to do things, but if you have volatiles like ice, ammonia, or methane buried fifteen kim down, it will absolutely get'em out into the atmosphere, right now, and that's the idea.

Dad grinned at me. "Now I bet you've been wondering why we've been knocking around in the Prome for a month, on this long trek, and why we've been setting off so many seismics and doing so much listening to the seismics coming our way from all the chondreors crashing on the South Pole and all the mining going on up in the South Hellas. Well, funny thing. You know how everyone is always saying—when they're trying to pretend a crash ain't coming, I think, and pretend it can't ever come—they always say that there's lots more out there to be found and there's plenty of big scoreholes and most of the surface of Mars hasn't even been touched? Funny thing—they're right as far as it goes, but they don't act like it—we do.

"The whole reason we're taking this weird route, through the Prome, to the Gather, is cause I think it's an area that has some of the greatest potential on Mars, and the guys at the Development Corporation all agree with me, but you notice we're the only ones out here— most ecospectors go where the others do, they don't really look for scoreholes, they look to set up next to someone and collect crumbs off his table."

So then he showed me what he had in mind, and posreal it drove all my disappointment right out of my mind. Dad pointed to graphs on the screen of that silly werp of his, instead of us just sharing a virtual—I reminded myself not to pick a fight with him about that—so we hadda lean our heads close together and I guess it was good we weren't in helmets. "For sure, the way that thing is echoing, from those shots we took earlier this year and from all the logged seismic shots I've put together on this, there's the right kind of structure down there, and the echoes are the kind you get off an ultra-deep gas pocket," Dad said. "Probably what we have here is just the deepest anyone's ever found CO_2. But the minimum size is such that even if it's only CO_2, it will still be the biggest biopotential that anyone has ecoactivated in a good long while, as sure as you're born, and that means more rubbies than we've recorded in the last few years put together.

"Now when you look at conditions thirteen and fourteen kim down, under the Prome, first thing you see is it's too cold down there for it to be water vapor or liquid water, and it's not ice cause it's clearly fluid—look at the way every transverse wave is lagged. But I ain't at all sure it's gonna be CO_2. To be that deep, in rock that old, it has to be really ancient. The orthodox theory says that carbon dioxide, especially far enough down so that there's plenty of water available from the rocks around it, oughta've mostly dissolved into carbonic acid and gotten carried away in groundwater, until the pressure got low enough and that pocket collapsed, and then the rocks oughta've packed up over time and we shouldn't have anything down there but fused gravel for the last billion years—*if* that gas was CO_2.

"Now, add to that—what does this structure look like to you, underneath?"

I stared at the charts and figures for a while, trying to let an impression form; Dad had been teaching me for years not to leap to conclusions, so though I had the idea right away, I kept looking for ways to reject it, but finally I said, "Looks porous or even broken. Which isn't uncommon considering that it's under broken crater rim—the whole Prome is what got thrown up when the meteor dug Hellas, right? So there oughta be heaps and piles of all sorta shattered rock down there, some of it forming long tubes and chimneys that go far, far down.

"And I don't see any bottom either, within the range that the echoes can reach—that's what you were getting at, right? That you have this coarse-grained, wide open channel that maybe goes all the way down to the mantle, or further, coming up under the basin rim of Hellas ... and formational gases have been leaking up through it for three billion years, then—until they came up against that upside-down bowl of nonporous rock. And the main formational gases—" (this was something I had learned in school that hadn't seemed completely useless) "—are water, ammonia, and methane, and ammonia is limward too active to ever have lasted all that time, and water would be solid."

"That's what it looks like to me, too, Teri. I think the stuff in the pocket might be mostly methane."

"And the size of it . . . oh, Dad. That's amazing. All the stuff they say about you, they'll be saying limward more of. That's just . . ."

Oh, Dad looked smug. You put that man down into that cavity he'd found, let him stew a few weeks, and you could've pumped smug out of it for a thousand years. He beamed at me as he said, "I looked, and I tried not to get all caught up in where everyone else was looking; 'where everyone else is looking,' is pretty much—"

"—'the formula for where everything has already been found,' " I said, quoting him.

He looked annoyed at first, then grinned, that big wonderful grin that always spread all the way across his face when he'as pleased with me. "Teri-Mel," he said, "you have been paying attention to your old man. Who'd've thought?" He reached forward and rubbed my head, scratchy where the fuzz was coming in—I'd been letting the hair grow out a bit cause Perry liked the texture—and I couldn't help it, I started to laugh too. Dad was always so hard to stay angry with.

The morning didn't seem so bad, after all, not at first. It *was* my favorite breakfast, and we took the time to enjoy it. We weren't on any pressing schedule, and it was 9 A.M.

before we set off. Despite having had most of my dreams ground up into skoshy pieces, first thing after getting up, I wasn't really in too bad a mood. You eat what they put in front of you, you know.

❦❦ **I stop the** recording for just a minute. God, it's late already. Past the time when Teri would have called. I hope that means everything's fine. Probably what happened is that she had to spend some extra time getting her party settled in for the night—chances are they have a lot of little kids—and then was just tired and decided to go to bed. Which would be the best thing she could do. If her fears are grounded, then the old acronym, the one that started with alcoholics and went to everyone else, remains true— HALT. Don't Get Too Hungry, Angry, Lonely, or Tired.

Thinking of drunks, I pour another drink, and think about why I stopped the recording right there. Maybe just because I like the early part best, when she's hurt but not hurting too badly. Maybe because I wish I'd known her in the time she's talking about.

I've been at this job a long time and I'm not sure

whether I can go on being profound, I think. And I imagine the advice I'd get from Telemachus Murray—contract's a contract, it's not whether you want there to be water in the rock, you eat what they put in front of you—and toss most of the drink into the sink, unconsumed, sit down, and reach to turn the recording back on. Just before I do, I remember: I stopped here because it's less than a minute before the first time Teri realized what was going to happen, which was the first time—far from the last!—I had to hurt her, and that thought makes me sick.

I retrieve the bottle, refill the glass, sit down, turn on the recording. If I have to eat what they put in front of me, I want something to wash it down with.

⚏ **Just before the** midmorning coffee break that we always took, I had another argument with Dad. It was a bad day for those; sometimes I didn't have any for months, and now twice in a day.

But he'as so wrong, Doc, he'as off on another love the froyks thing. I couldn't take it, just couldn't.

What do you mean how do I feel about having argued

with him? Is that something you need for the recording? *Something* I *need?* How?

But I thought I was already cured. You mean I gotta lose—what I just said is all the memories I'm gonna have? Doc, that's not fair! You said I was cured!

❧ **I fast-forward through** all my long explanations, and through her crying and shouting. There was nothing else to be done. I knew it, and she was smart enough so that I could explain it to her. And that was all there was to it.

But still ... I've had two of those unfortunate incidents, as they are discreetly called in most public records. I've lost three fairly important weeks of my life in them, including one divorce. All I know of them is my picture, talking to my backup and friend Cal, telling him everything; and then weeks of watching those recordings over and over. Like waking from having been asleep and getting a message from yourself.

I thought I had explained it clearly to her. I thought I always did to everyone. But most of the time, they don't get it till later, and then they cry and scream. I fast-forward through some more of Teri's anguish, and some more of my insipid ineffective comforting and explaining. She starts her story again. I've finished my drink, and I refill it, my eyes never leaving the screen.

☞ Yeah, I can do it now, Doc. Sorry I didn't understand before. Sorry I got so carried away. Pretty stupid of me all around, actually, and it does me no good. It's not whether you want there to be water in the rock, and it's not whether it would be good for there to be water in the rock, it's whether there's water in the rock. I know.

All right, so here's what Dad'n'me fought about. Like a moron I looked over his shoulder while he'as laying out our course for the day. Then something extra-stupid inside me made me say, "You're gonna put nineteen extra kim into today just to avoid a reservation that doesn't have anything on it yet?"

"Teri, the law says we don't cross that line without permission."

"There's not anyone even living in that reservation till six Mars years from now! And what the law says is that if we cross that line without permission, we pay'em a few credits! You'n'me've'ad pizzas in town for more'n that fine would cost us!"

"We're practicing, think of it that way."

"I already know how to roo," I said.

He got that stubborn, dug-in look—just like the one I get, Doc, you already know that look, I guess. "We follow the law. We have always followed the law."

A person with a brain would've stopped right there, bango, no more, don't let him hear another word from me. A moron like me just hadda say "I don't see why we hafta respect the rights of sideshow freaks, who haven't even moved in yet, over a stretch of rock and sand that we won't harm one bitty skosh by crossing it."

Funny thing. No kid my age has seen a circus sideshow. Truth is, the idea that anyone ever thought it was fun to go stare and point at people with odd medical conditions makes me sick.

But now and then you get ideas that, no matter how repulsive, just live on and on for generations, sticking like a dingleberry in the ass hairs of culture. Kids my age still use the idea to insult each other—just from the fact that some horrible part of us can still imagine doing that, and still knows how to mock the bearded lady, the midget, and the dog-faced boy. I'd bet you it had a lot to do with the way that the word "froyk" formed right away, from people reading "froid-K" and not knowing it was French, and grafting it together any which way—cause it sounded like freak and that's what those creatures are.

So if you're a roundito or roundita my age, when the subject is Marsform people, and all that land and resources they're getting for free, "freak" or "sideshow" are the words that come popping out of your mouth. Just as naturally as spiders lay eggs and slugs leave slime trails, I suppose . . .

Well, course that word was something that Dad wasn't gonna have in his family. A good-hearted man like Telemachus Murray wouldn't put up with it, period. He laid into me in a very I'm-the-boss kinda way. "That land belongs to them. Period. By treaty. And we are gonna learn to get along with'em, and learning to get along means mutual respect, which means among other things that you don't go across somebody's property without their permission. End of story. End of subject. We're going around. Is that clear?"

"It's clear."

"And the next time I hear the word 'freak' out of your mouth—or any other rude word for Marsforms—I hope you're a Full Adult so that I can give you a beating and have it be simple assault instead of child abuse."

The right thing to say would have been "I'm sorry," followed by "I was wrong," so it stands to reason, being I'm a moron and all, that what I said was, "It's a long walk for a stupid principle."

"How do you know something's a principle till it gives you some trouble, hunh? If you won't put yourself to some trouble about it, it's not a principle, it's just a comforting slogan."

"That's how I know this is not my principle, Dad. So I'm taking a long walk for your principle—"

So he yelled at me, madder than before cause I'd said

it wasn't my principle, and course I yelled back at him, mad as all hell because life was so full of disappointment and Dad never seemed to understand me at all, and we probably lost half an hour to that, with neither of us changing the other's mind, nothing gained.

But Doc, it was still nineteen kim to avoid trespassing for seven, and it was still a lot less than an hour's earnings in fines. Dad was still so wrong. See, we were in the Prome, which is so rugged that even the government could do the sensible thing and give that to the froyks. (We oughta have kept rights to the rubbies, though, if anyone was asking me.)

Now, the Prome, it's a pretty big area; we were just cutting the tip of a corner of it, where a long tongue of basin-rim smashed country sticks out about four hundred kim, just about due west, between 55 and 60 degrees south. Straight ahead of us was supposed to be the westernmost territory of the Austral Nation, just as soon as the Austral Nation had enough froyks to populate their territories— right now they didn't have a member over thirty years old and way more'n half of what they had was children, or puppies, or whatever you call the little ones.

After our visit to the broad crater where Dad thought he'd find his methane scorehole, we'd be turning back west and descending into the gentler (but still plenty rugged) ridges and channels of Mollyland. The trouble was, once they gave the Austral Nation the great heap of dirt that was the Prome, the next thing they did was worry that they might not have access to other settlements, so they gave'em a skoshy southwesterly hook of an "access corridor" into Mollyland—and the edge of that hook, only about seven kim wide where we would've crossed, lay square in our path.

So that was what it was all about, Doc, and as to how I felt, well, he'as wrong then and if he'as here today with us I'd still say he'as wrong and that's that. Contract's a contract but you can't make one with an animal.

But it was dumb, dumb, dumb to get into it. One of those arguments where if you think for half a second before you get into it, you already know everything about it—how it's gonna start, proceed, what each side will say, how it will end, right on out to the apologies and the forgetting about it. Only I guess I'm guaranteed to forget about it, hunh, Doc? Except that then this tape guarantees I'll remember. Hope you don't mind my saying, Doc, but your job is posreal weird.

Dad'n'me rooed along the broken top of a crater rim instead of on a smooth lava plain, me not speaking to him, him doing his best to ignore me. We ended up having to cross two extra gulleys to get to the foot of the crater that dented the wall of the crater we were interested in, near where a big massif that Dad had named Gateway reared up two and a half kim above the land around it. All so the froyks wouldn't have their wasteland walked on. I guess I never did understand my father.

⬡ Teri should have passed her FA the year before, or even the year before that. In my generation she would have.

Tantrums are no reason not to declare you an adult. Hell, to judge by the people I work with, they're part of your qualification.

Her Dad had a bad habit of telling his little girl the truth, too. Probably spoiled her for life. Just as well that if she gets her way she'll live out in the roundings forever, I suppose. She sure isn't fit to be back here among us.

I do hope that when she passes by Red Sands City, she'll drop by and visit. We can have dinner or a drink together, and just enjoy sitting in a room with one of the few other people that knows why we wake in the middle of the night and stare into the dark and hope to perceive nothing.

I reach for the bottle and stop myself for a moment; I'm just at *that* point.

But I'm off duty and nothing comes in for weeks at a time here—nothing in my line. The regular beat cops are coping with what frontier cities have been like all through history, so they have lots of petty theft and brawling and all that. But usually those aren't crimes people do for weird reasons, and that's what I am, the department of people who do things for weird reasons—where I make sure that their weird reasons are only weird, and not terrifying.

I think up a new title for myself: the officer in charge of the inexplicable. That's my job. The Grand Explicator.

Even when the weird reasons are not the bad weird reason, I'm sometimes useful. Frontiers have always drawn strange people, people who have been hurt and picked on for their strangeness all their lives, who just decide to flee from the cruel picking monkeys that make up most of the human race. Such strange people tend to run to where it's quiet. And lonely. And the loneliness will then make them weirder.

Of course I know a bit about that, too. Other cops avoid me because I don't seem like them in general and we don't have much in common. Besides, people like me are prime targets of memes and we've been memed and de-memed before, so people avoid us because of the human tradition of avoiding the unlucky. Then again maybe the real reason for avoiding me, and most of my shrink colleagues, is that we're lonely, and our loneliness has made us weird.

Not that we had any choice.

Hell, hell, and hell again. I pour myself another. Anesthesia. Greek for no feeling.

I'm already thinking like a drunk.

But, as I said, being a drunken shrink at least has a history, runs as far back as the profession runs. Which is pretty far if like me you count barkeeps, priests, and whores among the profession. Actually when I think about some of my colleagues I'm not sure they come up to that standard. Despising the profession is another tradition with a long history. I take a swallow and realize it wasn't a sip; well, it's been a month or more since I just plain got bombed, and here we go, eh? One for tradition, two for history, and as many as it takes for anesthesia. . . .

The first settlers didn't get here till 2014, still less than ninety years ago, and Mars already has too much history. Mostly it's the story of one long race to catch up, of the eternal discovery that it was later than we thought and that we only had a short time to get things in order before the next onrushing disaster ground over us.

The early settlers, back in the twenty-teens, had been rushed out here early in Reconstruction, after the Eurowar. The bioweapons that were de-terraforming the Earth looked like they might well just sweep everything before them, and with billions dead and billions more at risk, the human race had to take every long shot there was. In the late twentieth century, Mars always hung about fifteen years of development in the future, and nobody ever started; Mars was possible by 1985 in 1970, and by 2000 in 1985, and so forth. Then our idiot species, trying to win a war that wasn't about much of anything, had gone and really broken the biosphere, maybe for good, and as engineered plagues and blights and nightmare weeds and pests had spread over a planet whose climate was thrashing out of control, it had gone from "we must get around to getting to Mars someday" in 1994 to "can we get there fast enough?" by 2004.

Everyone, from Pope Paul John Paul, almost the only symbol of hope there was, down to every farmer in Asia who got up each morning to see how much more of his family's food supply had been lost to Tailored Rice Blast, from the plutocks in their private fortresses to the vags in the ruins, felt the desperation of the postwar years in their guts, uncertain whether the human race was about to lose its birth planet to all the bioweapons turned loose in that great planetary orgy of mutual murder. For the next twenty years, humanity struggled to make sure there were enough places where we had some chance of surviving, as the Earth's ecology continued to reel all over the graphs like a drunk who had already tripped and was about to fall headlong.

Ultimately, it had not quite fallen, whether because space-based industry and food production had relieved the pressure of human demand, or the Earth's environment was marginally more resilient than had been feared, or for some reason we didn't quite understand even yet.

Out here on Mars, the desperation was as deep but the hope was greater, and maybe that contrast made a difference. The people who came up here from Earth as adults—all over fifty years old now—refer to Diaspora One—the founding of settlements in the solar system after the mut-AIDS Die-Off of the 1990s and the Eurowar of the early 2000s—and Diaspora Two, the movement of millions of refugees out to the space colonies at the end of the War of the Memes, in the early 2070s. Native Martians like me talk of four waves. I guess it all depends whether you're pitching or catching.

The First Wave came out here to die at a rate of fifty percent every three years, back before 2025, and the few of them you still see have faces set in stony cold endurance even now. It's whispered that they ate their dead; I believe it. I've had two First Wave rogees, and I don't think I could have understood less about them if I'd tried to psychoanalyze a giraffe or a rock.

My parents, and Telemachus Murray's, were Second Wave; these were the adults from the transfer ships after the bloodless mutinies of the 2020s. They were sad people who laughed now and then, and in my younger years I had a lot of them as patients, mostly for depression, for which thank god there was a pill, because most of them had seen the Die-Off and the Eurowar and then been thrown out of their comfortable homes on the transfer ships, and mostly they just wanted to put their time in and die. I learned not to talk to them unless they wanted to talk (at which point it was my job to let them unload their horrible stories on me) but mostly to just give them the pills.

The Third Wave, much bigger than the first two put together, were Mars's first real optimists. To this day you find that towns like RSC, founded during the Third Wave, are more lively and have more sports teams, performance spaces, dance clubs, and bars than the older cities. The Third Wave were the ones who scraped together enough during the Gray Decade to try to get a fresh start out here; they came from a jobless Earth of ruined hopes to a place where, as they said, at least there was always work.

The Fourth Wave was the Second Diaspora: the post-War of the Memes wave. Good people, lots of them; some as traumatized as the First and Second, some as free as the Third, but lots of them.

People make all kinds and sorts and orders of distinctions between them, and there are plenty—I see them all the time. I came here at age three, with my folks, so for practical purposes I was a Third Waver, and to this day my accent will get me a table near the kitchen and the slowest service in the universe in any restaurant in Wells City or Marinersburg. Then from later in my life, there's a scar on my left index finger that I got from breaking a bottle over the head of an uppity Fourth Waver, some idiot just off the transfer ships, during those years in my late twenties that I don't really remember at all, back when I spent too much time with the regular cops and not enough time staring quietly out the window and thinking.

Nowadays I do more thinking but I don't have a window. After the Sunburst, I'm not sure how many Martians ever will. That might become a defining mark of our culture, at least till the air is thick enough. Something that bridges all four waves and their descendants . . . if anything will. I suspect that when the Grand Fleet comes in, three hundred years from now, the descendants of the First Wave will still think the descendants of the Fourth Wave are riffraff and newcomers.

Probably there will be no Fifth Wave, ever, unless the Grand Fleet brings it. Everyone on Earth is running the Resuna meme, which means they are all perfectly happy with One True, so they aren't going to decide to leave (unless it sends them, and they'd have to get past the watchers on the Moon and the dozens of guardposts, all orbiting the Earth a few light-seconds out so they can't be memed, all at least nervous and most downright trigger-happy, and then past Planetary Defense here, and past the militia wherever they landed).

Even if unhappiness were still possible on Earth, there's much less to be unhappy about these days, anyway.

Under One True, Earth is recovering rapidly, and more species recreated from preserved genetic samples are being added to its mix every year. There were celebrations throughout both the individual and the memed parts of the solar system last year, when the recovery projects on Earth brought back tigers, moose, polar bears, and sperm whales, the first wobbly babies emerging from the incubators, forerunners of what would some day be wild populations again.

Mars is a living world, now, not dependent on Earth any more; human colonies dot the asteroid belt and reach as far in as Mercury—well, they did, and they will again, as soon as the suriving colonists get out of the hospitals, the rescue crews finish restoring the facilities, and the robots finish digging the newer, deeper colonies. Hell, there's at least two hundred Mercurian survivors here on Mars, in long-term care, that have already applied to move back as soon as they're well enough.

There have been human settlements on Titan for fifty years and there's talk of reaching all the way out to Triton soon. And even though Earth is one vast hive mind under One True, just the same, life is finding its way back, and if the grip of Resuna is firm, it's also light, and the people there are conspicuously still human. Despite all the chain of human disasters that began with President Bush being found dead in his bed in 1993, and ended—well, maybe they haven't, let's not tempt fate by saying they have—despite a century of nightmares, we're on our way back; killing off humanity has proved harder than it looked, so hard that even humanity itself has not managed the task.

Damn, we're a great species. I toast us in the mirror,

pour another one, and let myself run through all the evil I've seen, and in no time at all I've reversed my opinion completely; we are all vicious devils in the ugly bodies of horny monkeys. I drink to that, and to my clear-headed perception of it. I know from past experience that I can keep this alternation going for several hours, and still manage to stagger home and call in sick tomorrow.

But I don't want to. What I was doing, was replaying my way through the recordings of Teri's interviews with me, because of that message I got from her. I need to slow down on the bottle and get on with the viewing. I put the cap on and put it back into the worktable drawer, out of easy reach; then I click up the next part on my screen. I should check the clock but I don't. I already know it must be completely dark outside.

❧ **So is today** another talk-about-nothing-that-matters day, Doc? I kinda liked doing that yesterday. I guess I like to talk more'n is good for a roundita. Especially when the subject is anything I feel like and I'm with some poor guy that has to listen. No, don't try and tell me you wanna. If you really wanted to they wouldn't hafta pay you, would they, Doc? I mean it stands to reason.

Well, okay, if we can talk about anything here, today I wanna talk about methane. If you want rubbies, you really can't beat methane. At least the government figures its value really high, so the Development Corporation pays plenty for it, and all those smart guys're supposed to know.

To begin with, it's a powerful greenhouse gas, and its spectrum of absorption is different from carbon dioxide, so it picks up and traps warmth that goes right through CO_2, so that's one effect you get paid for. Secondly, it's way lighter than Mars's CO_2 atmosphere, and it floats upwards and builds up in the upper atmosphere, insulating the surface and helping it get warmer, like a pot on a stove warms faster and boils sooner if you put a lid on it. And third, they pay for it cause when it goes away, by reacting with oxygen, it turns into water and CO_2 and both of those are rubbies in their own right.

So methane does nothing but good, it's the best of all the common rubbies, and releasing a big methane pocket, whether it burns or just leaks, will get enough money out of the Development Corporation to set a family up forever.

The Promes is about as rough as any country on Mars, or at least as any country that anybody goes to. It's a patch of smashed and twisted land where all the stuff that was dug up in the impact that formed the Hellas Basin got thrown. Then sometime long after, a bunch of magma shoved its way up here and there and made massifs—the one we were passing just south of, that afternoon, which Dad was calling the Gateway, stretched way up into the sky above the horizon.

When I called up the virtual werp on my faceplate screen and checked, Gateway Massif was 2600 meters above areode, and it was higher than that above us cause we were going down into a deep, sixty-five-kim-across crater on the south side of it that was probably 300 meters below areode at the bottom. Dad had laid out a path that took us up one steep crater side and down another, then we would follow the ridgeline of the crater we were after, and late in the day start our descent, trying to at least get into the area that would have sunlight in the morning. It was almost the equinox, heading into autumn in the Southern Hemisphere, and right after Gather, everyone would be heading over to the railroad spur that ran southeast from Red Sands City, to head north for the spring and summer up there. Dad hadn't wanted to leave a potential scorehole this rich for someone else to beat him to next spring, so we were gonna try and get something going in that crater while we had the chance.

Rooing uphill in broken country like that was challenging, but it wasn't anything new to either of us, and we made good time, pushing on to get out of the most broken-up areas before night fell. Mostly it was just making sure your feet touched down on reasonably hard ground or on boulders too big to flip. For the hour before and the hour after lunch, we went up and up, that huge massif to our right, the broken wall of a partial crater to our left. They say in school that the more craters there are in a stretch of dirt, the older it is, and I guess this stuff was really old. Crater walls ran into crater walls, and lots of them were mostly choked with debris; even the places, here and there, where some volcanic rock had pushed its way up, were noticeably weathered more'n most of what you see on Mars.

Still not speaking to each other, though I know I'd gotten over the fight and I don't think Dad was really mad, either, anymore, we stopped to sit and drink some water, and eat a quick half-ration, when we topped the edge of the smashed crater-in-the-side-of-the-crater wall, and looked down into the deep valley in front of us. Usually on Mars the horizon's just a skosh over three kim away—you can roo to it in twenty minutes. I checked on the virtual werp and from up here, we were seeing crater wall more'n eighty kim distant, and to our right the dark wall of Gateway Massif flung itself a full kim higher into the sky than we were, steep and fierce. We took a long time on the half-ration—I was having tomato soup, when you're getting close to a Gather you tend to have all your favorites—and contemplating the space in front of us, when Dad said, "And doesn't it seem like we're the only people in the world?"

"It does," I agreed.

"Bet it'll seem even more that way after we get down into the crater. What do you think?"

"I think if we're gonna try, we'd better get started."

"That's the girl I raised."

It had been a peace offering. I was glad he'd made it.

Sometimes crater rims are really awful for rooing, if they've pitted and collapsed badly, but this one wasn't bad at all. We headed southwest, retreating from the Gateway

Massif and descending the long curve of the crater wall; according to the satellite pictures Dad had, in about two hours there oughta be a long, gentle slope down into the crater that we could descend safely.

The sun swung round behind us, getting far to the north now that fall was here, and continued on westward, so that by the time we turned northwest to make our descent, our shadows reached fairly far up the slope behind us, and we hadda dim faceplates quite a bit cause the sun was full on our faces. At least it had been an easy pathway—we'd barely hadda take an APS fix all day, not like the way it was down in flatter country.

I had more or less shoved the whole disappointment of Dad's decision to the back of my mind by that evening, when we stretched out on an east-facing dune, and I looked back up that long, long slope that we'd just descended and watched the first stars rising.

Then I realized it was time to com Perry and break the news to him. He'd be disappointed and sometimes when he was disappointed he got sulky and angry and was no fun or support for me at all. For a moment I thought about just waiting to tell him the bad news at the Gather, but that seemed unfair to him and cowardly besides. So I swallowed hard and commed him.

But even though there was bad news and we'd hafta face up to it sooner or later, that didn't mean I hadda lead off with it. When he first came on the com I asked him how his day had been. Not that there was gonna be much news, really. His family party was now just walking toward the Gather in Mollyland, with no more stops to make. But whatever news he had would keep me from having to give mine.

"Eahh, you know," he said, sounding awkward and bored as he always did when there wasn't some direct purpose to the conversation. "We rooed and rooed and rooed, bounced over some stuff, set off a few seismos just to see if there was anything interesting—there wasn't—"

I could have told you that, I thought. Dad was always saying that Perry's whole family tended to just try things aimlessly rather than figure them out, and I was always annoyed cause Dad was right. After we were married, Perry would hafta learn to do a little thinking in advance.

He had warmed up a skosh and was actually describing his day, but just as I had expected, his news was no news. "We checked the magnetometers and the background radiation to see if there was anything there, and zip," he said. "We seem to be crossing rock that's barren right down to the core. But this South Hellas country is so crowded that we've seen two other parties just today, off in the distance. Used to be you got south of Red Sands City and there was nothing, and now the furthest railhead away is six hundred kim. And I guess they're gonna let a contract to have some roads thumped down into here, and set up some ranches. It's really getting crowded. It must be much nicer where you are."

"Thank you," I said, though I knew it wasn't intended as a compliment. Perry never gave compliments. I did keep hoping (in vain) that he might be teachable.

"So you still have one more stop to do?" he asked, though he'd probably known that for a week.

"Dad thinks there might be a good place to try a deep driller, where there's some kinda interesting seismo stuff. Very near the Gather, actually, in a straight line, though there's more'n you want to see of rough country between the site and the Gather, so we'll probably make it to the Gather the second day after we deep drill. I'll tell you all about it at the Gather, win or lose."

"Do that." Then he didn't speak for a while. He wasn't too much of a talker. He liked ecospecting, and could talk about that some, but the other things he liked were food and sex and he hardly talked about those at all, whether they were good or not. "Uh, we're gonna hafta spend some time together at the Gather."

"Of course, silly."

"Oh, yeah. Um, right, I am being silly." There was another long pause.

So we had run out of the pleasant, easy part of the conversation. Time to show some guts. I swallowed hard and explained about how I was gonna be stuck in school for another year. When I'd finished, I waited to see if he'd be disappointed, angry, frustrated, sad . . . I was betting on all of them.

So of all the stupid things to say, Perry said that well, it might be good for me, and I asked whose side he was on and that just seemed to confuse him, and pretty soon everything each of us said was irritating the other, and in no time at all we were clicking off; the last thing I said was that I'd com him tomorrow, and he didn't even say that much.

Well, I figured, Perry wasn't too good at expressing feelings, and it kinda made sense, in an awful kinda way.

He couldn't tell me he was hurt and disappointed and that two more seasons—that would be a whole year on Earth, just about—was gonna be a long, long time. So feeling all that frustration, and being the guy he was, knowing that he'd be putting up with a long wait . . . course, he got all sullen and uncommunicative, and picked a fight with me.

Understanding him perfectly, however, did nothing for the fact that I really needed a good cry, and I didn't care whether the monitors picked it up or not, cause it had been a long day, and I was tired, and I was limward disappointed, and Dad was for sure already asleep—he was always like a dead man two minutes after he lay down—so I had no company but the bright stars, moons, and satellites that dotted the pitch-black sky above. I clamped down hard, trying to hold it in, but it didn't hold very well, so I just switched off all sending on all the com channels, and let myself go, sobbing and shaking there in the sand.

"Teri?" Dad spoke softly.

I clicked my voice back on. "Yeah?"

"Are you all right?"

"No. But it's not serious. I'm just crying."

"Is it about—"

"Yeah." I tried to make that sound as final as possible.

"I'm sorry."

"I know. I just hate it, so I'm crying." I paused and then some impulse made me say, "I talked to Perry and it didn't go so well."

"That's almost a surprise," Dad said. "Did he get upset?"

"He didn't say so, or say anything, but I could tell. I

can always tell," I said. I seemed not to be crying as much. I started the face wipe inside my helmet, getting the mess cleaned up.

Dad said, "Well, I guess that's to be expected."

I wanted to say *Yeah, course, cause you're an old pig-head,* or something like that, but I'd been working so hard at understanding everything, all day long, that I guess I wasn't up for spite or silliness. "I wasn't really crying cause *he* was upset." I said. "Posreal. Really I'm just kinda shaky because of plain old tiredness and delayed disappointment. I'll be okay. You can go back to sleep."

"You're sure?"

"I'm sure."

Alone with my thoughts again, I felt all cried out. I commed a light-classics music channel that I liked. Of course it was like something out of some corny film to put on the light classics while lying here in the Martian sand, so far from anyone and anything, looking up the magnificent crater wall with the Southern Cross hanging high above and the Magellanic Clouds close enough to touch, but if ever there was a night for it, this was the one. I turned a skosh so I could watch the chondreors come in—they were still crashing a few of'em on the CO_2 glaciers around the South Pole.

The impact was 2000 kim away, but chondreors travel fast and high up. Here in the high latitudes, up beyond fifty degrees south, they entered their final approach almost bang overhead and then glowed all the way down to the horizon, a bright silent fire in the sky that lasted about six minutes each time. It wasn't as impressive as it had been a week back, when we'd actually been up working close to the Antarctic Circle and the chondreors had been going from horizon to horizon in almost nine minutes, but the stately progress of the great fireballs from the zenith southward across the sky, one or two in an hour, each with its long golden tail, was still one of those things that could make me ask myself how anyone could ever stand to be a sitter.

I lay there and let the peace work its way into me, under that bright sky full of stars with the chondreors marching across, listening to *Appalachian Spring*, with the program set so that it would fade down in a few minutes. Just as dawn came up, it would return to full volume with the *Canon in D Minor*. There are times when the world is a corny place, and about all you can do is harvest the corn.

The looming crater wall in front of me brightened as Phobos rose behind me, a sliver now, waxing as it went, on its slow way east. The little low communication satellites, forever changing orbits and moving to better positions, so that I could see a rocket motor flicker now and then, shot past the lower moon, like courtiers in a dance around a queen in one of those stupid shows they put on at school.

For an instant the night sky merged into the music and both merged into this dream, beautiful to the limward, where all the stars, moons, and satellites danced to the music, before, at last, I dropped into sleep like a chondreor into the sea, my mind fading away like the flare behind it.

From the moment we planted our first pingers the next morning, we knew something good was gonna happen.

You hafta have the first couple of pingers planted on solid ground, a couple of kim apart and far back from the pocket, so that you have a really good basis for comparison to feed to the AIs when they're coming up with the imaging. When we planted our first pinger, we were already over pocket; it rang like a bell. From what it told us there had to be at least a seventy-meter depth of gas-filled space way down there, 13.8 kim below the surface. We ended up re-climbing the crater wall halfway, planting a pinger a full kim east of where we'd slept, to get even one over real solid rock. Even if this pocket was just CO_2, it was gonna be the biggest scorehole in a long time for us.

And, like Dad said, no one had ever found CO_2 at that depth.

For the rest of the morning, we were both on continuous APS, rooing all over the landscape. We each started out with twenty pingers, and normally we'd have planted them at half-kim or kim intervals. The pocket under the ground was so huge that we ended up setting pingers at six kim intervals on an eighteen by twenty-four kim grid, and even if you roo at a good steady eight kim per hour starting right at sunrise and taking no breaks, that's still twenty stations to set, and each of us had a good forty kim to cover, all told, between getting our survey benchmarks set, getting all the pingers down, and then getting out of the area.

Once we had the pingers set and did our first few echo tests, the analysis clearly showed the optimal target—a place where a big chamber reached three hundred and fifty meters closer to the surface, and it looked like there was one smooth ceiling more'n a kim across. The highest spot on that roof was limward closer for Dad, so he was the one who rooed a few kim back into the target area, placed the beacons, and then APS'd to the exact spot to stencil down the bullseye. We still had about two hours till impact when he was done, plenty of time for him to get a safe distance away, but not nearly enough for the two of us to rejoin each other, so we sat down to wait till the show was over.

At least it was a chance for a good, full chargeup. I spread out my whole 200 × 100 array of solar collectors, all ten panels, on a sun-facing hill, and plugged in. I stretched out and just enjoyed the feeling of perfect air flowing over me, of venting all the tanks and cleaning them completely before filling up with fresh condensate, and of having as much electric power as I wanted, to enjoy everything. I even switched on the power massage and the muscle warmers and let myself get completely relaxed.

I know there are ecospectors who use times like that to read, or watch entertainment programs, or play games with other people on the net; for me, just the pleasure of looking right out through the faceplate and not having to glance at the edges for a single readout, and of knowing that all the reserves, power, oxygen, and water, were going up, not down, was a pleasure to be reveled in. I stretched out on a big flat rock, facing the impact spot, and luxuriated better than anyone I know except Pywacket, the cat they have at school.

(And Pywacket is a professional—he practices constantly).

It was about an hour and a half past noon when Dad called on the satcell to say that he was sitting comfy, too, and added, "We're at about an hour ten to impact, Teri. When was the last time we did a deep driller?"

"Last Southern Spring, I think," I said. "That deep ice deposit. Quite a while, anyway."

"Well, if I'm right, this is gonna be the biggest show anyone's had in a long time. You got your camera on?"

"Yes, Dad. And I closed my faceplate before I left the tajj."

"No need for sarcasm. I just wanted to make sure we have all the pictures we can get. You don't get bragging rights like these every day."

"Fair enough," I said. "As long as we're triple-checking, we meet up on the rim afterwards, due south of the impact?"

"We do, and thanks for rechecking."

There wasn't anything else to talk about really, so I just lay back to enjoy the warmth and all the optional things you can have with abundant suit-power; I assumed Dad was doing the same. Every year, as the oxygen content of the atmosphere continues to increase, exosuits hafta work a bitty skosh less hard to get lox into your storage tank; when I was a little girl it had seemed to take the whole day for a small child's pack, but nowadays, with the whole 200 × 100 spread out if you didn't move much, you could have a full charge—water, lox, fuel cells, and batteries—in about an hour and a half.

No matter what happened right after the deep driller hit, we wouldn't be moving for a while; things hadda settle out before it was safe to go in and pick up whatever pingers had survived. There were always secondary collapses, breakthroughs, sinks, and all sortsa things for a while after. You never could tell what might spread along a fissure, so the best thing to do was to be in the middle of a good solid slab of rock, which is what my exosuit's built-in pinger was saying this was.

It was such a nice afternoon, and I had been scrambling so hard that morning to get everything placed, that I almost drifted asleep while waiting. I came out of my half-doze with a start and checked the time; still ten minutes to go, so I set the alarm for one minute till and let myself drift, but I no longer felt like sleeping. I ate a suitration, and drank water, and then it was time.

The thing you never get used to is that there's no visible motion; a deep driller starts into the atmosphere at ten kim per second or so, and picks up maybe two more kim per second by the time it impacts, so you don't see an object descending, you see the white-hot streak of superheated air that expands outward from where it just passed, ending in a sun-bright ball where the normal-matter parts of the deep driller have instantaneously vaporized. A bright line in the sky connected to a bright half-ball on the surface appears instantly, the way a painting in a dark room does when someone turns on the light; one side of a blink it's this way, other side it's that.

Then the surface shock wave arrived, rolling like the big slow waves on the Boreal Ocean do after a chondreor strike in the sea. The surface sand around my little island of rock roiled and fluidized for a few seconds. Subsurface rock heaved up in a moving ridge two meters high that rolled under me. My little boat of rock rode it out just fine, though quite an impressive crack opened up half a kim in front of me, zigzagging over the horizon back toward ground zero. I checked my radar; nothing solid, so far, had gotten thrown into the sky, so no need to take cover.

The horizon erupted.

Methane'll burn at very low concentrations of oxygen, even just what's in our Martian air. This was thousands of tons of methane shot into the atmosphere like a blast out of a cannon, driven by the heat and pressure of the neutronium expanding back to normal matter, and all of it had just rushed through a tunnel hot enough for rock to run like gooey soup. A mighty column of blue-white flame reached up, according to what my camera recorded, just over eight kim into the sky, and at its top a cloud began to form rapidly; each molecule of methane, when burned, releases two molecules of water and one of carbon dioxide, and it was cold up there; the water was freezing out and falling back as snow.

The smaller shock wave arrived, making the ground buck and dance for a second time, just as the first big puff of cloud appeared at the top of the blazing pillar. When I looked up again, it looked like a welding torch, swathed in streaks of white cloud, blasting against the pink dome of the sky, topped by an immense, spreading, roiling cloud; even as I watched the icy clouds were stretching out to cover the blue aureole surrounding the sun.

It was about as close to perfect as a deep driller shot gets. I became aware of a noise in my earpiece, and realized that even with my external mikes turned off, the rumble had been so intense I had been able to hear nothing else. Now that I could hear my earpieces again, I heard Dad shouting "Eee-*yah-HU*!" over and over.

Just like that, we were rich.

❧ **So many times,** I've played this recording and wished the story ended there, and that there was no reason to listen to it except for Teri's voice. It was the biggest day of Teri's brief life-as-an-adult up to that point, I think. She was finding her emotional maturity and also finding out that you can be very mature without getting rewarded for it, and while still being quite unhappy. Her bigotry was normal for a roundita of her generation; the ecospectors had been given the roundings with the understanding that they would make a living from it, and their remotest descendants would, for terraforming Mars was supposed to be a very long-term project. The success of the Mars-forms took everyone by surprise, but once it was realized that humans could adapt to Mars better than they could adapt Mars to humans, that Mars could be "finished" in two centuries instead of twenty-five, there was no chance that the impossibly expensive project would be completed. This was sad and regrettable, and it would mean that the promise of "down to your remotest descendants" wouldn't be kept—and this in dealing with people who worship contracts.

I shudder when I think about what that's going to mean in a few years, when it becomes clear to everyone, and not just the smart ones.

I'm loose and comfortable and feeling warm, but not terribly drunk. I consider whether I want to see the recording of yet another session before I record a message to send back to Teri. Perhaps I can compromise . . . certainly I'll feel better if I just eat something. And there are plenty of places still open. I could go get a big slab of tank-grown steak, and follow it up with a load of potatoes and vegetables . . . this is sounding better and better.

And it's not like I need to play the next recording. It's one of the ones I played most often, back when I was the main investigator into the "unfortunate incidents" as bureaucratic tradition dubbed them. I wondered what other things in history had been called unfortunate incidents— the Crucifixion? the burning of the library of Alexandria?

Hiroshima? Probably all of them were called that by somebody doing the paperwork, I would think.

I get up from the desk, lock a few things up, emphatically including the bottle, and toss the glass into the washerslot on the wall. I wonder if that gadget reports, to anyone, that there is frequently liquor in the wastewater.

Then I lock the place up, not sure whether I'll be back before tomorrow—I can just as easily com or message Teri from home—and start down the escalators; there's a Kwame's that fronts on the park that serves pretty good barbecued steaks and chops, and the idea just keeps seeming more appealing.

It seems strange to me that Teri and her father never even remotely discussed just retiring with a scorehole that size. Neither of them would have had to work another day, ever, nor would any of their descendants. I sometimes wonder what might have happened if that thought had occurred to them and they'd acted on it; they might have been inside a city when the Sunburst hit.

Maybe I just wish I'd gotten to meet Telemachus Murray.

But hardly any Martian would give up working just because of being rich, and the few that would wouldn't be rounditachi, and if you could find a roundito that was willing to be idly rich, it wouldn't be an ecospector. Mars isn't that kind of place; just because you're rich, or famous, doesn't mean you stop or even especially take it easy—you want the respect of your neighbors and fellow citizens too much.

⬡ **Doc, today, if** you don't mind, let's skip the starting with what doesn't matter, and just pick up the story. I agree with you that that was a pretty good trick to get me talking, but I'm getting better and better at telling my story, and I think from here on out I can just tell it. That's gotta be better for you, anyway, to get to skip the preliminaries, right? I mean it stands to reason.

So, anyway, once we knew there wouldn't be big rocks out of the sky or many more major fissures opening up, Dad'n'me rooed around to the south edge of the crater. There was still two hours of daylight left and we figured we might as well get somewhere comfortable before we set up the tajj for the night; Dad had a lead on a spring and that might even mean a warm bath, which is so nice to do *before* you get to a Gather.

I waited to bring it up till it was pretty clear that this next half hour, just descending the outer edge of the crater, was gonna be a nice easy one, more or less just bouncing down the hill. We rooed two-footed like little kids most of the way—little kids who had just become bazillionaires.

"Dad," I said, "Let me ask you something. Since you

and me are rich now, it would take a long time to spend all of it, wouldn't it?"

"Teri, thanks to the magic of compound interest, I don't know if we *could* ever spend all of it. Certainly not the way we live."

"Well, then, if I married Perry, and the two of us partnered up and worked hard at ecospecting . . . even if the bottom fell out, so that we didn't earn a millicredit, not even gross, for years . . . well, we'd still be in business and working, wouldn't we? So it's not so important to be able to take another job—"

"You're right," Dad said. "My guess is that low end, this scorehole's worth three million credits, and high, maybe as much as twenty; six to eight is what I'm guessing. Your share is half that, and a little two-person operation like you and me have doesn't cost even ten thousand a year to keep going, counting food, medicine, gear, and exosuits . . . so if you and Perry wanna be ecospectors, and nothing but, well, I guess you're set. That does change some things." He thought for a second, took a running leap, and went up a cliffside, half running the last steps against it, a little trick that he'd taught me ages ago. I knew he wanted to see me do it, so just to be a skosh annoying, I took a harder leap, springing off a boulder, and made it in one bound. "Nice landing," he said, cause it was.

"Why'd we just do this?"

"Takes out two kim we'd otherwise've hadda go, around a canyon down below us," he said.

Well, that was Dad; he wouldn't walk on empty land cause the froyks had a title, but he'd do all kinds of bizarre physical things to save some steps. Posreal I never understood that man; probably I didn't need to, anyway. Not to love him or for him to love me.

"Can you give me the rest of the day to think?" Dad asked. "I think you're right and you'll be able to marry Perry at the Gather. And we'll work something out. But I wanna think for a while, before I say anything definite. Probably it's all gonna go the way you'd like, and chances are that I'm gonna say that to you sometime by the end of the day today . . . but I wanna think and digest and get it set in my own head that what you've got in mind is the best way. Would that be all right?"

"You're gonna try and come up with some reason for me to finish school," I said. I tried not to whine cause you never know when they're listening.

"I am. And to be honest, right now, I can't see one. But if you give me a chance to figure things from all sides, and to weigh it out in my head that there really isn't any better way than what you wanna do, and so on, then once I've gotten that settled into my own mind, you can have my whole-hearted consent, as long as you pass that FA. So you've got what you want, Teri. Just give me two zilties to adjust."

"That's fair," I conceded.

"Then let's get the day's rooing done, get down to that spot where there might be a spring that we were looking at the seismics on earlier, and maybe get there a skosh early so we can enjoy the tajj, or so we can decide to push on, which- ever looks better to you and me when we get there. All right?"

"All right."

The problem wasn't my lack of education. It was Dad's. Just exactly cause he hadn't seen much of it he had way, way too limward a respect for it. His great-grandfather Cornelius had been one of the Second Wave of settlers, the people off the transfer ships, and had actually been a college professor, Ph.D. and everything, back on Earth, before the Die-Off and the Eurowar and all that stuff. My grandfather, Philip Murray, had been born on Mars fairly late in his parents' lives—he had a brother and sister he never met, on the *Flying Dutchman*—and he had grown up with just a standard CSL school education plus two years of tech school, and, I think, always felt inferior to his father and to his older sibs.

Anyway, Dad had left CSL school as soon as he and Mummy had passed their FAs and married; it was back when they were screaming for ecospectors and the Development Corporation paid him a big bonus for doing that. So the amount of schooling in the Murray family had been dropping for a century, and if it had been up to me it could have dropped clear to zero.

Mummy's people, the Tharsisitos—there were just her parents and my aunt Callie—had never been much on schooling one way or the other, but since she'd died when I was seven, we'd mostly lost touch with'em. For sentimental reasons, I guess, we used them as our teeper, and got mail rockets from their launch site every couple of weeks, but we never talked or wrote about much except the next order or the last one.

The Tharsisitos had been ecospectors for a while, but they had moved to Goddard and set up as teepers, though the business was hard-pressed to support them and Callie. I saw them whenever we passed through there, every couple of years; as far as they were concerned, whatever schooling I got was strictly irrelevant. So was anything else I did. Dad said Mummy had made him promise that he'd never make me visit them, but me'n'him did anyway, whenever we passed that way. I liked Callie and felt sorry for her, stuck with those parents of hers.

The whole time as we bounced down one steep slope after another, every few leaps, I was struck again and again by how much money we'd just made. Now and again, too, we'd hit some place where I would look back and see that huge, still-spreading cloud. I wondered if snow was falling in the crater yet.

Just in case of a fight with Dad, I'd better wait to talk to Perry till this evening. That wasn't an easy decision, but at least it gave me something to look forward to. I was bursting to tell him. We could hold the ceremony the second or third day of Gather—one nice thing about doing anything with rounditachi, it doesn't take long to put anything together—and then buy our tajj and gear on the fourth and fifth, be "at home" for the required visits on the sixth, and be out in the roundings, on our own and starting life . . . nine days from now.

After so much waiting, I couldn't quite believe it, but there it was. I wanted to dance and sing across the rocks.

A year or two ago, I guess I'd've pestered Dad more during that day, but I was working hard on this silly and pointless maturity thing, cause now I *posreal* needed to pass the FA.

That afternoon, he was usually at least a half kim in front of me, which meant he was thinking hard and dinwanna be interrupted unless I broke a leg. I figured that obsessive honesty of his was forcing him to conclude that most of the facts and logic in the case were on my side. I even managed to bite down any impulse to remind him that it wasn't whether you wanted there to be water in the rock, or whether it would be good for there to be water in the rock . . .

We leaped and scrambled down the crater wall, not so much rooing as just using the rocks to stop us from plunging all the way to the bottom. It was such broken country that I was reflexively checking APS every few minutes, and more'n once I found myself already a hundred meters off course, sometimes having wandered in the wrong direction within steps of the last APS fix.

There was still an hour of daylight left when we hit the badlands that formed the last part of the Prome's slope down into Mollyland.

The badlands had been fretted channel country before terraforming. Much of the surface soil had been deep clay. Thicker air and released water had brought rain and snow and even thunderstorms and tornadoes to Mars for the first time in many millions of years, and all the new erosive forces, where there had only been wind before, had found that area easy to cut into. Underground streams were triggering collapses; broad plains were being dissected in just a few years by swift young creeks; canyons that had mostly filled up with windborne debris were scoured clean, and their debris deposited in great fans of soft sand.

It looked very much like the badlands in the old flat-screen movies they showed us in that stupid "The Frontier Tradition" unit in CSL school. I wondered if enough of the water formed by the burning methane would land here and make these channels flow with water; this might be much worse country to cross if every one of these little gullies was a creek. The place was tough enough now; I was shooting APS fixes almost constantly, and it seemed like the way was constantly running out from under my feet and hiding over the nearest hill.

We had gone at almost twelve kim an hour down the crater wall, but in here we were lucky to get three. We had less than an hour of daylight left when we reached the place Dad had picked for our camp.

"Well, Teri, do you wanna push on? I'd rather sleep in the tajj tonight." Dad's voice over the suit-to-suit startled me after so many quiet hours.

"My vote is with the tajj, too."

"Good, then. Check your APS—we're here."

I did. Sure enough, we were only three hundred meters from the spot he'd noted—a cluster of protruding rocks, ten meters high or so, that might offer some shelter if we got a duststorm, with seismics underneath that indicated a possible spring.

A wonderful thought crossed my mind. "Dad, did you save your APS fixes the whole way in?"

"You know I always do; I've got APS fixes going back twenty years, Teri. And you'd better have all of yours, too—I hope I taught you right!"

"Well, I do, in fact," I said. "And I was hitting APS about every two hundred meters or so—it's a huge file."

"I was too, Teri, it's way too easy to get lost in there. What's your point?"

"Well, it stands to reason that we didn't do all our APS fixes at the exact same times. And I was noticing we didn't take on too much rough country here in the badlands— that was a good route you laid out. So I bet if you combine our files, what you have is enough points to map out a trace and thump a road up to the crater wall. And there's enough fixes on both sides of it that from there they could bore a tunnel into the crater. So they could thump a road and bore a tunnel that didn't cross any reservation land at all, right into that crater—where all that water and CO2 are forming. Remember we looked back and saw that Gateway Massif's south side is already snow-covered? All that's gonna drain down into the crater next spring. There's gonna be all kinds of little lakes and ponds and wide flat country with soft dirt under it. Now, if they thump in a road and bore a tunnel, they can open up the whole country to ecospectors. Which means there'll be swarms of'em working around our gas hit, and we'll get secondary royalties on everything they develop back there. I'd bet that in ten years they'll have a city started in the crater wall, and a rail line through that tunnel, and you'n'me'll hafta hire people just to count our money."

Dad whistled; I hate when he does that on suit-to-suit and I can't understand why he won't lose the habit. I whistled back at him to make his eardrums meet in the middle, like mine just had, and he said, "Ouch, right, sorry. Teri, I don't know how I overlooked that . . . I hadn't gotten any further than figuring we had the biggest scorehole in three or four Mars-years to our credit. And here you've figured out how to make it pump money for the next hundred years. We can have an AI do that proposal up, it's so simple, and have it over to the Development Corporation before we go to bed tonight. And if it gets fast-track approval like I think it's bound to, they'll have the road and tunnel in there before next spring, and the first parties'll be in before the equinox. That crater's eighty kim across and right now there's not another claim in it; five thousand square kim of perfect-for-development territory, and we'll get a cut of everything they do in it, probably six percent of everything that depends on our scorehole and then a percent and a half, maybe more, for whatever depends on the road. Don't you forget to tell Perry that besides a cute little girl, he's getting a business genius."

I felt so happy and hugged that it took me a second to realize what he'd said. "So you're gonna—"

"Oh, yeah. No real way to argue against it now. There's one thing I want you to look at, but it's not really a change in your plans, per se, more of just an enhancement you might think about, if you don't mind. I'll tell you about it after dinner. But feel free to say no—I'm expecting you to—and don't feel like I'm pushing you to say yes. Like the teepers always say just before they skin you and hang you out to dry, no obligations."

At the campsite, it was still sunny. This late in the fall, with so much water in the air to settle the red dust, the aureole of deep blue around the sun was bigger than I'd ever seen it, almost a quarter the width of the sky, and the shading from white around the aureole to delicate pink to deep red at the horizon was compressed as if the expanding aureole had jammed it all together. I wondered how long before a Martian was born who never saw a really red sky. A thousand years? Ten thousand? Or if they weren't really gonna finish the job, would those froyk descendants Dad thought we'd have still see skies like this?

When you get those deep skies, you don't get a long

twilight, like you would on Earth; you get a sky dark enough to see bright objects in the daytime. I looked up and figured I was seeing a personal record for bright objects in daylight. A chondreor streaked over, its brilliant white head leaving a trail of orange as it raced for the pole. Phobos and Deimos were both visible, along with two of the low-flying satcell relays that streak around supplying efficient relays and APS, all bright as spangles on a red velvet gown, and I could just pick out Pollux rising, a dim little bright spot in the glare, and—"is that Jupiter just rising?" I asked Dad.

"Hmm, check the almanac. Skoshy too bright."

His tone and the way he wouldn't quite say the word told me what it hadda be, but I did call up a faceplate screen and check the almanac anyway. Of course, it was Earth. Mistaking it for Venus or Jupiter is such a common mistake in people older than me that, in our psych class, they used to cite it as an example of a significant slip of the tongue. So many people on Mars have such a horror of Earth, because it's all held by One True and because the whole Fourth Wave of settlement—probably the last wave we'll ever get—was refugees from One True. As a result, somehow or other, people often manage not to see Earth in the sky, even though it's the next brightest natural body after Phobos and Deimos. We're Second Wave, on both sides of the family, and even Dad and I sometimes slip that way; I knew a few ecospectors of Fourth Wave descent who gave up the roundings and took a job in town, just cause they couldn't stand to see that bright light in the sky. It's not like saying "Earth" is dangerous, the way "let override let overwrite" would be, but a lot of people don't like to remember it's there. They prefer it far away and in the past.

"Hey, Teri, stop staring at the sky and drop a few pingers, I think we have something here," Dad said.

I hurried to help, and in zilty we were looking at a great sonar profile; "I'd bet that's artesian," I said. "This alone would make it a profitable day, let alone the highway we just marked, let alone the scorehole. For some reason we just seem to be on a roll of solid luck."

"Well, those always change," Dad said. "Looks like it's only about ten meters down at its top. How much daylight do we have left?"

I checked the almanac again. "Twenty-six minutes. That's time enough to make a few kig of blasting compound—"

"Just what I had in mind. I'll spread out the sheets and you power up the synthesizer. Let's say make up three kig of carbox slurry, shape it into a meter tube with a deep tip well."

We used explosives all the time, but if we had tried to carry as much as we needed for a season, we'd have been weighed down pretty badly, not to mention prone to abrupt disappearances into clouds of pink mist. Fortunately, the raw materials of explosives are the raw materials of life. While Dad was spreading out and hooking up the solar collector sheets, getting our full array arranged to catch the late afternoon sun, I programmed the synthesizing equipment to produce what he had ordered—three kig of cryogoop, carbon dust and liquid-almost-solid oxygen, which it made by extracting CO_2 from the air, splitting it, and chilling the oxygen. The synthesizer put the mix into a meter-long tube, about three centimeters in diameter, with a deep concave cap at the business end—a shaped charge, one that would direct most of its force in the direction of the "well" at the end. The tube itself was made of an explosive plastic, and would be consumed in the milliseconds after the explosion.

It was almost dark when the tube rolled out; I clipped it to the igniter wires and checked to see how Dad was doing. He'd fussed and fiddled until he'd placed the drill hole right on top of the dome that lay just a few meters below our feet, and he'd bored a two-meter hole there, vitrifying the sides with a welding laser and then adding a skosh of epoxy, so that it would be smooth to slip in the shaped charge and then harden to hold it. We made sure we had a good connection to the detonator, and slid the charge into the hole, letting it drop to the bottom, and hardened the expoxy around it with a trickle current.

By now the shadows were long and the hole was just a small dark circle on the ground in front of us; power coming in from the solar panels was zil, and we were on battery.

"Figured we'd run out of time," Dad said, "so I guess we'll just use sand for packing, maybe set a big rock on top. Oughta do the job."

We pushed sand into the hole until there was a raised dimple where the hole had been. The sun was now fully set, but with Phobos in the sky, we could see well enough without headlamps. I picked up a middling boulder, about eighty kig, and set it on the dimple. "Think that'll do it?" Dad asked.

"Just has to keep the force going mostly down," I said, "and not fly too much itself. Yeah, it oughta be fine."

"And I hate to ask this but—"

"Yes, Dad, I made sure I placed the charge with the business end down." Just once—one stupid time, mind you, just once—I had put a shaped charge in upside down, and when we'd detonated the packing rock had gone sailing into the sky on a bright jet, and Dad'n'me'd hadda run for cover while rock chunks dropped from a kim or more all around us. Stuff like that happens when you're eleven years old, you know, Doc? He was never gonna let me forget that. Every time he mentioned it I wanted to scream, but I was trying posreal hard to be mature.

"Well, then let's back off and do it."

We moved to a comfortable spot perhaps fifty meters off—you never know what these things are gonna do so it's best not to stand right on top of'em—and Dad said, "You wanna blast it off?"

"Uh, I'm not a little kid, it's not a big deal."

"Didn't ask if you were a little kid. Asked if you wanna set it off. . . ."

"Well, sure," I admitted. He handed me the detonator control; I checked it, armed it, looked at the packing rock so as not to miss whatever might happen, and squeezed the trigger. There was a very bright flash and a bang I could hear mechanically, through the helmet, as well as through the mikes and earphones. The big rock seemed to wobble and then fell into pieces; darkness welled up around where it had been.

We walked up and found gushing water, already freezing at the edges in the ferocious cold of night. Dad got a couple of flow measurements before it skinned over with ice and the ice plug began to grow in it. "That stuff was cold," Dad said, "which makes sense when it gets this close to the surface. But I bet if we leave a thawer on it when we go, tomorrow morning, and it gets to run all day, it'll carry up some heat from some deep thermal sources, and we'll have a good running spring here."

"Yeah," I agreed. "And for right now there's plenty to restock our exosuits and the tajj. Which we oughta start setting up right away."

"Which *I* oughta start setting up right away. You've gotta com that guy of yours, with some real good news, and you've been sitting on top of that news way too long. Now get on it, Teri. Your romantic mother would never forgive me if I made you put this off to do more work. When you're done talking to Perry, I oughta be all set up, and you can just come in and join the family celebration. Go have your conversation and the tajj and everything'll be all set up when you're done."

It's like crapping; you can't actually see or hear anything in the exosuits, but it feels more private to be out of sight. So I went around behind the rocks, making sure I was on the uphill side in case the flow turned out to be strong enough to start a stream tonight, sat down in a comfortable sand pile, set my com for satcell, and called Perry.

"Hi," he said, "how'd the deep drill go?"

"I'm rich," I said, and told him about the size of the pocket. "It solves most of my problems. I won't have to do that last year of school if I just pass the FA—"

Perry shrugged; his face in the little com window projected on my faceplate was hard to read, cause it's always a bit distorted by the curve, but perhaps he was just having a hard time getting his mind around the magnitude of the scorehole. "So that whole country is gonna be opening up—"

"Well, not with winter coming on, not till the next Southern Spring, but yeah, a big share of that methane is gonna be ice and CO_2 slush on the south side of Gateway Massif, and once it starts to melt, there's gonna be streams and ponds and a whole big world of work to do. And they oughta have the road thumped and the tunnel bored by then. It's the biggest scorehole of Dad's career, and the first real one of mine, and I think probably a few hundred ecospectors are gonna be working that country for the next few years."

"I gotta tell my family—we were looking for something new to tackle and so much was looking played out—"

I was startled; had he forgotten what I had just told him? "*We* can be working that country," I said, "there's still plenty there to be brought up—"

"Oh, uh—hey, I wanna hear everything in detail, but we're west of you right now and we still have daylight, and it's kinda rough country so we hafta get moving. See you at the Gather tomorrow?"

"Sure, course, we oughta be there by late afternoon." I wanted to insist that he take a zilty or six and have a proper talk with me—we hadn't had one in what seemed like ages—but when you need daylight, you need it, and you always need it when you're moving with little kids the way that Perry's family was, and so I bit it all back and said, "Okay, I'll talk to you then, and you can hear all about how brilliant I was."

"That will be great. Bye."

I said, "Love-you-bye" quickly but I think he clicked off before I got it said.

I sat on that rock, feeling awful cause the conversation had run so short that I could probably have done my whole share of the work on the tajj, but I couldn't bear to talk to Dad yet. Obviously something was posreal wrong with Perry . . . or I was really immature and not accepting plain necessities, like his family needing the daylight. . . .

I hated myself, but I called up the almanac, and for the very first time ever, I checked up on something Perry had told me.

He was east, not west, of us, where it had already been dark for at least half an hour. And it wasn't broken country at all; it was the kinda easy slopes you find all over Mollyland. They were in a big gentle valley, smooth country anyone could've crossed if they'd hadda keep walking in the dark. And Phobos was up, so there was plenty of light. I waited five minutes and checked again. They hadn't moved. I checked the status log at central. They had registered as camped for the night, forty-five minutes ago.

He had lied to me.

Knowing Perry, this hadda mean bad news he dinwanna deal with over the com. So whatever we were gonna talk about tomorrow, I wasn't gonna like it.

I sat there looking up at all the bright lights in the sky, and at all those stars—the atmosphere had cleared further with nightfall, frost pulling the water out of the air, water condensing on the dust and dragging it down to the surface, and now it might as well have been the pure vacuum of space. Earth-and-Luna, Phobos, and just-setting Deimos and Mercury blazed away in the night sky, and the stars were visible down to sixth magnitude easily, so the sky was thick with'em; the Milky Way looked almost solid. The satellites were everywhere, and the dim cometlike shapes of incoming chondreors still in space.

As I watched, a chondreor entered the atmosphere, brightening as it came in and streaking over the horizon, temporarily lighting the whole landscape to as bright as a cloudy day; high up, probably on its first aerobraking pass. They usually brought'em through the atmosphere three or four times before crashing'em into a bed of frozen volatiles.

The instant it had gone over the horizon, the sky had gone back to black, and the stars, moons, planets, and satellites had sprung back into being. It was so clear I could count thirteen Pleiades.

I was delaying, and I knew I was delaying. Dad would ask, and when I started crying, cause I just didn't know or understand what was going on, he'd be awkward and gruff and inept, and limward skoshy comfort. I would probably cry myself to sleep, and then tomorrow I'd be dragging my feet all day, afraid to get to the Gather and get the bad news. And it would come crashing down on me no matter what.

I was muttering "I want . . . I want . . . I want . . ." over and over to myself, unable to think of how to finish that sentence. Posreal I wanted just to not have to deal with any of this, and that was just plain not on the menu, no matter how much I slipped the waiter and the chef. Feeling like I was being a shitload more mature than I wanted to be, I stood up, and walked, not rooing at all, slowly around the rocks, past the steaming spring—looked like as deeper water came up to the surface, it had been warm enough to keep a flow going, and a steaming creek had formed, gray with mud in the yellow pool of my head-lamp, not more'n a meter across so far, winding its way out over the plain, already more'n a kim long, halfway to the horizon, crawling toward a dry channel like a blind snake, leaving piles of ice at every bend.

Dad had set our tajj on higher ground, between two rocks. He'd done it smart, I thought, and left the solar array spread out, with a tap pipe down to the spring, so that soon as the sun was up in the morning all the recharging systems could run full-out; probably the spring was warm enough to get us some power from the heat pump, too.

We'd at least be going into the Gather with everything redded up to go when it was time to leave; Dad always pitied the people who arrived with tanks, cells, and batteries near empty, spending so much of their earnings on a recharge, having to make time during the Gather or right after to get back to charge. It was one of those millions of petty points of pride he had, expressed as a sigh, a raised eyebrow, or taking a skosh too long to begin a sentence with "well . . ."

As soon as the airlock light indicated that I could, I raised my face plate, opened the door into the tajj, and smelled the rabbit-noodle casserole cooking. I was home and we were rich, and it seemed like it shouldn't be all that hard to be happy.

I dinwanna talk about Perry, not yet.

The place was almost twice as big as it usually was; Dad had unfolded the other module to generate the auxiliary tub room, with its meter-deep hot pool. "I decided I wanted to smell nice *before* I got to the Gather," Dad said. "I don't really wanna hafta start soloing again, so I thought at this Gather, I'd better do some shopping for company."

"That's posreal good, Dad." I'd been pushing him to start looking for someone for some years; I worried about him being out in the roundings all by himself while I was stuck in the useless ordeal of CSL school, but he never did any serious courting, just went to the rent-a-bitch a couple times every Gather.

"Besides, it would just feel real good to feel clean, and after the cold water in that surface reach worked its way out, that turned out to be a hot spring. Or as hot as Mars gets, you know. The thermometer on the heat pump is saying about three ten K, which means you could stick your arm in it, direct."

"You've got the heat pump on?"

"Oh, yeah. We're running off it tonight; power to spare, so we might as well have a hot soak after dinner, and really exfoliate."

I said it sounded great. It's always kinda scary stripping out of my exosuit, cause the habits of a lifetime in the roundings scream that systems can fail at any time, and I might not be able to get zipped back up in the exosuit fast enough. I even felt that way inside the dome at Red Sands City. But exosuits, fine though they are for living in, are not so good for bathing, and it was kinda nice to get the few extra kig off after all the walking that day. I hooked all the pieces into the protolyzer, positioned so I could get back into them in a hurry, and did my best to not worry about it.

"Now," Dad said, as he loaded up the big steaming plates of rabbit and noodles, "I figure we oughta *enjoy* this meal, and then, since my idea for why you might wanna get some more schooling isn't gonna upset you or me, whether you say yes or no—I think you'll mostly like it even if you decide not to do it—we can talk about that while we soak and scrub. So for right now, let's just enjoy the food. Wash up if you need to and then it oughta be cool enough to eat."

I could smell that he'd made real coffee again, too. I guess he was planning to get more at the Gather for his "private stash," what he called the little sack of coffee beans he carried around for special occasions, when the reconstitutor just wouldn't do. We'd had our last mail rocket three weeks back, so he must be running low.

I scrubbed my face and hands in the fast-filling warm pool, and by really scouring my face I figured I got it a more even shade of red, which might hide the fact that I had been crying a skosh better, if Dad ever got around to really looking at me. I couldn't quite believe he'd missed it; normally he was pretty on top of stuff.

When I knelt at the table, I thought maybe I wouldn't cry in front of Dad at all. A good cry might have been satisfying but I posreal needed to keep working on that maturity score for my FA.

I picked up my chopsticks and carefully composed a bite; when you eat through the suit port as often as an ecospector does, you don't take real food and real dining for granted. Warm, satisfying food, with all that good smell and taste, lifted my spirits limward. I was feeling pretty human by the time I'd finished the first plateful.

Dad'n'me mostly talked about what we needed to do and who we needed to see at the Gather, putting schedules and appointments from our common virtual werp up on the wall where we could both see it easy, and tapping in ideas and corrections from the pads beside us. We had dozens of new product demonstrations to make it to, and it always took at least half a day to see all the new Mars-forms in the life development pavilion; there was even gonna be a talk by a rep from some company that thought they'd solved the problem of coming up with a good pol-linating insect for Mars, some sort of hibernating drag-onfly/bee as far as the prospectus went. "Almost looks as if they're claiming to have found a way to make an insect soar instead of flap," I said.

Dad shrugged. "That's been a dream for a long time. It was always right around the corner when I was younger. The corner just keeps getting further away; far as they can tell there's no genes for it in the Bear Regions of any in-sect, and they can copy genes but still nobody can write them."

The presentations were easy to pick—just a few good ones, few conflicts—but it wasn't so easy to get the whole social schedule together. There were always so many peo-ple we needed to see for a meal, or coffee, or something, that we hadda split up just to cover the territory. Every-body always has to do that. There still aren't that many ecospectors (there's not even that many rounditachi), so everybody's several different things to everybody—out in the roundings the same people are your relatives, friends, business prospects, co-contractors, or partners or future partners.

So you hafta stay in touch, all the time. At every Gather, someone in your party's gotta see each of all them, once or twice, depending on how close you're connected, and then course some people are just pleasant and you wanna see'em more, anyway ... I'm told that in larger families the problem gets even worse as you figure out who rates a visit from the eldest child, who from one of the heads, who from a younger child, and who from an attached relative. At least Dad and me could only be two places at a time, and since he would be the head until I got FA, for each given time we just had to pick two of the possible meetings and send Dad to the more important one.

It was limward complicated. I knew one family where brothers had kept a common household, the oldest kids were twins, and a grandpa and a great aunt were in there in the mix too, so it had four heads, two eldests, two attacheds, and about half a dozen—it was hard to count, those people bred like rabbits—mixed and assorted children. They always got to the Gather site two days early just to get all their planning done.

"All right," Dad said, after we'd been on the social problem for about a half hour, "we have one more multiple visit person, but it's Kindness, and he's about the easiest one to work things out with. Now he gets two visits, and he's already agreed to be at that dinner the Wangs are throwing, and the Wangs are top of the list of our single visits, so I think I see a way here."

"How did the Wangs jump so far up our list?"

"They're some of the best big-group-leaders out there—they've conducted parties as big as fifty families through some two- and even three-season projects. So if our plate is warm with them, maybe we can talk'em into creating an enterprise to open the territory around the big gas pocket, especially since there's gonna be a road back there thanks to my brilliant daughter. The Wangs are about the best people I can think of for doing that kinda job."

I was scanning their record and said, "You're right. Hmm. And you haven't worked with'em since I was about three, that's why I didn't remember. All right, you're right. The Wangs' dinner is a 'gotta,' then, and besides, it does get another visit in with Kindness. Besides, they're all old friends and you'll like seeing them."

"It'll have to be *you*, Teri. I've gotta get drunk and wild with an old set of co-contractors from that forest project I did back before you were born; there's a big royalty stake still riding on that, and it's been a long time since we've all been able to be together at once. So it's you at the Wangs' dinner, and then I'll get a few drinks with Kindness late the next evening. Stupid, isn't it? He and I met the year you were born and we've been close friends ever since, and both of us know that we'd still be good friends even if it was twenty years before we saw each other again, so it would be no big deal if we didn't quite catch each other at some Gather, but we hafta meet twice.

For that matter if we met three times people would figure we were going back to being partners, even if we just felt like meeting three times. So stupid."

I rolled my eyes. "Sheesh, Dad, that's so simple and dumb that we study it in school. It's important to do it because you and Kindness are showing everyone else that your friendship can be relied on, cause if they wanna make you an offer that involves the two of you co-contracting, or even re-partnering, then they need to know that you all are still tight, so that when they bank the deal they won't hafta worry about you splitting up, or fighting, or one of you buying out and taking vital skills with him."

"Can't they take our word for it?" Dad asked. He had a stupid little smile that was so posreal exasperating.

"Dad!"

"Just proving to myself that whether or not you will admit it, you did learn something in school. Once upon a time, anyway. And that point is also, by pure coincidence, relevant to the offer I'm gonna make you."

He almost tricked me into wanting to know right away, but I saw through that maneuver and held my peace. After a moment he shrugged and we went back to working out the social schedule, but my mind kept wandering. With teasing like that, I knew that Dad really thought he had something, but I couldn't imagine what.

At last, we were just eating the food cause it was good, and wishing we had somewhere inside to put more of it so that it could keep rolling in over the taste buds, and the social schedule was looking reasonable. We'd traded confirmations with pretty much everyone, and we had managed to get the required number of meetings with everyone we posreal hadda meet with, almost everyone we oughta meet with, and even a few of the people it would just be nice to meet with. When we'd rechecked twice and were both satisfied, Dad said, "Well, then, the pool?"

We tossed the dishes into the grinder, skinned out of our wickies, and were in the warm water almost instantly. Dad had found some nice pumice in the area—you get plenty of it on Mars and it doesn't take long to find—and soon we were scouring ourselves, and each others' backs, like we were trying to take all the skin right off. When we were done with the first round of scrubbing, Dad added the salt, and we both stretched out to float for the first round of soaking, leaning our heads on the tub pillows so that our ears were out of the water and we could hear each other.

I watched the steam roil up to the condensers in the upper surface of the tajj, and the clear tubes there pulsing with the purified water running down to supply the protolyzer, recharge our tanks, and feed the hydrocatalyzer that was filling up the fuel cell tanks. I thought about the tajj walls, thinner than your skin, and beyond them all those kim of dark air, too thin to breathe, to the next tiny tajj, and all the empty kim of Mars, waking up slow after a good ninety million year sleep, dotted with its wide-scattered tajjs, like a handful of pepper thrown onto a whole city's solar collector. And above all the tajjs, and the open Martian desert with its skoshy moist islands of forest and grassland, all the emptiness between the planets . . . all closed out by just the thin film of the tajj roof, close enough for me to splash with the bathwater if I wanted. . . .

"Teri, are you falling asleep on me?"

"Long day," I admitted, "and sometimes your thoughts just run away from you. Sorry about that. We were gonna talk about this idea of yours for getting me to undergo voluntary torture."

"Well, that's not how I'd put it, but let's see if maybe, just maybe, I can't interest you in more schooling. Remember you don't hafta say yes, and I'm not even really expecting you to, but I'd sure appreciate it if you'd listen seriously."

"I can at least promise that much," I said, meaning it. I was miserable about the whole subject of Perry, and I sure needed something to take an interest in, instead, and though there might be hardly a less interesting topic than school, at least it was a topic that had nothing to do with Perry. If nothing else, *Perry* would see to that.

And the thought of how big and empty it really was out there, for some reason, had given me a serious case of the creeps. So even though it was all about an idea I posreal hated, just this once, if I had to, I could listen till blood ran out my ears.

"Well, then, let me lay out how I came to start looking for the idea that I found." He put his hands behind his head, on the headrest, and arched his back to float a skosh higher; skinny as he was, he always hadda salt that water limward to float at all. "To begin with, even I realized that there was pretty well no point in having you finish CSL school. So I thought about it and asked myself if there was any reason for you to go to school at all, and I came up with just three reasons that really do matter to me. First one was for you: I wanted you to have security, in the sense of not going broke and starving, and we sure took care of that today, didn't we, Teri-Mel?"

"Sure did," I said, and we both practiced our whooping, which is limward better in a tajj together than it is out in the roundings where it comes at you over headset. Probably a silly way to spend our time, but you don't get rich every day, and the idea was still new and fresh and nice to us.

"Now, thing two I wanted, I wanted you to have the better kind of security you get from being able to change jobs or learn a new job whenever you need to. And even though the scorehole just made that whole thing irrelevant, when you come right down to cases, all the same, rules change and situations develop, and having skills you can sell is always a good thing, because nobody with a salable, essential skill is ever posreal broke, you know?

"Not that there's much reason to worry about going broke, course, not now. I can't imagine there's gonna be any change that would ever take that pile of money away from you, or your rights in that valley, but you know, you ask some of our older Fourth Wave people and in the 2040s they were living in some house on Earth that their family had been in since forever, and they'd lived through the Die-Off and managed to keep the place through all the shit after the Eurowar and managed not to lose it to the government or some PSC during Reconstruction and they'd kept it through the whole thing—and then boom! The War of the Memes comes along and overnight the family is refugees, and a few years later when One True was taking over, they were lucky to get off Earth with a set of clothes. And I'm sure there were people in places that don't exist anymore, like Holland or the first Supra Berlin, who thought they were set up forever. What was it that old time politician said—the thing they teach you in school—"

"It was Henry the Ninth, Dad, I know the quote you mean. The Surgeon King, when he came aboard the *Albatross,* and said it was better to be alive, poor, and in scrubs than dead, rich, and crowned. So you thought maybe I'd go to school just to have that backup skill you keep worrying about?"

"Naw, I was trying to be honest with myself, Teri, and the fact is that you're a first-rate ecospector, all on your own, and chances are that when the shakeout comes, it'll shake out the lazy, the dumb, the inflexible, the unimaginative—and the unlucky. The only one of those you'll ever be, Teri-Mel, is unlucky. And against that, nothing closes the door. So I think you're about as safe as you can be. Besides, doing what ecospectors do, you pick up a lot of other skills—you'd be employable with your math, or half a dozen of your manual skills, anyway. I just can't imagine how you wouldn't be able to earn a living, unless the whole world turns upside-down."

"So reason two is out, like reason one?"

"It is."

"So what was reason three?"

"Reason three was the most embarrassing, cause the truth is it's really just me. I'd like my daughter to have a diploma or a certificate or something cause I never did. It's dumb, but it's sure as death the way I feel. Fair enough so far?"

"If you're making the case for more schooling," I said, stretching again in the warm water, "somehow I'm not getting it."

He pushed off the wall, ducked his head under, blew bubbles for a while, and came up gasping and blowing and rubbing his face. "Oh, man. In theory people could get along without this. Which shows what's wrong with theory. Well, so what I thought of, finally, and oughta have thought of ages before, was what does Teri want? What would attract her to do something like go to school? So I started hunting through all kinds of sites and texts, and bingo, there it was. Something that might enhance what you really want, rather than compete with it for your time. Have you heard that RSCU is gonna start having technical certificates and majors?"

"I can't imagine that I'd wanna go to a university, Dad, that's six more years of school, even if they let me in, which with my school record they wouldn't do, specially since I'd need another year of CSL school to qualify. But what are those things?"

"The exact solution to the problem you're having, Teri. There were even some articles by the Ministry for Education that explained that people like you were always scheduled to be turning up right about now, right there in the plan, and that's why they've created these programs now.

"See, ever since Reconstruction started, after the Eurowar, in every generation we've hadda hop people from one demanding job to another, over and over and over. Teach somebody to be a cop, then an engineer, then a teacher, then maybe a medic, back to a different branch of engineering, and it has to be a person who won't complain or fuss or try and hang on to the old job. That's why people like my grandpa and Phil Comasus and them developed the whole CSL system in the first place, because what it does is stimulates the meta-learning abilities; it gives you a handle to tackle any new subject and teaches you to enjoy and seek out difficulty."

"But Dad, I hate learning."

"What's the best part of *Crime and Punishment*?"

"Aw, I read that outside of school, I just wanted a good story—"

"How is Hamlet like Raskolnikov?"

"See, that's why I hate school. That's a stupid question cause every possible answer is either trivial, so that it disappears when you look more closely, or else it's buried so deep that by the time you get to it you've lost both stories—"

"How do you know that every possible answer is that way?"

I couldn't understand why we were talking about school stuff, let alone stuff I'd had a couple of years before, in the middle of all this, but on the other hand it was such a dumb question, posreal I wondered if Dad'd ever been to school at all. "Cause the primary transform for decoding either character pretty much has to be the transform to verisimilitude, I mean that stands to reason unless you're being deliberately perverse or doing countersemiosis, and from verisimilitude it's at least a second order (maybe more) transform to any thematic structure, which is where you would find any similarities that were meaningful, and at that point the junction of similarity you have constructed is at least three degrees away from both works and any bridge between them has such a low probability of intent that—*stop laughing at me, asshole!*"

He laughed harder, and I reached out and grabbed his foot and tugged hard enough to pull him off the headrest and into the warm water. Then we had a really adult splash fight followed by ducking each other under the water in a mature kinda way, ending up with a lot of giggling that revealed our full emotional development. At least, if the monitors were following me, that's how I was hoping they would see it.

Then it seemed like a good idea to scrub each other's backs again, and scrub ourselves generally, and see how much dead skin we could take off. At the end of that process we were both pink as boiled crawfish and to judge from what my skin felt like, and how hard I'd scrubbed Dad's back, by all rights the water in that pool oughta have been soup. "A skosh more salt soak before we take it to fresh?" Dad asked.

"Sounds good. Now what were you laughing at?"

"Somebody who's got all the basic CSL skills and uses them well and thinks she doesn't like to learn just cause she doesn't like school. Talk about your elementary confusions!

"And also it just fit perfect with that article I was telling you about. It said society always produces the type of kids it *needs* in its schools, and not the kind it wishes it needed or the kind it says it wants or the kind it thinks is ideal.

"So for example, back before CSL, in those old things they called high schools, mostly they needed people to move paper around and kiss each other's butts, so they taught some kids to make blah-blah noises like administrators. They also needed kids who were going to do actual work, but they had too many of those, so they kept the rest of the kids locked up to keep'em off the labor market. They taught the first group to make vague noises about any subject that came up, just like the noises in the media, and that that was what knowledge was; and they taught the ones they were warehousing that learning anything was for snots. And they got just what they needed, a bottom group that never learned anything (because they had been taught that they didn't want to), and a top group that never learned anything (because they thought the blah-blah noises were all there was to know). It even reinforced, because the tops thought the bottoms were stupid since the bottoms didn't make blah-blah noises, and the bottoms thought they didn't like learning because they didn't like blah-blah noises. It worked just fine for pretty nearly everyone."

"And *that's* what we're going back to?" For the first time in my life I was glad to have gone to CSL school.

"Naw, it was just an example of the way that every society always makes the kids it needs. Up till about 2000, they just didn't need anybody very smart or capable— what they needed was people to buy stuff and follow rules."

"Too bad you weren't around, then, Dad, you'd've been good at making blah-blah noises."

"You're probably right. Okay, so then we got that whole one-long-crisis from the Die-Off to the Fourth Wave—about seventy years of pure shitstorm that turned the world over—and everyone hadda adapt, adapt, adapt, and just to keep the species going, you needed people who would learn anything, and use everything they knew, all the time. You not only couldn't afford to be stupid, you couldn't let your neighbor be stupid.

"But—here's what the article said—that only works in an unstable world where everything changes all the time, and we're finally moving into a stable world again, like has existed before, and we might be in it for maybe a century if we're lucky.

"It said that this current generation in school is gonna not like school cause they don't see it having anything to do with the real world—because for the first time in generations, we've got a 'real world' anyone would wanna live in. For most of the past century life outside stunk and any idiot could tell that it did and they wanted to stay in CSL school, where it was interesting and you had friends and there was something to do, and sometimes for physical safety and food and a warm place to sleep.

"The article was trying to explain your generation to mine, and that was one thing they said, that where most of us saw a world outside that was pretty nasty, and felt like we hadda leave school too young, and we always missed it, most of you see a world where people are doing things and making money and accomplishing all sorts of things, and you wanna be out doing that, and you're not very patient with school. Or much of anything else, I could've told'em. So we're going to be moving back to a more narrow style of education that has more to do with what you like and want and less to do with what the world needs. I don't think we'll ever go back to the institutionalized moron factories that they had in the twentieth century, but there just ain't any point in turning out somebody who can hold sixteen jobs in his life when they're gonna go into one and stick to it. It'll just make him unhappy in the one he's in, and maybe bad at it.

"Now, back when your great-grandpa was a college professor back on Earth, very few students took a general college degree. In fact what they got was either a specialty in some academic subject, like math or literature, or else certification in some useful trade, like engineering or lying."

"They didn't have certification in lying!"

"Ha. The first place my grandpa taught was a program in something called 'communications.' Look up the curriculum sometime and tell me that's not a degree in lying! But more seriously, that was part of how they got so many people to stay out of the labor market—I know it's hard to believe, but back then they actually had a labor surplus—and spend so many extra years in school, by offering 'em a chance to study something that was supposed to get 'em a better job later, or make 'em better at the job they got, or maybe just help 'em look better to someone who might give 'em a job. It was a pretty crazy time in history, economically and socially, so it wasn't necessarily real clear what the purpose of it all was. Some of the old video gives you the impression that everyone was at school in order to dress fashionable, get drunk, fuck, and jump up and down and yell 'whoo!' Makes as much sense as anything else, really, I mean as a way to pass the time before they let you have a job. But the point is, back then, people didn't spend their college years doing a bunch of general knowledge, how-to-access-information, and advanced CSL courses; a student who was gonna be a doctor studied biology and then medicine, a student who was gonna be a lawyer studied politics and writing and law, and so on."

"Sounds limward limiting to me," I said. "What if a doctor needed to know some law?"

"Then she paid a lawyer to know it for her. That's what they mean in your history books when they talk about a 'quasi-permanent division of labor.' Now the thing is, *if* society has enough people and *if* society's needs are stable—instead of a series of crises, which is what society has been coping with since President Bush came down with mutAIDS and the Die-Off started—well, basically, if you're having more or less normal times, and people don't hafta tear up the rule books and do something new six times a decade—then that quasi-permanent etcetera is actually the most efficient way to do things. It doesn't really pay to have a bricklayer thinking about how to route a railroad line and what the likely genetic sequence that makes Tailored Rice Blast so contagious is. It just makes him an inefficient bricklayer who daydreams, at best, and at worst it may mean that you've got a talented logistician or a geneticist being wasted laying bricks. If the world is going back to a more normal kind of rhythm with people having a much better handle on what the next decades will be like and how things are going to go, then you really, really want specialists. Not necessarily *narrow* specialists, of course, that's asking for social disaster, but at least masters of their trades.

"So that was what a major or a tech certificate was; usually a major meant you did a scanty, abbreviated version of a general college degree so that you could spend lots of time studying one particular subject or discipline, and a tech certificate was something you got in two years where you did nothing but directly study the things you'd use on the job, and become really knowledgeable about that." He stretched out, arching his back to float high, and said, "We could turn the water to fresh, or we could reheat and stay in a while longer."

"Definitely reheat and stay in. Well, I hafta admit that if someone held a gun to my head and said that I hadda go to school, but I could get a tech certificate or finish CSL school, I guess I'd pick the tech certificate. Same way I'd rather have a broken finger than a broken arm."

"I figured that was how you'd react," Dad said, smiling. "Let me just tell you the rest of it, then. The deal is this. RSCU is gonna offer a two-year degree in ecospecting. It's open to anyone who's passed the FA, and from what I've seen these past couple of days, you're sure looking like someone who could pass it. The emotional part too, I mean. No question in my mind, anymore, posreal; you always had the brains and you've been handling all kinds of stress well."

My eyes stung for an instant; I wondered if I oughta tell him what a bad time I was having over the issue of Perry, and how vague the whole horrible business was. I ducked down and rinsed my head under the water, letting the cloud of warm bubbles rise around me, and came up wiping my face and blowing air and water around. "Well, thanks," I said.

"Just as accurate an assessment as I think I can make," Dad said. "You're gonna pass FA, I think, though a few days back I wouldn't've thought so, and so you'll be eligible. Now, the way it works is this. You actually spend about three quarters of your time in what they call a field school, somewhere out in the roundings, helping planetologists and genecologists and all the rest of them develop the data that we all use. I'm not sure how much field and how much school that is, but it's gotta be better for you than the classroom. It's more or less what you and I do, except instead of looking for what's profitable, and developing resources, what you try and do is find what's interesting and not yet known, and develop a body of information. The quarter of the time you do spend in RSC is mostly in advanced science and math classes, which you always liked anyway, to develop a deeper understanding of your fieldwork. So you get some advanced planetary history but it's all about why certain fossils are found over aquifers, and mineral chemistry but it's all about what's in the rocks that might be useful to an ecospector, and a pretty thorough grounding in molecular genetics but it's all about looking in the Bear Regions for the junk code of Earth plants and Earth animals, to find those ice age, high-CO_2, or high-altitude sequences in the DNA, and matching it up with Mars, which you got from applied climate modeling and meteorology...."

The funniest thing was happening to me, and I didn't know how to handle it. Now, I like money, and I like success, and I had never before felt as good as I'd felt earlier that day hitting a planetary-level scorehole. But I always wanted to know why things were the way they were, and I spent tons of my reading time in the field, and my spare library time at school, reading up and keeping on top of the scientific literature and the new ideas in engineering. So the idea of two years spent mostly out in the roundings, just exploring and learning all I could, not having to worry about making money . . . with real scientists right there to answer questions and classmates who would think the same things I thought were fascinating . . . it seemed like an invitation to go live in heaven for a while.

Yet at the same time I knew that Perry would never go for it. Sure, he had his FA, and I guess his grades from before he dropped out of CSL school were okay, but when you came right down to it, out of the whole big bunch of reasons he liked ecospecting for, and all of my talents that he valued, not one of them were the kind of thing they do at a university. He liked bouncing over the landscape, trying any old thing to see if it worked, jumping rocks, blowing holes in the ground, moving fast and gambling on luck.

One of the few times Perry'n'me had had a real quarrel was the one season he'd spent with Dad'n'me, cause we liked to spend a long time setting and moving pingers and getting a picture of what was under our feet, and Perry figured you could just blast a few wrong holes if you had to, and you'd get something eventually, and he couldn't see why we were spending so many hours working on the difference between pretty good and optimal.

Perry might be able to see why you might wanna be able to identify the fossil of a skweejee, the Martian "walking squid" that had inhabited so much of the last flowing water on the planet, cause you found them above aquifers so often, but he'd never, never have understood why you'd actually wanna know anything about the skweejee except that there was likely to be water under it. He'd see that forecasting a sandstorm might be a useful trick but he wouldn't see any reason that it was appreciably better than just having your tajj in good order and always knowing what side of a rock to pitch it against.

And, I realized, it seemed too much like I was already losing him. Somehow we weren't connecting the way we had before. Calls had been getting more strained and . . . well, the problem was clearly that we had already spent too much time apart.

Now, knowing Perry, I couldn't possibly get him to go to RSCU with me, or to pay attention if he was there, and anyway even if he married me after I'd been through the program, I hated to admit it, but he'd never listen to anything I had to say, no matter how well founded it was—and he wouldn't care about nine tenths of what I'd know.

It seemed very unfair of school to finally get sort of attractive, just when everything with Perry was such a mess.

So I was all set to just tell Dad that it had been a nice try, but school was school as far as I was concerned, when I started to cry like a little girl, wailing like I was dying.

Dad was there right away—when was he ever not?— holding me, soothing me, saying "It's all right, no one will make you do anything, and I'm sorry I brought it up—" and that was so silly, so far from what the actual matter was, that I just cried harder and hung onto him, and finally I blurted out the whole awful mess of Perry.

Dad sat and listened quietly to me, the way he always

did when he took me seriously, and when I had blurted it all out, and cried a while longer, he said only, "Well, I'd been wondering, Teri-Mel. Wondering a lot, actually. You didn't come in and tell me anything about your call, and more'n that, there we were mapping out a social calendar, and you didn't even mention that you'd need some time for your wedding, or your honeymoon, or to receive guests, or anything. I figured you'd tell me when it was time."

"I guess it was time, then," I said, feeling small and sad and very tired. "And for all I know it's gonna be fine. But you know, our schedule has been up on the net for hours, and Perry hasn't sent me a note asking about getting married, either, and . . . well, it doesn't look like he's gonna, does it?"

Dad sighed. "I'm afraid that no matter what, you'll find out tomorrow, anyway. So let me mention that I did leave one blank time in the calendar—the time for you to take the FA. And I want you to take that exam, Perry or no Perry, cause you need that for your life and your career, regardless, okay? And even if your heart is just squashed as flat as it can be, I expect my daughter to pass with flying colors—I don't mean I'm telling you to, I mean I know you will. You got that?"

"Got it," I said.

There wasn't much else to say, so we finished our soak in silence, switching on the salt-recoverer after a while to freshen the water, then toweling off, checking and cleaning boils on each other, putting back on the exosuits except

for the helmets, and sleeping comfortably, breathing tajj
air moistened by the still-full tub. It didn't seem like there
was any good reason to hurry to this Gather, so we didn't
set a clock and we didn't plan to hurry in the morning.

Well, now, that was stupid. And very unprofessional. I went off for my steak, and had it—a very good
steak, too—and while I was having it, decided it would
enhance the experience if I added a few glasses of wine. So
I did. I took a few things to get that out of my bloodstream, but they don't all work right away, so course what
happened then was that I staggered home and fell asleep
on the floor in my bedroom. When I woke up in the
morning, the alcohol scrub had prevented a hangover, but
that process takes immense quantities of water, and I got
up and practically drank the sink dry.

So now I'm here in the office and there is, at the moment, as is the case most days, nothing to do that actually
needs doing, unless I decide to record a reply to Teri right
now, and I still don't know what to say. Otherwise my
inbox is empty—dusty, really, it's been weeks. Red Sands
City has about fifteen homicides, a hundred assaults, and

maybe thirty rapes per reporting period of 335 days, and few of them require the attention of a shrink; burglary and so forth never do.

(As for why we have that silly reporting period, a skosh more than half a Mars year, I remember we had to go to six separate conferences over in Marinersburg to settle what the reporting periods would be—a Mars-year, an Earth-year, a Mars-season—but that was complicated because with its elliptical orbit, Mars seasons are not uniform in length the way Earth's are—finally what was settled on was to use half a Mars year, because . . . well, mostly because no one wanted to go to any more meetings about it, and the bosses were demanding a decision. They wanted a well-justified one so we put some time into making a bunch of things up.)

I've been in this office for ten minutes and I'm already thinking about that bottle. This is not good. I'm a controlled alcoholic, or that's what I tell myself anyway, and the line between controlled and not controlled is easy to cross.

In some ways, I wonder more about what happened to Teri before the big incidents than I do about what happened after. Major shocks and an emergency . . . that takes no explanation, just as you understand why, if you hit a rock hard enough with a hammer a few times, it goes to pieces. What's harder to estimate is what all the freezing and thawing of millions of years before did to it first. Was it actually full of hairline cracks all along? Or had it already sloughed off every weak part? Would you have needed half as much force behind the hammer to shatter it, or did you just barely make it work at all?

More to the point, was Teri ripe, somehow, for what

happened? And if so, how many others of us would be or might be? How vulnerable is the whole population of Mars? And what makes people vulnerable, anyway? Genes? Seeing your mother killed in front of you? Sudden change of fate? An unhappy first love? A mildly incestuous attachment? Being human? That's what the bosses in Marinersburg would really like me to be able to tell them—how many people do we have to keep an eye on? But they want to know that from me, without telling me what they already know. . . .

It's a crappy analogy, anyway, really. People, of course, are not rocks, and events are not hammers. And I am not a drunk and I am not unprofessional. I decide not to rewatch the interview where she told me about getting rich and all of that. One of the reviewers wanted me to explain why I didn't ask about the "obviously incestuous relationship" with her father, and I ended up explaining for the fiftieth time, "they took a bath together. Every family in the roundings bathes together," over and over. "Washing is not foreplay, especially not when your back is dirty," I remember saying on the com, and getting back "I have never allowed any part of me to be dirty for one moment, and I don't see what my personal life has to do with this."

I decided I'd better not invite him over to bathe.

RSC is getting to be less of a frontier town, just as Mars is getting to be less of a frontier world. There's less ignorance and less crudity than there was, but more bone-deep stupidity out here now. There was a memo yesterday that said that someone at the Bureau of Nomenclature was considering setting a standard so that all the names that

were given to all the land on Mars back before anyone had
visited would have to take precedence over what people
called them now, so that any ecospector who wanted to
buy a map of the Prome would have to remember it was
Prometheia Terra and that Mollyland was Malae Planitia
and so on. After twenty years here at RSC, I can't even
remember what the Hellspouts were originally . . . and the
idea that someone who did all the work turning an expanse
of rock and sand into a country would have to call it by
the name some scientist who probably died a hundred
years ago in the Eurowar would . . . or take the rules that
say that, if I send Teri a message that's just encouraging
and contains some advice, one friend to another, I have to
report it just as if I were still counseling her and still in-
vestigating the incident . . . or the rules that say I have to
be in my office when there's really nothing to do and the
most productive thing I could do would probably be a
long walk and sitting out in the park for a while. . . .

A frontier is a place where everyone works because
there's so much to do. Even if what they work at is being
whores or gamblers or killers, they work. The last thing
that's needed is more work, so on a frontier you don't
have bureaucrats to make more of it. Mars used to be the
human frontier, and Red Sands City used to be on the
southern frontier of Mars . . . but right now, just a Mars
year after it all happened, already there's a Telemachuston
with sixty settlers down in the Terimel country, and it just
elected its first town council, and the train will be going
there in another Mars year at most. And Telemachuston
isn't going to be a frontier town for twenty years, the way
RSC was. It will be lucky to be a frontier for five. So it

wouldn't be worth putting in to move there, once they can afford a shrink for their police department.

Most of the settlement of Mars is yet to happen, but it's going to come fast, now. Figuring most people live to be 110 or so these days, I'll live to see it when, about 2150, we don't have any roundings, just preserves and parks and the Nations.

Frontier vanishes, stupidity rises, make-work takes over. The natural succession is coming on, as naturally as ponds became meadows became forests on Earth. I'll miss so much. I'll miss making decisions on the spot, and the don't-bother-me-unless-it's-on-fire attitude my first bosses had, and criminals who might be vicious but were seldom really stupid, and victims who wanted to get back on their feet and get going again right away. I'll miss its being okay to have a bottle in my desk.

This used to be a good place to be a shrink and a cop.

I wonder if they're going to need shrinks when they resettle Mercury. Hell, I never go outside anymore, anyway.

I might as well watch some more recordings before I get back to Teri, since I still have no idea what to say to her.

When we woke up, the sun was just coming up; habit will do that for you. Dad had left the pool filled and warm all night, so we had the lovely warm wet air to soothe our noses and lungs. We ate our plates of corn beef hash with poached eggs on top—doubles, what'd we hafta worry about conserving for, we had unlimited money and could go shopping later that day—in the warm pool. After that we scrubbed once more to be nice and fresh as we got back into our wickies and exosuits.

When I think about it, it's a skosh strange that so many rounditachi sleep out in suits so often. The tajj is pleasant, and taking down a tajj and folding solar panels takes almost no time; after all, families with young children hafta do it every single day. We dumped the hot water from the tub out on the sand and watched as it ran down the gentle slope, leaving a trail of crackling white frost behind it, to join the stream that now meandered over the horizon. "Hey, check the satellite pictures on what developed overnight," Dad said.

I did, and then immediately went to much higher magnification as I realized that we had truly, though acciden-

tally, made something special. Our skoshy spring had
found its way into an ancient dry wash about fifteen kim
away, forming a lovely little waterfall at one lip that was
already framed in ice formations, and then, cooled by mix-
ing with air, and slowed by the broader floor of the wash,
it had formed an ice dam across a narrow point, and was
now accumulating into a perfect little lake in the bottom
of the wash.

"Probably won't freeze to the bottom even in the winter," Dad said. "The areothermal source seems to be pretty
hot, as we know from having pulled power out of it all
night, and besides it's pretty salty. If you were using it
regularly for drinking water you'd wanna desalinate a
skosh. We didn't really notice because when we freshened
the tub, the extractor took out the natural salt along with
the salt we put in."

"Perfect place for modified brine shrimp," I said, "and
maybe after there's enough percolation, we could put in a
few of those salt-resistant pines. . . ."

"It would make a beautiful place," Dad agreed. "And
the falls and the lower gap are lined up eastward. Every
time Deimos comes up, you're gonna have it shining
through the gap and onto all that ice around the falls. It'll
be a honeymoon spot in another fifty years."

He probably kicked himself, but hearing that didn't
bother me. It was true. And besides, it wasn't exactly clear
that my honeymoon was canceled. Yet. Just posreal im-
probable.

So that the subject could get changed, I asked, "So how
high is that ice dam gonna go, and where will the water
go once it overflows?"

"Looks like it has five, six more meters to go," Dad said, "and the lake will be half a kim long. There's a low spot, a break in that northern ridge, where it will probably get an outlet, and then it'll flow down from there into the old river bed. Probably not enough water around yet to keep it going so it'll probably just be a wadi for the next few years, till there gets to be enough local rainfall to extend it down to the sea. Or there's a broad low spot down below that might become a sebkhet. It's hard to tell, not knowing what the structure's like underneath."

"But anyway, it's yet another country we've opened up," I pointed out, "A small one, but a good place for a town—it's on the way out of the developments in Mollyland into the crater—hey, what are we gonna call the new wet country in that crater, anyway?"

Dad laughed. "Well, I'd've thought it would've been obvious. There's already too many Murray Rivers and Murray Lakes everywhere, and I've stuck 'Telemachus' on so much of the landscape that some people might get to think it was the name of the planet. So it's gotta be the Terpsichore Valley—"

"There already is one," I said, "all the way north, that drains down into Chryse, the one Uncle Kindness named after me right after I was born. He'll be hurt if you give that name to a bigger one."

"Hadn't thought of that," Dad admitted. "What do you suggest?"

"Well," I said, "I was thinking we could use my nickname, cause there's nothing out there called the Teri-Mel anything, so we declare that whole big crater to be the Teri-Mel Crater, which is going to turn into plain old 'the

Terimel country' pretty fast, and that will be fine. And since you stuck me with the names of two muses, I figure we can name things after the muses' specialties—dance and tragedy. I thought maybe we could call this wadi, or creek, if that's what it turns out to be, the Dancer Wadi, and that beautiful little canyon can surround Tragedy Lake, which I guess makes it Tragedy Canyon."

"You know how many folk stories are gonna grow up around places with names like that?"

"Limward nicer ones than grew up around the Asshole Sebkhet or those twin mountains they call Barbara's Knockers," I pointed out. "At least mine will be romantic!"

Dad laughed and said, "All right, I'm sending in all three names."

We made excellent time that day without really trying; eastern Mollyland is easy going. It might have been nice to visit the new Tragedy Canyon but we would've had to go far out of our way through badlands; it was limward better to just get down onto the plains.

We were coming from the south and east, so we saw no one till we were very close to the Gather site. That was fine with me; I dinwanna start gossiping just yet, and I took some pride in our having been working wilder land than most of the rest had.

The perfect Gather site is a two-kim crater in a broad gentle downslope, and we were coming down that down-slope, which was mostly firm-packed sand with the usual scattering of stones and small boulders, interrupted by only the occasional low rocky ridge. It was perfect country to roo in, and we bounced and bounded like a couple of little kids in a soft-floor gym, racing and playing with each other all morning long.

It had been a long time since Dad and I had done anything like this together. Now that I thought about it, it was kinda strange. When I had been younger, after Mummy had died, there had usually been no one to play with but Dad, and playing is the most natural thing to a kid, so it didn't seem odd that he played with me. Little kids, or at least happy well-cared for little kids, are like kittens that way—everything and everybody is something to play with.

As I'd gotten older, I'd drifted out of playing, which, again, was the most natural thing in the world. Ten-year-olds play and fourteen-year-olds don't. Usually, I mean, it depends on the kid and the circumstances. But Dad had played with me when he was in his thirties, and had seemed to like it.

I wondered, now, sitting on the warm black rock out-crop and gulping down tea and wafers, whether he had missed it when I stopped playing? Maybe that was why my friends who were young marrieds were always com-plaining about all the pressure from *their* parents to have children right away—their parents wanted someone to play with.

I asked Dad about that and he put his head back and laughed and said, "Oh, yeah. It'll be all I can do to refrain from calling you during your honeymoon and telling you to hurry up."

"I don't know if I'm gonna have a honeymoon—"

"Didn't say with who or how soon, Teri-Mel. But you're more'n average pretty and you'd make a posreal talented business partner and as of yesterday you've got money and as of this Gather you'll have a rep. If Perry is gonna be a damn idiot about it—and so far we don't *know* that he is—you'll hafta keep the rest of'em away with a stick. Just don't use too big a stick and remember to drop it when the right one turns up. Cause you're right, I'm coming up on forty, getting to the point where it would be fun to have grandkids. And also because the job of raising a kid with Murray genes, well, really only somebody young, vigorous, and slightly dumb, with no idea what they're getting into, oughta try that. You wait too long, you might get too smart."

For the last hour and a half to the Gather site, we leaped and chased along, light on our feet despite our full tanks, as if we were kicking the planet away beneath our feet. The compressors kept having to ramp up the oxygen enhancement, the exosuits popped out the back fin to cool us, and the water-recoverers filled practically to the top, but it felt limward *great,* not like work at all.

The sky was a clear deep pink with just a red rim on the horizon, the aureole around the sun was a shade of blue you might see in fine china, the temperature was probably about ten below freezing, one of those beautiful warm days you get in early autumn close to the pole, and as long as I didn't think about anything before or after exactly-right-now, I had every reason to be happy.

We covered the hundred kim to the Gather pavilion at a near-record speed for us, and arrived with an hour of daylight left. The first sight of the pavilion arching up into the sky like a mountain always gets me, no matter that I've seen it nearly every change of season since I can remember (except a few times when I was being unavoidably educated).

I'd been at Gather sites a few times during the weeks before when the volunteer crew grew the pavilion, and that was always fun. We'd start the first week growing and spreading out the huge solar collectors, many kim wide. Then we all drove the little carts to and from the big machines, grinding up half a mountain of rocks and dirt to make materials. The second week began with placing and growing towers and cables, laying them out on the crater floor, and ended with spraying the whole thing with the foam that, once it was fed with rocks and dirt, self-reformed into ultralight molecular-weave fabric. Then we dumped loads all over it and powered it up, watching it eat rocks, dirt, and water like a huge amoeba. The last couple of days before the arrivals were due, the air and water plants would draw all the power from the solar array and fill their tanks to the brim. Finally, trigger day would come, and thousands of cables would begin to pull on hundreds of towers, which would all rise from the crater floor under the great canopy as air thundered in through dozens of tunnels, and in an hour it would all go up in one vast billow of iridescent silver fabric, a sudden small mountain rearing into existence over the ancient crater.

I hadn't seen that in a couple years. Dad had preferred to do his vol time taking kids to and from school, which had been another effective way to make it more likely that I would go for each successive year.

The pavilion raising had been two days back; the official Gather opening was tomorrow in the morning, so maybe two-thirds of everybody was already here. Now the pavilion stretched up from the ancient crater in arcs, peaks, and curves like a forest of gigantic tajjs, or like a volcanic dome of magic silver, two hundred meters above local surface level. As we drew closer, it just kept getting bigger, and the mind just kept readjusting for scale; that was the effect it had on everyone.

We came in from the up slope side. The last five kim was along one of the narrow lanes between the great fields of solar collectors that stretched far past the horizon. One way that Gather always paid for itself was to drastically overmanufacture; all these collectors would be cut up and sold to some industrial project in a couple of weeks, and the money would go to the Gather's trust fund.

We arrived as the big freight lift was getting ready to depart for the inside, just before they closed the gates. The freight lift would have made a very nice-sized warehouse all by itself, but it was still crowded; we were sharing our ride with a few thousand tons of meat and vegetables fresh in from the city greenhouses, a mountainous pile of crates from Aregene that was probably their ready-to-go stuff for the big store they always had at every Gather; a load of office furniture for the administrative offices; six fuse-dozers; a boxed-up opera stage; the bleachers for the softball games; and about a hundred mixed people, maybe twenty- or thirty-some parties in all.

The big lift descended slowly into the ground—we were going about two hundred meters down, half a kim horizontally, and then about thirty meters up. It took a few minutes, but no one was in any hurry; everyone was too busy trying to find people they knew on the lift, or talking about what might be in what box, or trying to be the first to share some gossip. Rounditachi spend almost all their time in the same small group, except for the ones who are all alone. A Gather is thousands of people starved for human company and determined to get it right now.

Through the tall windows of the freight lift, the fabric-filtered sunlight of the inside of the pavilion came in, and the light slid down the windows in front of us; in a moment, the sides were sliding up the framework on all sides, and we had arrived.

We were in the warehouse-receiving area, close to where we needed to be, so we hurried to our campsite, and found everything in order. Dad asked me to handle setting up the tajj. He wanted to go see about getting us an hour in a trade booth to promote expeditions into the Teri-Mel country—he hadda go in person to do some greasing up, cause last minute booths are a *big* favor that you only get by calling in lots of long-standing favors, and some of those will be the kind of favors you don't talk about over the com. "You wanna get precise about it," Dad said, "some of the favors, what they are is *not* talking about things, on the com or anywhere else." So he was gone real quick.

I stopped a passing robot cart and got 180 kig of General Construction Mix, the black powder that was formulated to feed a growing structure exactly what it needed in the most accessible form, unfolded the whole tajj (something we almost never did out in the roundings), threw the mix onto the tajj, and plugged it in. Normally it takes about twenty minutes for a tajj to pop up and open, but with the right materials mix and unlimited power, it happened in five.

By tradition, nobody wears an exosuit or wickies inside the Gather pavilion. After all, there are plenty of shelters around, in case anything goes wrong, and in a space that big things can't go wrong all that quickly—it takes hours for a blowout to have much effect. So once I had stripped and scrubbed and thrown everything into the protolyzer, I pulled out the rented clothes-grower, tossed in some sand, let it capture skoshy air, and while it got its raw materials into order, started looking through the catalog.

The difficult question was, should I try and look nice for Perry, since it was quite possible that everything was just a misunderstanding? Or dress businesslike, in case I hadda be grown-up in public about something awful? Or look good-but-grown-up to remind him about what he might be losing (or make him happy about what he was keeping)?

I remembered that Dad had always quoted something my great-aunt said in one of her rare letters, about always being dressed hot to break up, so that the stupid man would feel like a fool for the rest of his life. I think she got it from her mother-in-law, if I remember that family legend right, and the occasion was either a divorce hearing or having caught her husband at something. I never paid as much attention as I ought've to family stories.

But, anyway, always dress hot to break up? That seemed like a good rule. So I settled on a thin white bandeau that showed most of what I had (not much—it just doesn't run in the family), and a nice shiny bright yellow modesty patch that showed plenty of cheek, and let it go at that. I was old enough for platform sandals but wore'em so rarely that I was awkward in'em, and if I needed to turn on my heel and stamp out, I dinwanna fall on my face.

Perry had never liked cosmetics, so I just touched my lips with clear gloss, lined the outer edges of my tan mask with a deep-brown striper, and called that good.

I could have commed to find out where he'd be, but that might tip him off that I was coming, and besides I knew Perry and his family well. His father'd be selling the thick, rich, cilantro-heavy guinea pig chili that had been a family boast for three generations. Perry and the girls, on this day before opening, would all have been drafted into chopping up peppers, garlic, and onions. So I headed for the back side of Chowhouse Row; just by walking along and keeping my nose open, I found the right booth fast enough, because nobody in the world who has smelled that wonderful stuff could ever mistake it for anything else, not even in a street full of great food.

I hesitated a second at the back door. Why had I not commed first? Was I trying to catch Perry at something?

Hell yes.

Whatever I was about to learn, I wanted it to be blatant. I wanted to have the whole story behind everything, right now. I knew I might not like whatever the answer was gonna turn out to be, but since I had made up my mind to get the whole truth in one big kill-or-cure shot, surprising Perry might help.

I swallowed hard. I reached for the door plate. I just hadda take a deep breath, and—

The door opened. Perry was there, holding a big tub of chopped vegetable trash. "Uh," he said, and then repeated, "uh."

"I missed you too," I said.

He leaned forward and gave me a skoshy peck on the cheek, not at all like the mauling, clutching, tongue-to-tonsils kisses we used to give each other on first sight, and with a bucket of garbage between us, it wasn't even a very good peck on the cheek. "Where've you been? I started looking for you as soon as the Gather started—"

"We just got in," I said, "and I came here to find you."

"I've got some news," he said, "and I'm not good at this talking thing, and I need to get my news out, so I guess, um—"

"You oughta start talking," I said.

He gulped, and said, "Um, we connected with the Letitia Family for this last season, working a bunch of frozen CO_2 veins way west of here—"

"I know," I said, "you and I talked almost every night."

"Um. Yeah." He didn't speak for a long breath or two.

Finally I realized I didn't want to just stand there forever, and said, "Just tell me. Tell it your own way. I won't interrupt again."

"Well, the CO_2 veins were not the hottest thing in the world, you know, but good enough to turn some profit, and even though it wasn't a lot of money at any one time it was still a big job over time—I know I told you all that as it happened too, like I said, I hafta tell it all or I can't keep it straight in my head what to tell you—"

Dad had always said that only a liar needs time to get

the story straight. My heart dropped like a stone.

"—but anyway, it took weeks and weeks following veins under the ground and drilling and blasting and shoving in heaters to get it all flowing, and um . . . well, you know how it all is, working partners all the time, sharing a tajj all the time, you get to know someone pretty well whether you . . . well, sometimes you actually start to really wanna know someone pretty well. Well it happened I was out there with—"

Ruth Letitia, who I'd known for a long time—we'd been in some sessions of CSL school together—came barging out of that back door and said to him, "Now, look, if you won't deal with this, then I'll have to." She looked angrier, at me, than I'd ever seen anyone before. "We've been married for four months and it's high time that you stopped calling him every night and bothering him and begging him to—"

She stared at my face. I felt sick and ready to faint—I think. I was too bewildered to have much memory later. Parts of my brain were whirling around and saying, *that's why I always called him and not the reverse no matter how long I waited* and *this is why he changed the subject whenever I mentioned the future* and even one distant part that said *but we talked each other through masturbating just last week!* Maybe she saw all those thoughts crossing my face. An evil part of me especially hopes that somehow she saw the last one.

Ruth's head snapped toward Perry. "You said you told her. Did you tell her? Did you tell Teri? You told me you told her." Her voice was flat and calm and frightening.

"Uh," he said, and cleared his throat. She hit him, hard,

with her open hand, really a push but she threw it like a punch, making a hard whump on his bare chest. He winced and she slapped his face.

"You didn't tell her," she said. "You told me you had told her right after you proposed. Five weeks before the wedding. A *long* time ago."

(I did the arithmetic and realized that the two of them must have gotten together within a couple weeks of the last time I had seen Perry in the flesh.)

"I was gonna."

Apparently that was the wrong answer, cause she hit him, again, a roundhouse slap that anyone could have ducked, but he just stood there and took it.

When she turned back to me, I doubled my fists and brought'em up to protect myself; she was twice my size but I wasn't gonna let her thump on me like that without thumping back.

She stared at my hands for an instant, as if wondering why I had grown them. Then she looked at me very directly. For just a zilty she was my old school buddy. Quietly, almost tenderly, she said, "I know it's a mess and a surprise and all, but go away anyway. I don't want you around him. He's got some kinda thing for you and we're married now and he shouldn't have. I can see he never told you, and I'm sorry. It wasn't your fault, but go away or there will just be more trouble."

I turned and walked away, fighting myself the whole way, probably walking jerky and awkward as I tried not to run or to roo. Behind me, I could hear Ruth's voice plunging to a growl and then crawling up to a shriek, over and over, punctuated by the thuds of her hands on his chest, shoulders, and back.

I realized, but didn't turn around to confirm, that she was heavier than when I'd seen her last. And she'd gained most of it around the waist. I guess some families don't get their daughters a reversible and some girls can't use implants, or something like that. I mean it stands to reason, since out here in the roundings, as they say, accidents are the leading cause of people. I had a feeling that I'd be hearing some gossip about the whole situation soon, or at least seeing people shut up and change the subject when I approached.

I turned a corner. By now I could only pick Ruth's voice out of the crowd noise with effort, and I willed myself not to make the effort. I walked another couple of blocks, all posreal calm, nodding and smiling to a couple of people I knew, then turned two more corners before I dared to look behind me and confirm that no one was there. Then I spent a few seconds figuring out which way the tajj was— fortunately not in any direction that would have forced me to retrace my steps—and ran there as fast as I could.

The best thing about being at a Gather was there was no airlock to slow me down. I went right through the door, letting it seal behind me, and threw myself face first on the bed in my room; another good thing about Gathers was that you could grow your tajj to its full size, so I had a separate room with an actual bed. I put my face down into the newly generated pillows to smother the sound, since the fabric wall was all that was between me and the alley. Then I just let go and howled.

I hadn't cried like that since we buried Mummy. It went on a long time, and by the time I got up to pull the privacy flap closed, it was pitch black in there, the light no longer filtering in through the pavilion roof and the transparent top of the tajj. They must have turned off the street lamps hours ago.

I went back to the bed, stretched out, and let the hard sobs come now and then; in between I lay there wiping my face and thinking of nothing.

Finally, after all the stars had gone out and the universe was a thin scum of barely warm iron contaminating a vacuum, and God had died of old age, boredom, and loneliness, a slight cough behind me announced that Dad had come home.

I had settled down to the low miserable keening that drives people crazy to hear—it was starting to bother *me*—and makes your throat sore, just about the most wretched sound human beings make. I said "come in." The lights came on, and I rolled over and saw that he had just stepped through the privacy flap. I bounded forward and more or less threw myself into his arms. He held me the way he had when I had been a little girl, or when I'd had nightmares for a year or two after Mummy's death, cause that had been so sudden—a rock out of a cliff we were climbing had dropped a very long way, and none of us saw it until Dad shouted "Look—" and didn't even have time to say "out" before it bashed in Mummy's faceplate and sent her plunging to the bottom, half a kim below. I still sometimes saw that in a bad dream now and then; the first year after it happened, I saw it every time I closed my eyes to sleep.

And just like then, with his arms around me and his voice breathing "It's all right, it's all right, it's all right" into my ear, I just clung to him, buried my nose in his chest, and went limp.

Finally, when my breathing had slowed and I was holding on quietly, Dad rubbed the back of my neck and said, "I heard about Perry. From someone that saw that whole thing with Ruth. I hurried home as soon as I heard."

"So everyone knows."

"Probably, but you can bet that most folks think that Perry is the asshole in the story. I don't think anyone will even mention it to you, unless you invite them. You know rounditachi, Teri; they know all they need to know. You can hold your head up anywhere."

"Maybe. My friends can call me 'the proud idiot' or something."

Dad hugged me tighter. "Teri-Mel, when you do find the right guy—and you will, you will, even if it doesn't feel like it right now—and you move out, I'll only get to laugh a tenth as much. Well, if it makes you feel better, Perry isn't gonna have even a reputation as a *proud* idiot. He never impressed any too many people to begin with, but since you liked him I tried to keep my feelings to myself. It's gonna be a relief not to hafta defend him any more, to anyone, especially not having to do it in my own thoughts."

"That'll be a relief for me too."

"I never did think that boy could have had enough brains to betray or exploit somebody; to do that, you hafta have room to hold two ideas in your head at once, and my impression was that he didn't really have room for one."

I snorted, though it hurt my nose after all that crying. It seemed funnier than it really was, cause for so many months Dad had been so careful never to let me know he thought that Perry was dumb as a rock, and yet I'd known anyway, and resented him for it. Finally being able to just say it must have been a big relief to Dad.

Almost as much a relief as thinking it had been for me. I'd been trying to tell myself it wasn't so for a long, long time. But once I thought the words "Perry is not awful smart," all sorts of things I hadn't been able to understand about him, and had worked out these really complicated explanations for, became amazingly clear. And very simple, like Perry himself.

I realized I might not have been as impressed with Perry as I had thought I was. In fact I even felt a skosh sorry for Ruth. I finally pulled away from Dad's chest— the most comforting place in the universe—and wiped the wet mess from my face.

"That *is* my favorite shirt," Dad said mildly, "and you could use a hanky, you know."

"Sorry."

" 'S'okay. You're still not quite back with us, I don't think. You've had an awful shock." He grabbed a kitchen wipe and very gently and tenderly cleaned my face. I shut my eyes and let him. It felt so good.

"I'm so sorry," he said, again, and I whispered back, "thank you."

Then he sat and listened while I told him what it had been like. Sometimes I yelled and screamed and sometimes I cried, but he sat there and listened, held me when I wanted holding, just listened when that was what I needed.

It must have taken a couple of hours all told but I don't think he ever yawned or tapped a foot or looked around the room.

Finally I was just sitting on the floor of the tajj, talked out, cried out, and raged out, ready to just be quiet. Dad tossed his shirt into the hopper for the clothes-grower to grind up and recycle.

"Sorry about that, I know that's your favorite."

"A new one'll grow in two minutes, it's not a problem. But I'm kinda worn out, Teri-Mel, and—"

"Sleep, Dad, I'm okay now. Thanks."

"Wake me if you need me." He hugged me again and went back to his own room to sleep.

Despite all his patience and kindness to me, I couldn't help thinking that Dad had looked tired, old, and discouraged. I made myself a cheeseburger and fries in the reconstitutor, took a quick shower, and kinda fell into bed. Being in bed without an exosuit felt funny, just as if I were at school, and kinda scary; I almost got up and put on my exosuit to feel more secure.

⬡ **In the morning** I woke up tired, feeling like I'd been poisoned. Everything around me seemed heavy and dull, and all I wanted to do was stay in bed. But Dad told me that he wasn't about to let me sack-rat. "You'll like yourself better, sooner, if you get out and around right now, before you have too much inertia to overcome. Get out, get around, give people the impression you've already shaken off the dumb son of a bitch and six more like him. Don't fall in love again right away, don't get into brawls, don't go places where you think Perry will be, but other than that, just go places, meet people, see things. Here's your schedule for today . . . you've got a lunch, two coffees, tea, and that supper with the Wangs and Kindness. I got your FA delayed a day on account of emotional stress, but you're gonna take it first thing tomorrow morning."

I felt like whining, but preferred not to hear myself whine, so I just said "Right, Dad," washed my face, put on my bandeau and patch, and went out to confront the world.

I had hoped to find somewhere quiet to just sit, but other than my own tajj, where I couldn't go cause Dad would know I had sack-ratted, there was no such place. Gathers are about meeting people.

So I braced myself and wandered around, saying hi to people. Friends, especially my own age, would squeeze my arm and tell me they were sorry for what had happened to me. Acquaintances would be sorta awkward, perhaps. But everyone was extremely nice. I guess Dad was right—a vote had been taken, and I had been declared Not the Asshole.

By time for lunch, I was actually looking forward to meeting with some of my school friends. Danielle, Calliope, Urania, and Miriam were children of families that had worked with Dad and Mummy, and as very small children we had often been in the same tajj. Now they were possible future business contacts. Or that was our excuse. Actually it was pretty nice to see everyone again, especially since Calliope had graduated, Urania had dropped out, and Miriam had transferred to a school in Goddard, so even if I went back to school in a few days, I would only be seeing Danielle. Like always, we went to the Djevernik family booth for Sweet and Sour Rabbit on a Stick, and overate and got our faces all sticky, just as we had at every Gather since we were eight or so. That meant having to go back to the tajj to wash my face.

Dad wasn't there, so after scrubbing I spent skoshy mirror time and decided that I'd try one of the new looks just coming in; some women were starting to wear dresses, just like in the old movies, and they had some nice light-weight material that wasn't warm or binding or uncomfortable, so I fabricated a knee-length, sleeveless shift, from the front part of the catalog, a nice looking thing that didn't seem too complicated. Skoshy practice revealed that it wasn't all that easy to remember to keep your knees together and to make sure it didn't hike up too much, but I figured that with most people running around practically naked by comparison, a look up my dress wasn't gonna make anybody's day. And the dress Danielle had been wearing had been just *amazing,* so beautiful and unusual, though she'd discovered that dresses are anything but well-suited to eating messy finger food like Rabbit on a Stick.

I was actually out of the tajj, strolling up the street, enjoying the glances from the guys and the conversations with the women about the dress, before I realized that I'd had about an hour of not thinking about Perry at all—and it had felt just great.

The rest of the day went by in the blur that Gathers do—seeing all sorts of people, leaving business cards everywhere, inviting people to come to our booth on the last two days, admitting that yes, Teri-Mel was Dad's nickname for me and that I was who the new country was named for, and answering questions about what the satellites were seeing (the answer being that the plume was still burning huge and bright and water was snowing out all over Gateway Massif, and the whole country was re-forming too fast to keep track of). It was fun to be the center of attention, and, I admitted to myself, it was also more fun to get the attention and not have a big, good-looking but silent guy (silent, I could admit now, cause he wasn't quick enough to amount to much in a conversation) trying to drag me away from it so that we could "talk serious business" by which he meant "have serious sex."

Next guy, I told myself, will be just as good looking, ten times as smart, and not serious at all.

That night was the dinner with the Wangs. Besides me and Kindness, Earl and Myrtle Foucault were there. They were among the very small minority of people who still practiced cybertao—it was hard to imagine, now, that anyone did, it seemed like part of ancient history, like Napoleon or Jesus or President JFK Jr, but in fact the oldest people still alive had been born *before* cybertao, and had seen the whole rise and fall of the Stochastic Faith, from its start in the early 2000s till it included half the human race by 2025 till it was pretty well gone by 2070.

Give the cybertaos one thing, though, they had had a real tradition—I guess they had thought they would last as long as Islam or Buddhism or Christianity, and so they had been all systematic and everything about laying down all sorts of customs that they thought would last for thousands of years. It made it fun to visit their houses— they did so many quaint things in such interesting ways— but it didn't seem to get them any converts.

Earl was older and affected a more transparent helmet than most rounditachi, with a bigger faceplate; as a result his mask went most of the way up his forehead and all the way down to his upper lip, and he had deep grooves and liver spots in it. He wore his light brown hair long, three centimeters or so, and had a sun-streaked forelock—hard not to stare at. Dad'd hadda tell me, when I was younger, that Earl didn't look weird because he was cybertao; *so don't go getting bigoted about cybertao because of Earl. Earl's not weird because* cybertaos *are weird, he's weird because* Earl *is weird,* Dad had said.

He had met Myrtle at cybertao services; she was a quiet woman with big horsey teeth and full red lips and enormous blue eyes, whose face seemed skoshy too small for all those features, like she got stinted on the blank spaces. She laughed limward more'n she talked, like everyone was real funny, and she particularly liked anything Earl said that sounded like he might have been trying to make a joke. This probably accounted for why they seemed to be such a happy couple.

As cybertaos went, they weren't bad company; they didn't try and push it on you unless you gave them a conversational opening, and you could avoid giving them one.

They talked about as much as I wished Kindness O'Hart would, and vice versa. His name told us all that he'd been born somewhere in the 2040s, the Gray Decade, and back on Earth, cause that was when and where prank names had been so in vogue. (There was a girl at school whose grandma was named Pussy Galore, after some obscure fictional character, and my mother's father had been named Uranus Pootz at birth, only changing it to a nice, normal Ajax Tharsisito after his parents had both died.) But his name was the only clue, really, to Kindness's age. He was one of those ageless people—could have been an old thirty-five or a young seventy.

Esther Wang was trying to get him persuaded that he oughta start looking for a permanent partner—he hadn't had one since he and Dad and Mummy had been partnered, way back—cause according to her he was getting to be too old to solo, since things could happen to you out there, and without a partner, you might just disappear without a trace. "Where with a partner," Kindness pointed out, "I can be buried in a carefully marked grave, which I'm sure will make a *big* difference to me. Sure, things happen, and it's good to have a partner who can go for help if I'm unconscious or lying there in pain, but for almost all situations, satcell is more than enough. The added risk isn't that much. And I like to be able to get some thinking done without having anyone around to interrupt."

"What do you think about?" Walter Wang asked, setting down a plate of real potatoes and a boat of gravy; it was his second trip to the kitchen to reload the serving dishes. People who don't often eat real food eat it with passion.

Kindness stared for a moment, one of those thousands-of-meters-over-the-horizon stares that some adults get when they think back too far, into the Meme War and the Gray Decade and all the other ugly shit that happened long ago on Earth. That was another reason to be glad Dad was Mars-born—he didn't really understand that stuff either.

"Well," Kindness said, after the pause was getting interminable, "I saw a lot of sad and evil things, and a few wonderful and good ones, that I like to turn over in my mind, and try to see the good in, or at least see some way that they weren't so bad. And I look for reasons why. And sometimes I just enjoy having a whole day when I don't think in words. It's basically a way to look for some peace."

Earl cleared his throat importantly, and Esther and Walter exchanged glances, obviously looking for a diversion before Earl could launch into one of his sermonoids (that's what Dad called 'em—he said cause they were too small, and not quite similar enough, to be real sermons, so they were tiny sermon-like objects).

It was perfect that the com chimed just then.

Esther Wang looked up and said "On screen," putting it on the big screen above the table in their tajj. A red and blue ball pattern appeared, and she was rising from the table even before the voice intoned that this extraplanetary transmission had been cleared of memes. "Oh, it'll be from Judy, my sister on Earth. I hope you'll all forgive me, but I'm gonna take it in the bedroom. I won't have any concentration at all while I'm worrying about Judy—they were gonna have to evacuate her, and her family, from the Mohawk Valley for the third time. They thought the ice dam was done with forming and breaking and re-forming, and apparently they were wrong again. So the last I knew they were getting ready to move out on short notice, and maybe lose that house again, and I just want to know that they're all right." She nodded again at all of us, not really checking to see if it was all right—after all, what could we have said anyway?—and bounced through the doorway into the other room. The whisper of an obscurer came up, blurring anything said from that direction.

"Well, this will be a while," Walter said. "She's not going to be able to resist recording a reply to Judy. And she hates having her cooking spoiled by sitting around waiting, so she'll be madder at me if we don't proceed. Anyone want thirds, fourths, whatever we're on?"

The food was wonderful but everyone had already had plenty, so we finished what was on our plates, paused to assess any room we had saved, and then contemplated the possibility of orange sherbet and coffee.

"This must be strange for you," Earl said.

Walter shrugged and continued pouring coffee. "Well, Esther stays in touch with Judy, just cause those two were always so close. And it's not as bad as you might think. I knew Judy before, and when you watch her messages, she doesn't really seem all that different from anyone else. It's not like it was in the first few years after the Second Diaspora, when One True was controlling everyone really tightly and they didn't speak at all without consulting their personal Resunas. Those early messages from Judy were kinda weird and spooky, and of course everyone from Earth remembers back to the original One True, where everyone running it had the same personality and the same reactions and just did what they were supposed to do like ants in a hive or robots on an assembly line. I mean, all the old stories were true. One True really did do things like send long files of kids marching across minefields and into machine gun fire, or capture somebody that some big-shot scientist had a crush on and make her his sex slave to get at him, or just volunteer a couple of hundred people running it as medical research subjects. Purest form of good-of-the-whole evil the world ever saw, and I spent most of the war fighting for the Freecybers, so I saw plenty.

"One True was so bad that when it decided to go emergent instead of single-brain, even the original Resuna was actually an improvement—at least you could see individual mannerisms again, any time One True wasn't giving its full attention to the individual unit. But nowadays most Earth people are just visited by One True—yeah, visited, that's what they call it, it sounds like Judy was having it over for coffee or something—now and then, maybe a few times a year, usually on their birthdays for some morbid reason, and their Resunas stay quiet unless One True needs something, or unless they ask for them to help—"

"Help," Kindness grunted. "Yeah, I guess it looks like help, to be taken over and operated by the meme, to someone who runs Resuna."

"Well," Walter said, "I'm not defending it, you know, but after what all happened in the War of the Memes, there would be billions of real basket cases out there—probably the great majority of the Earth's population—from what they saw, or what was done to them, or what they were forced to do. And with Earth's biosphere in full thrash, they can't afford to have billions of patients to take care of; they need everyone up and working. Now, I'm not saying that One True is the thing they should be working for, or that Resuna isn't controlling and manipulative, or that the whole thing isn't evil, but I am saying that if people couldn't just turn everything over to Resuna every time they get too distressed, that you'd have a planet of screaming lunatics there, and that with Resuna, they're managing to get everything pretty well rebuilt. I wouldn't want it here, but I can understand why there are people glad to have it there, and even, I guess, why they don't trust anyone who isn't running Resuna and plugged into One True. Almost exactly the same way that we don't trust anyone who is. It seems weird and abnormal and besides you understand the way you are, so you want other people to be the same way. If you see what I mean.

"Anyway, if you watched Judy on the screen, you'd

never know there was anything different, let alone wrong, with her; she's the same old Judy, except with perfect courage, perfect calm, and perfect focus when she needs it. God forgive me, every so often when things aren't going so well, and I think about being able to just say those four magic words and get through a day with no stress, always doing the right thing, I even envy her a little. So no, it's not that weird having her and Esther messaging each other all the time. They were always close, and they'd miss each other so much if they couldn't, and Judy's just not that different than she was before."

"Hunh," Earl said. "I've got a brother on Earth, but we didn't have what you call a happy childhood, and I don't think Resuna would let him talk to me—certainly he's never tried calling me. But there's times every now and then when I wish I could talk to him. He's the only one that remembers some things, you know, all the little family inside jokes from when we both were little, and that might be kinda nice, to talk with someone who remembers."

"At least I could find out where you got some of your silly nicknames," Myrtle said, and laughed.

Kindness sighed. "Well, compared to One True itself— the old One True, that ran one full copy to a brain— there's nothing spooky at all about Resuna, at least not on the surface. People say that's just a matter of memory space and processing time, that because Resuna is just your local connection to the big emergent One True, it leaves you much more brain to be yourself with, but I really do think that the emergent One True is different from the old one-to-a-brain version. I talk to old friends, now, who are running Resuna, maybe once an Earth year or two, and I'd have to say that the people I talk to are different than they were, but not necessarily in a bad way. Very often Resuna stomps down people's worst sides. People are made by what happened to them, and what happened to people on Earth for about three generations was bad enough that you don't necessarily want people who were made that way to be running around doing what comes natural."

"So," I said, "How is it different? I mean, how is Resuna different from One True?"

"Like I said, it's not," Walter said. "One True used to run one to a brain, now there's just a single One True and it runs on all the brains running Resuna, but no matter how you look at it, a meme controls the person running it, that's what a meme does, after all. The big difference is that when it's Resuna, it doesn't take up quite so much space, so the person still has the same basic desires, and the same memories, and all the things they did when they were unmemed, and unless they say lolo—"

"Lolo?" Earl asked.

"The abbreviation for the four words."

I'm not sure how effective that was as a way to stay away from them—I immediately thought "let overwrite, let override."

"Anyway, Teri, when Resuna is in effect, rather than running background like it usually does, things in your mind are sort of like the way things are in the city during a power failure or a pressure breach—everyone is posreal calm and reasonable, and does exactly what they need to do.

"And as for One True...well, the current version doesn't reside in any one brain, it's basically a conversation between all those billions of Resunas talking with each other in background whenever they're not needed, so who can really say what it thinks or what it's like? It doesn't seem to kill people just for convenience, or force people into things, or just erase personalities and write what it likes on top of them, the way that the old version did. At least if it does it we don't hear about it, and I don't think it does that kind of thing often. That's good, I guess.

"Or like I said it's better than the way One True used to just grab a brain and do what it wanted. Back in the War, One True would just decide to take a position away from us, and send a whole platoon or company at us, no retreat, no prudence, just go forward until killed, and keep doing it till we caved in. I don't know if the present One True does things like that, but at least since there's no war, and no other competing memes, I don't think it does it quite so often."

Kindness nodded. "The Freecybers seem to have changed it—right at the end of the war, when One True had almost won but it seemed to be slipping away as the advanced Freecybers were spreading around the globe, it was adapt-or-die, and one way memes are not like people is that for them, that's not really a choice. They always adapt. You could see that groups of Freecybers working together in loose local networks were smarter and more flexible and faster than a team of identical One Trues under a single master controller. And the whole secret of the Freecybers was that they were so tiny compared to other memes—for a long time nobody minded carrying one because all it did was protect you from big controlling memes, and even late in the war, when Freecybers started actively grabbing people, they mostly grabbed people that wanted to fight on their side.

"Which is another way that Resuna is very like the old Freecybers. Most of the people on Earth probably really *do* want to work for the recovery of the planet and to get things onto a sustainable basis, and mostly they *do* understand that everyone has to cooperate and play fair and do more than their share and receive less. What Resuna does, besides giving One True a place to be, is let everyone do that together, without all that trauma and stress they remember getting in the way, and make sure that no one even worries for a second that other people might be cheating. Sorta like socialism the way it was meant to be."

Earl shuddered. "My folks were socialists and that sure isn't what they meant."

Kindness shrugged. "I could just as easily have said it was very Christian or very democratic. People have always wanted to share generously and always been afraid that if they did, they'd get taken advantage of. Justifiably afraid, at that. Whether you call it Christian charity or democratic generosity or socialist justice, that's what Resuna gives you—from each according to his abilities, to each according to his needs, *with no cheating.* The fact that Resuna is a small, helpful part of your personality, instead of a huge overriding controller of it, just keeps the yoke from chafing, but plenty of humanity likes their nice comfy yoke, so naturally they seem just like always when you talk to them. Because they are just like always—except nicer and politer and less stressed out."

"You're talkative tonight," Earl said.

Kindness shrugged as if he were losing patience. "Well, I like being out here in the roundings all by myself, to get my thinking done. Happens that some of what you're talking about is things I've done a lot of thinking about." He smiled at me. "And this probably bores poor Teri out of her mind. She knows that Earth got taken over by memes, and then just one meme, and that everybody here is afraid of memes, but I bet she's never even talked with or seen a memed person."

"They won't let us see films of them in school. Parents think it would be too frightening for the kids."

"That must be great," Earl said, waving his spoon for emphasis. "Not to know anything about them, directly, I mean. I hope we never, never, never have any kids on Mars who know anything about memes."

The noise suppressor shut off and Esther came back in. "Well," she said, after all our worry, it was good news. They were able to save the whole Mohawk Valley this time. It turns out that for some years there were crews up in the hills building levees and dikes and a diversion channel to take the whole mess right under the Alleghenies and into the bed of the Old Hudson. It's even helping to sweep some of the silt out of New York harbor, and Manhattan and Long Island are temporarily islands again. So it all got solved; One True was just not telling them all about it because it wasn't certain that it would all get done in time, and it was thought to be less stressful if everyone was redded up for a full evacuation right from the start.

"Other than that, it was just the usual—she's sending along a few of my mom's recipes, which I wanted to try for a little food booth next Gather, just to see if anyone still likes those flavors, and she couldn't remember the rules to Red Rover, Run Sheep Run, or skipball—those were games we played when we were kids, and she wanted to teach her kids—and that was about it. But I bet all of you out here spent the whole time grilling poor Walter about the fact that I still talk to my sister."

It was near enough to the truth for all of us to start a bit, but Esther Wang didn't seem to be angry, or indeed even very concerned. "Really," she said, "people worry too much. You need a tight feedback loop to get a meme into a brain; you can't just ram it in there, you have to incorporate it with the rest of the mind, and to do that you've got to talk in real time. One True has never even been able to take over the Moon, just because of the second-and-a-half radio lag. That's all the protection you need. And radio lag from Earth to out here is sometimes twenty minutes and never less than four. One True is never going to get any memes installed here unless it manages to bring a brain, or a computer, or a recording, here physically, and that's what Planetary Defense is there for. So much of what people worry about is so silly."

Walter's jaw was working hard, and I had a feeling this was an opinion that wasn't supposed to be expressed outside the Wang household, and maybe not inside. "But you wouldn't want your own copy."

"Well, no. It's much too hard to get rid of it. But on the other hand, I remember Judy when she was younger. Real bitch. Self-destructive. Mean and hateful and hard to live with, and I felt so sorry for my brother-in-law. Now she's a full-fledged pleasant reasonable human being. So if you want me to say that Resuna actually hurts people, well, you really can't prove that by Judy."

"We've gotta keep them out," Walter said, in a total non sequitur, "till the ships get back and settle everything."

The room got posreal cold, and all of a sudden Earl and Myrtle were remembering a late-night drink they were supposed to have with someone, and Kindness was noticing how hard it was to stay awake this late at his age. I really did have a mixer I could go to, my first time single in a couple of years, so I like to think that my excuse at least sounded more convincing than theirs. We were all out the door in zilty.

✦✦ **What a lot** is wrapped up in that little word, meme. As a word, it's about 125 years old.

Once upon a time, long ago and very far away, a scientist without much grasp of philosophy set out to cut a figurative Gordian knot. Much as Alexander did when he cut the real one, he got all sorts of applause from people who didn't understand that the whole point was to untie it, and that demonstrating that you could cut a rope did not demonstrate any superiority over the knot-tier, any more than punching a grand master in the nose makes you the better chess-player; ever since then philosophy has been fond of the Gordian knot metaphor, because it covers cases like Sam Johnson kicking that stone so nicely.

So the word meme persisted as an annoying way to label an argument without answering it, every bit as annoying as Freudian terminology, neurotransmitter explanations, sociobiology, and the Briggs-Meyers were in their day. If you don't want to answer someone's argument, or (more likely) you can't, you say that they believe what they believe because they have that belief which is nothing but a belief that they got from somewhere, only you use some synonyms for "belief," and you claim to know what thoughts they didn't voice, and you finish up by making the somewhere a disreputable enough place to discredit the whole thing. As in, you don't agree with me because you are authoritarian, and authoritarianism is nothing but anal-retentiveness, which you got from your mother having paid too much attention to your poop chute. Or as in, authoritarianism is nothing but a dysfunctional drive to mate by force which you got from an inferior set of genes that hasn't worked its way out of the modern population yet. Or in the case at hand, as in, because you've got an authoritiarianism meme which you caught by listening to another authoritarian (more or less the way you'd get a cold if he sneezed on you).

I hear the door close out in the corridor; the last person other than me has gone home. I pull open the drawer, get out the bottle, and wave a salute to the mirror. God, I look like too little real work, too much evil work, too little rest and too much idleness. Naturally my face looks like hell. During her recovery, when Teri got to know me for the second time, she used to suggest that I just have it ironed.

I miss her.

The alternative to all the theories that explain too much—and therefore can never be refuted—is behaviorism, which explains too little. As to why Aunt Edna thinks the bugs under the sink sing to her, behaviorism offers the helpful note that the investigator's notes say that she says that she does.

Every prosecuting attorney, and therefore everyone who works for any prosecuting attorney—such as me—has to be a behaviorist to work well. This is part of why I am such a lousy scientist and content myself with being an artist. If I can show that Ted did whack Bob with an ax until such time as Bob's head did separate from his shoulders, and that Bob was clearly established to be alive until and including that moment when the which said axe did strike his neck, and that Bob was dead afterward or shortly afterward, together with the coroner's statement to the effect that very likely the cause of death was decapitation with an axe, then we need know nothing of Ted's genes, memes, or toilet training, and it is a waste of my time and the taxpayer's money to ask.

The first glass goes right down, no problem, and a little click happens in my brain. I put the bottle away, look up at the ceiling, and think . . . but maybe those old meme-guys back in the twentieth had a little bit of a point. Be careful what ideas get loose in society, because no matter how stupid they are, you never know when some idiot might try to make them happen—it had happened often enough in the past, with dumb ideas from free markets to theocracy to people's republics. In this case, "meme" had become slang among the socially-impaired group that makes up so much of the world's technical staff, meaning "unoriginal idea" or "idea I do not like, to which you adhere despite my disapproval, for reasons I do not care to understand." And this became a part of the vocabulary of technical people generally, and of one technical person in particular.

And in the fullness of time, that technician or engineer or whatever he or she called itself (such people generally want to be precise about their titles, because they suspect that to almost everyone they are just the smart one in the white coat), whose name we do not know but who we think was cybertao, grew up and became a mercenary in the War of Papal Succession when that colossally extravagant folly erupted in 2049.

Earth, which had gotten itself back together, almost, thanks largely to moral suasion from Paul John Paul, had honored him in death by tearing itself apart. The cybertaos didn't care who was pope, but they saw a chance to get into an argument, and I've never known any cybertao who could resist that.

And this one very clever cybertao technician achieved a piece of mischief that had been sought for decades. If a computer virus—that was the term they used then, I know what a poor description it is, but that's what they called the limited-to-one-system memes of the time—were smart enough, it could figure out what was on the other side of an operating system boundary, and port a version of itself over. Naturally when our anonymous technician came up with this "universal virus" (the original term, the same way that automobiles were once "horseless carriages" and radios were "wireless telegraphs"), which was called Good Times in particular, the name given to the general class of which it was the progenitor, probably by its creator, was a name familiar from reading bad pop science—"meme."

To a meme, a human brain looked exactly like a very big massively parallel processor, and in the first few years of the war, there was an amazing plethora of direct-to-brain and brain-through-eye military hardware around. It didn't take long for copies of Good Times to learn how to cross over . . . or for the other contenders in the war to devise other memes . . . and in a couple of years, the War of Papal Succession became the War of the Memes, and the memes began to kill each other off, until finally one big fat one sat astride humanity, like the last survivor in a roomfull of cannibals: One True. Which for reasons fully explicable only to itself, discovered that it preferred to live as an immanent presence in a network of minds, rather than wholly in any one mind; and so it brought out Resuna. And One True, through all its Resunas, looked and saw that the world was itself.

I pull out that bottle again. Radio lag is the barrier that memes can't cross; a meme can talk its way into your head but not if you have time to think. Praise the Old God and Albert Einstein, Earth is quarantined by radio lag, because the light speed limit is not just a good idea, it's the law.

The cap comes off smoothly in my practiced hand. One more for this. I feel no twinges and no guilty conscience, no self-hatred for what I'm doing to my body and spirit by being an alcoholic. If I were running Resuna, it would be trying to save me from myself, making me feel that drinking was wrong, calling me quietly away from the stuff. I consider, idly, whether to go shoplifting on the way home, or to pick a fight with a stranger. Nothing has caused anything to wake up to protect me. This is good, so far. Whether it's an effective trick, I don't know. Most of us do it though. (That little observation indicates a tendency toward behaviorism, either because my rigid father inclined me to behaviorism, or because those with a genetic predisposition to behaviorism (which gave them some advantage over predators or in finding mates ...) became behaviorists, or because I have a behaviorist meme.)

An applied semiotician would notice I have just formulated the sentence "I have a ... meme" after engaging in behavior intended to keep memes away. I always hated applied semiotics seminars. I got top scores without studying, and I did some postgrad in it, but I remember now, I always hated it.

When One True got the Earth, Mars got nervous. Because there's dozens of ways a meme could come to Mars, or anywhere else. It could be carried by someone emigrating from Earth, so we stopped all trade in people. It could be carried by a little unit no bigger than a basketball on a solar sail no bigger than the side of a tall building, so we put in the orbital patrols to stop those and burn them as they came in. It could be wrapped up in a long video message, so we only allowed short ones and we randomly altered things to screw them up.

Or it could already be here. Somebody might have screwed up. Somebody might have been a traitor for money or some other silly reason. There might be someone memed, walking among us, and the meme might be clever enough to keep hiding itself.

Until the host did something different from the usual. That's where I come in. I'm the cop in charge of things different from the usual. Oh, sure, I pick through the nasty ooze that is the brain of a child molester, and I shine bright light into the inner dark crevices of a wife-beater, and all that. Now and then I establish that someone is pretty normal except for killing a couple people for money.

But in every case, every time . . . even when no law has been broken . . . when another cop gets a crawly feeling on the back of her neck, or when he finds someone who is weird in an unusual way of being weird . . . they call me. That's why there's always a shrink to call, no matter how remote you get, out here.

I raise the bottle, pour the final glass of the night. Here's to One True, god of permanent employment. And here's to its puritanical nature, for as long as I treat myself badly, I know I have not acquired a copy of Resuna. The henhouse is still being guarded by a big, mean chicken, and not the fox.

And it's still an open question whether the chicken is big and mean enough.

I swallow it; it feels good; and I decide that Teri can live one more day before I write back. She said it was urgent but she did say I could have a few days. Tonight, early bed, and a big anti-hangover shot. I contemplate seeing if I can get some kind of VD somewhere, and detect no immediate rush of self-preservation.

⚿ **I'd gone to** mixers with Perry, now and then, because I liked to dance and he liked to stand sullenly in the corner and watch other girls' butts. It was kinda fun, discovering how many things I had always known that I could now admit to myself.

Roundito kids don't dance all that well, and you donwanna know about roundito grownups. Nobody gets much practice. But everyone has fun.

If nothing else, I at least got the feeling that there might be a guy, or two, or six, that would be willing to replace Perry. I'as gonna have a social life, and there would be life after Perry.

The dance wound down, with just a few insistent romantics who hadda have the experience of being thrown out. There were a few parties going on, mostly thrown by young marrieds without kids, who had the energy and the time to be up late, and attended by people who were trying to become young marrieds. But for the most part, the pavilion was closing down for the night. It was almost midnight.

I went back home feeling tired and sorry for myself, and, to tell the truth, skoshy sniffly about Perry—I think mainly cause it was late and I was tired.

The next morning I woke up, feeling seriously all right. Dad had been off visiting with some half a dozen guys he knew from the early days of ecospecting, to swap lies about the big dust storms and the big scoreholes of the early years.

Dad was one of those lucky people that hangover pills work perfectly, or better than perfectly, on. He got up at dawn, the same time I did, bright and chipper, like he'd been drinking fruit juice all night.

So since we were both up early, and the Kiwanis was holding a pancake breakfast, and we'd promised so many people we'd see them there, we went to that, loaded up big plates of food, and gobbled those down.

If you get there in the first hour—make a note of this in case you ever go to a Gather, Doc—they still have the pancakes made from Marsform wheat flour, ground right there at the fair, and I don't know why—it can't be any sentimental attachment because I never encountered Earth wheat—they just taste limward better than the ones from synthesized flour that you get all year round. Don't ask me to understand or explain it, but the little bacteria in the tank just never quite make flour the way you get it when you grind up wheat.

After we had stuffed ourselves, we circulated, talking with everyone. We had a great time, not to mention getting a bunch of additions to our optional nice-to-see list out of the way, freeing up time for more in the next few days.

Plus it's so much better to get there early when thousands of little kids haven't already been and the tables are not sticky.

When it was all done, Dad said, "Well, there's a week left in the Gather. Are you bearing up okay? Would you like for me to arrange for us to leave early? Someone else can take the party of kids in to Red Sands City for school."

"You know," I said, "I've always loved Gathers, and Perry always complained about being at them. If *he's* got a problem, *he* can leave early." Ruth might make sure that happened anyway.

"Murray family attitude coming out again, Teri," Dad said, grinning. "How much time till you take your FA?"

"About an hour and a half."

"Nervous?"

"Not by comparison. I think the worst thing that's gonna happen already did. And I'm feeling pretty redded up. I should be free about noon, when I've got lunch with the Rodenskys—they're posreal interested in putting together a big group to seed Tragedy Canyon next spring, and maybe found a town there. That would sure make the crater open up faster."

We stopped, called up our virtual werps on the little pocket remotes that we carried when we weren't wearing exosuits, and projected a screen onto some smooth white ground. "Looks like you've got a few hours this afternoon, broken up with some coffee now and then," Dad said.

"Did you have something in mind?"

"Well, one of those culture gangs is coming out to perform for us peasants. Symphony, jazz, some dance, and a poet or two. And a softball game outside—the Red

Sands City, Lowell, and Korolev teams are all coming out
to play some exhibition ball with some pickup teams here.
So there's a lot to do and see. I know it won't be as much
fun as wandering around making big eyes, the way you
spent the last two Gathers—"

Something about Dad's tone made me look up at him.
"Dad, were you lonesome when I was with Perry all the
time?"

He shrugged. "It is not the job of a teenage girl to
keep her father company."

"That's not the question I asked."

"It was my answer."

"Dad—don't ask me why, but just for the moment I
want the truth out of you."

"Now, that's gonna really screw up family tradition.
Well, all right, Teri, yeah, I was lonesome all the time at
the last few Gathers. It was nice to see the old crowd and
answer all those questions about our scoreholes, and all
the usual stuff, but in the first place, I missed doing all the
fun stuff cause don't ask me why but there's something
hardwired into men, so that we need an excuse to do fun
stuff, and I didn't have my daughter to be my excuse. I'd
be standing around looking at a new growable drill and
wishing I could go see a ball game, or I'd be checking out
a strain of lichen when I wished I could go see the ballet
with you. I know that's pretty stupid. There's all kinds of
fun that men don't have unless we have women or children
around so that it will be okay for us to have it.

"And when we tried to do things with Perry . . . well,
when you guys first started out, he was always all over
you. Now I know you're a free citizen and I don't feel

like you should hafta accomodate yourself to my comfort, and I know that kids have sex with each other pretty much whenever they get the chance, which thankfully isn't often. I know all that. But all the same, I had a hard time with the idea that this guy was having sex with my little girl, and you know how young men are, they hafta keep that stuff in the father's face. So I wasn't comfortable, and I was having to work so hard to like the guy since he was important to you. And then after he finally got a skosh calmed down . . . well, he didn't like doing the silly fun stuff. He didn't want to go look at the landscape painting contest or try out funnel cake. He mostly wanted to check prices and go to meetings about subcontracting. Posreal businesslike boy. Which is what I used to say to myself so I wouldn't think, 'what a *lump*.' Well, I figure, I do enough business, at Gathers, to stay in business, and that's all the business I want to do. I don't hafta be one of the great ecospectors of all time, I just want to—hey, that's funny though."

"What?"

"Well, I *am* one of the great ecospectors of all time. And so are you. We just hit the second biggest methane pocket ever, and it was by far the deepest. And then on the same day we opened a highway into a five thousand square kim development basin, and set off a warm spring that'll create a major oasis. Basically we opened up the Prome. Nobody thought there was anything that size left out there, or any project that big to do. Teri—we're legends!"

I started laughing. "Oh, well, look at it this way.

Perry's gonna be a totally different kinda legend. If he'd've behaved himself, he'd've been marrying into all that. As it is, him and Ruth's gonna scramble all over the rocks, punching holes and setting off bombs, without too much planning the way he likes it, for the next few years, the poor bastard. I wonder if he thinks about that."

"Ah, let's hope for his sake that he's so in love with that girl that he never does think about it. Serious-minded men like Perry sometimes just eat themselves up inside over missed chances, and the one that got away, and should've-would've-could've. Especially they do that if they're short on imagination. And I know you're good and mad at the boy, and it's a relief to me to not hafta pretend I like him, but the world won't be better if he's out there stewing in his disappointment and anger and stupidity. Especially not taking it out on a wife and kids."

"Dad, if you get any more noble, I'm gonna puke. Tell you what, I'll just hate him."

"Fair enough. So do we get to go do all the fun stuff this time?"

"You bet. Hey, there's time before my FA if you want to go see some of the exhibits of new Marsform animals. We really ought to do that anyway."

So we did. As usual, most of the "new" stuff was just variations on existing Marsforms, and though Dad'n'me liked seeding work well enough, it wasn't as much fun as drilling or releases or any of that, and now that we were rich, it didn't seem like we limward wanted to go out there and spend weeks planting trees or releasing bugs. We'd still be valuable but we could concentrate more on the fun part of being valuable, so we really didn't need to see Aregene's new Chryse Glory kokanee; it looked like every other stupid salmon we'd ever seen.

The exciting thing was always to see the posreal new Marsforms, the plants and animals that Mars had never had before. Aregene had a very fast-growing cold-weather bamboo with an extra-thick barrel filled with sugary oil. Supposedly it would help to pile up biomass along rivers, which was interesting in a businessy kinda way, as was the bug that would feed on the bamboo's leaves and supply fish food.

Aregene had the designer right there at the booth to describe it all and answer questions, so we stopped to put him through his paces. "So what's that bamboo do, ecologically?" Dad asked.

"It'll slow down water and trap soil. Right now runoff is still pretty much unimpeded and Martian rivers have way too extreme a flood-drought cycle and they're always too muddy. This will fix that, thoroughly and for good. Besides, if the bamboo takes off, we're redded up to go with this." He clicked up a picture for us.

"Wow, what are they?" I asked.

He grinned. "This is the one I want to be showing, but till we have some rivers with something to shelter them, we can't release in the wild. There's a few dozen of each of them already, though, in the pens at Marinersburg. The one on the right is an interim species because Mars just doesn't have air enough yet to support flight for anything big, but things do float better here, so what it is, basically, is a great big flightless duck with extra feathers for the cold, which somebody dubbed the duckasaur. And since it needed to be more of an omnivore to get enough energy, we equipped it for slightly better fish-eating and plant-pulling by reawakening the tooth genes in the Bear Regions. So you might also think of it as a dinosaur with the flavor of a duck and the meat-making qualities of a giant turkey."

"With those teeth, are they gonna be dangerous?" Dad asked.

"Only to fish, bottom-grass, and bamboo shoots. I guess it could give you a nasty bite if you provoked it, and the mothers will still defend nests because those genes are awfully hard to switch off, but normally, no, basically they've got the personalities of sheep. And they ought to make the Chinese community in Lowell real happy—they've been wanting a reliable source of duck for a long time.

"Now this one here is actually built from museum DNA—the base species is extinct on Earth. What it is, is a Marsform beaver. We took some advantage of the cube-square law and made it limward bigger, of course. Did you study them in school at all, Teri?"

"Uh, let's see, early North America, frontier tradition, beaver pelts?"

"That's the stuff," he agreed. "These guys are modified quite a bit in some more subtle ways; since they were cold-conditions critters on Earth, all we had to do was give him the high-CO2 bloodstream, extra-big lungs, and a somewhat more efficient metabolism, plus the usual low-pressure adjustments. They still make a good coat but their muscles are pork and they have no musk glands. The originals weren't much as eating, but these guys have near as much lean meat on them as the pygmy pigs they raise for meat."

"And they must eat tons of food to keep functioning on Mars," I said.

"They do. That's one of the biggest redesign projects we have going—if Mars is going to have Marsform humans and a lot of large animals, we need to make sure there's plenty of sugar and fat created in the ecology as a whole.

"Now, what the beavers do for the ecology is this. They have an instinct to cut down trees and build dams across rivers, and they live in brushpiles that they build in the ponds that they make. The ponds silt up and become swamps or meadows, and the meadows become stands of trees, and it slows the river down and cleans it up. And since as soon as it silts up they move and build another one, eventually you end up with forests spreading outward from the rivers, and with big slow clean rivers that hold lots of water and dole it out slowly, and all kinds of new niches to introduce things into. Really good way of building up biomass because of all the good stuff that sinks to the bottom and the slow way the stream runs. Here's a picture—artist's conception—of what a stream should look like after a hundred years."

It was just beautiful. The bamboo in the background was huge, maybe a meter across the trunk and fifty meters tall—it's so easy to make trees tall on Mars, especially if they can bend in our winds. In and among the bamboo, pine saplings grew, and scrubby underbrush trailed off into the dim spaces between the trees.

In the foreground, the water was greenish, and paddling across it were two of the duckasaurs; behind them, a giant beaver rested on its pile of brush. The sky overhead was a magnificent red arch just cut at the top by the blue aureole.

The rep clicked, and we saw a grassy expanse with the stream winding through it; the shapes of the distant hills, and some of the stands of tall bamboo, said it was the same place. "This is forty Mars years later."

Click. "And eighty." Now it was a tall-trunked forest with a swift, narrow stream cutting deep into the forest floor—and, in the background, two beavers beginning to fell the first bamboo for their dam.

"Incredible," Dad said. "Every ecospector is gonna want to try to do that any place the climate will support it. It's just gorgeous, and *look* at all the biomass accumulated here—just click through it so we can compare, if you don't mind—" he pointed to different spots between the the pictures. Of course Aregene was making the pictures look good, but ad pictures are regulated, and they do have to get a certified modeler in there to make sure that the picture honestly depicts what the numbers say, and obviously the numbers said that a beaver forest was going to accumulate a pretty incredible mass of duff and silt. "This is the kinda thing you dream about for the end result of a scorehole."

"Well, to get this to happen, other things have to happen first," the rep said. "Mainly we have to get enough bamboo growing. So for right now Aregene's priority, because it's what the Development Corporation will pay us the most for, is seeding and growth."

"How ready to go is it?" Dad asked, still sounding more interested than I'd have expected.

"We've got the bamboo in stock now, seed or seedling, we're paying a sixty percent premium for planting seedlings and they are acceleration resistant, so you can have them delivered by mail rocket. We even reimburse you a third of the charges for the mail rocket. Then as soon as we've got full-grown third-generation natural-seeded bamboo—that takes about six Mars years in all, it reaches full height and starts seeding at the end of the second Mars year—"

"Lifespan?" I asked.

"They've tried to take that out completely," the rep said. "As much as they could they stripped out all the limiting genes. Might be more or less like an Earth sequoia, but we're only claiming at least as long as Mars oak."

That was supposed to last about 125 Mars years, or 225 Earth years—not bad at all. "What do the beavers eat?" I asked.

"On earth, the inner bark of trees, plus any stray vegetation. What we did here is to fill the bamboo trunks with this stuff"—he held up a bottle of thick goop—"and that sticky goo in the middle of the bamboo is basically candy, though *we* wouldn't like it with all the antifreezes in it. Anything living out here in the cold, on short oxygen, is really going to want limward calories, and the bamboo will put it out in huge amounts. We've even equipped the bamboo to heal easily so that the beavers can open one up for food for a while, then forget about it, and it will usually grow over and refill. Just dealing with the basic big-Marsform problem—everything you engineer ends up having to eat constantly. That's another reason we like the bamboo—everything will be able to eat it."

"Nice," I admitted. "Your engineers must be proud."

"Yep, exactly what the Alice River ought to look like," Kindness said, behind me. I turned and he was pointing to a view of a river surrounded by mature Marsform bamboo, flowing down into what must be a very new beaver pond, since there were many felled trunks beside it.

Dad did one of those roundings-whoops that so many people seem to like (they're okay at a Gather, but on suit-to-suit they're *painful*) and pounded the old man's back. "You still love that river for some reason."

"Pure sentimentality. We all know how *that* goes. And I happen to know that there's a little area up on the Tharsis where there's a lot of square kim of Marsform drylands conifers, each sitting in its own carefully blasted pothole, cracking rock and digging in and looking more like a bonsai farm than anything because there's hardly one more than five foot—I mean, a meter and a half, I grew up in the old system—tall, and they're all twisted and knobby and it looks like it ought to be a haunted forest for munchkins, but I know a guy who's awfully proud of that."

"Guilty," Dad admitted.

I'd already been giggling because every time we did a northern migration we hadda stop off and see Leslie's Forest, which Dad had named after Mummy, their first big scorehole right after they got married.

"There's two streams running through there, now, did you know that?" Kindness asked.

"I'd heard there was, but I haven't been back since the northern stream started to run. How's it doing?"

"Real good. Winds all over the place, gets just about the maximum possible amount of water into the ground, nice slow flow, couple of little waterfalls. And I don't think it killed even thirty trees—it mostly runs in gulleys where you didn't plant. Beautiful little stream. I followed it most of the way up to the spring, going into that country, last time I was north."

"So how do you think our bamboo would do there?" the rep asked, getting skoshy anxious to get the homecoming over with and get things moving toward a sale again.

Kindness shrugged. "It'll be pretty enough either way. But with the extra stream, and there's probably room to start two more—it's on the artesian aquifer that comes northeast out of Chryse—yeah, probably a good idea."

"Your beavers, when they're introduced, won't eat *all* the trees, will they?" Dad asked, and I knew he was thinking that he wanted the place to stay Leslie's Forest, posreal, forever.

"No danger of that. In the first place, they'll be there no matter what, because they do migrate, so we had to be careful about building in a slow reproductive rate. And they don't use very many trees, and they'll prefer our bamboo because it'll grow along the streams. And because they'll be producing all those big rich soil deposits, you'll eventually end up with more forest, not less. It'll just have some meadows and ponds in it."

"Well, that might be all right." Dad and Kindness both took copies of the information for their werps, and put down reservations on bamboo seedlings. Officially they had ninety days to cancel, but I had a feeling that the Alice River and Leslie's Forest were both going to be visited in the next Mars year. Neither of 'em really liked seeding, but when it came to their favorite little patches of territory, my dad and Kindness were capable of practically anything to make it all bloom. I understood that, though, a little; I was already starting to think how well this would go in Tragedy Canyon and in the Terimel country.

And nowadays, Doc, I understand it completely. Have I told you I'm applying to lead a group up that way, this coming southern spring?

"So, what've you got backstage?" Kindness said. That was always one of the most fun things, once you'd made a deal, the rep could usually get you a look at a few things in the sample terraria—three years ago they'd had a Marsform baby woolly mammoth, beautiful in a weird looking way, the start of a zoo population that was going to be let loose twenty-five Mars years into the future. And everybody was talking about the Marsform dogs and cats that would be joining the froyk bands real soon.

"Ah, I wish we did." The rep sounded really unhappy. "But security held up all sorts of development projects that we were ready to start on. There were some weird sequences in the last stuff up from Earth, and they're afraid that One True is playing games again. It's been four Mars years since the last time it tried this trick, but I suppose it never stops trying."

"This is One True trying to smuggle copies of Resuna to Mars—?" I asked.

"Yeah, in the genetic material. All that unactivated, ready to go code, all those Bear Regions where we look for the genes from Earth's ice ages and high CO_2 periods and so forth, there's plenty of room in there to hide copies of Resuna. The idea isn't that we're going to accidentally make an animal that runs Resuna, but that the computers doing the sequencing or the genetic systems working out solutions might get taken over, and once it got onto a big powerful platform with enough links to other places, Resuna would be whipping through the rest of Mars in no time, and we'd have our own One True overnight. So anyway, they found those sequences which just don't quite look natural, but they tell me sometimes artificial-looking sequences can occur naturally—and until they know what those sequences are, they're not gonna let any of the plants or animals based on them outside of tight containment."

"Makes sense," Kindness said. "Glad you're careful."

The rep nodded. "Still, it's a disappointment to everyone not to have anything new to show."

Then I looked at the time and realized I hadda run for my FA. I left Dad and Kindness chatting casually as I waved off and ran like a maniac to get there in time. I had two minutes to spare when I got to the test center.

Is there some term for the opposite of a nightmare, Doc? Cause I've never had the opposite of a nightmare, but that's what it was like. I sat down and knew all my stuff, posreal and no having to get slippery, and was done with the academics in zilty. Then the maturity interview was completely different from every one I'd ever had before, they gave me this big teddy bear of a guy instead of one of the rude little rat-men that they had every time before, and he asked a few questions and got me talking about myself, and I didn't even know that that was the interview—about the time I expected him to tell me we'd be getting into it, he said that I might as well hang around cause they'd have scores back in a few minutes.

And when they did, I had passed by a wide margin. They updated my records, shook my hand, and just like that, I was a grown-up.

    It's stupid that it's not easier to make this call; I hear too many voices in the back of my mind, my parents asking me why I can't just take care of things by myself, my teachers implying that if I just thought about things more I'd know the right thing to do, my own beer mutterings about how no one ever seems to be able to do anything, just for themselves, any more, about what a dependent society we've become.

I admit the need for anesthesia and pour a shot. It's the middle of the second day since Teri's message; I'm sitting here watching all my old recordings, and I've started to realize that first of all I have this weird feeling of importance, as if, if, if, if . . . if I just watched the right piece of the right recording, I would suddenly know exactly the right thing to do—but I won't know anything till I find it.

That's a suspiciously ineffective thought. It rings of self-sabotage. I don't like that.

Then when I had that suspiciously ineffective thought, I had other thoughts right on top of it. The roundings are reopening fast, now; there aren't many rounditachi, not with so many losses during Sunburst, but there are enough. Teri's whole self-concept is bound up in being the best of the best rounditachi, and in being Telemachus Murray's daughter. If what we fear is true, she'll be set back severely . . . and right now she's leading her first group traverse, as well. Being removed from that—losing her first time as a full, not emergency, traverse captain—would make even a record as good as hers utterly stink. And then having had massive memory erasures and rebuilds afterwards . . . she'd have to start at the bottom.

Furthermore it has been known to happen that when you take too many memories, you take some talent as well. Sometimes talent is an ability to learn something thoroughly, but only to learn it once. We pulled a traumatizing mess of memories out of a talented amateur painter once and he never really even learned to draw again; I've seen a case not much different from Teri's that cost a young woman her talents for violin and poetry.

I hate things like that, and I hate them deeply. I don't want to have to see them happen again, especially not to someone I like, like Teri.

But those reasons all have an oddly slick, creepily well-formed quality to them. Before I can think of more, I grab my com and start talking. I call Cal, my oldest friend in the business, one of the backup consulting specialist shrinks at Marinersburg, and start talking fast. Maybe it's only nervousness that's making me stammer. Maybe I only feel confused and sleepy—actually I feel like telling him to forget it, actually I'm fine—or that it's all a joke and gee he should have seen his own face—maybe I just feel that way. Or if there's a reason for me to feel that way, maybe it's that I'm worried sick about Teri and I've been sitting up thinking about her, and drinking too much coffee trying to fight off too much booze.

That seems very plausible to me, and I feel so ashamed of having bothered Cal.

Those feelings frighten me so badly that I say "Hurry, please, please hurry," and he promises to catch the very next train and be here before the end of day. I disconnect before I can think of any more reasons for him not to come, and, shaking and afraid, pour myself a big one in a water glass and pound it down. I grab that emergency button on my desk and push it before I remember what it's for.

This is stupid. Now I can't get out of my office. I can't even make a com call out, even if I want a simple pizza. If I had just reported the message from Teri when I first got it, I would be able to come and go like a normal person. It's very unfair that it's too late, now, to do that; I want to call them, out there in the office, and explain how unfair it is, and have them unlock me. I could order that pizza.

It's a good thing there's a bathroom in here.

No pizza, but there's a nice big water tumbler of whiskey. I look at the clock and try to figure out the exact minute when Cal will walk in.

Nothing else to do, so I might as well watch more of Teri's recording. It's coming up on the sad parts, pretty soon now, not much left till it gets sad, but I'm a big boy and a professional shrink—hell I was dealing with sadder shit before I was twenty—and I know I can handle it, so I take another sip and start the recording playing again.

I really like that kid. I feel so sorry and sick about what's going to happen.

⚅ **The rest of** that day, between social calls, Dad'n'me just kinda got caught up with all the stuff we used to like to do before Perry had come into my life. We saw some of a ball game. Dad loved those for some reason. Even though out in the roundings, often with nothing to do at night, he could have watched all the baseball and softball that he wanted, he never did out there, and he never really followed any of the teams. It finally occurred to me to ask him, and he said, "Oh, well, it's pretty simple. Your great-grandpa was crazy for the game and sort of passed it on to all his children and every grandkid he could get close to. I guess I wasn't all that susceptible, because the game really doesn't do a thing for me, but I like sitting in the bleachers. Makes me feel like a little kid hanging out with Grandpa, again."

So we did all the art and culture stuff, and all the hanging around with old friends, and we contrived excuses to meet people accidentally so it wouldn't count as part of the required visiting structure. Everywhere we went, people shook my hand and hugged me and welcomed me to being a grown-up.

By the end of the day, after I'd gotten back from a mixer and he'd gotten back from having wine with Kindness, as I stretched out in my bed (it still felt so weird and dangerous not to be in my exosuit—sometimes I wondered if that wasn't one of the things I hated most about school) I had the strange thought that Perry had more or less vanished from my memories and feelings, and that I was myself again after a couple of years' absence. I decided I liked myself and I'd have to see more of me.

"Dad," I called out. "You still awake?"

"Yeah, Teri. What's up?"

"Uh . . . about that ecospecting degree. I was thinking. Since I got my FA and all . . . and since, well, I was noticing that I don't understand half the things they say in the ads for the new Marsforms. Is it that way for you too?"

"Been that way for a long time. Want to come sit in the main room for a bit, if we're gonna talk?"

"Yeah. Hey, let's reconstitute some popcorn and cider."

"Contract. I was skoshy hungry myself."

After we'd settled in with the snack, I said, "Now here's what I was thinking. That field school doesn't sound nearly so bad, and they say it's three quarters of the time, right? And the fact is that I want to stay an ecospector, and having to know all this tech stuff is only gonna get worse. I mean it stands to reason that if there's so much now there's gonna be more later. And I might even be kinda interested in what they have to teach. I'd posreal like to know how those real scientists out there know all that stuff they pass on to us, and what they do with the field recordings they buy from us, and like that. So, uh, since I don't hafta finish CSL school, anyway, I'd like to um . . . well, I'm gonna apply for that program."

"Let me get my werp so we can get your application sent before you sober up," Dad said, his eyes twinkling.

⬤⬤ **"If we could** just make the memory cut right where we made it before," I say to Cal, "and of course everything afterward, basically it would be all right. She'd lose some later memories that were pretty sad, and she'd lose some important parts of her life—almost a year of it, actually—but at least she'd have some direct memories of the days leading up to all this. It still kills me that we had to lose her last happy times with her father. I know the orthodox thing to do is to take the whole preceding period of susceptibility because stuff can always regrow on it, but think of what a shock she woke up to before, and then think about how much worse it'll be if we extend the memory loss further back—bouncing right from a happy time of her life to this. Not to mention we might lose a lot of maturity that was very hard for her to get in the first place. If we start the cut later in her life . . ."

Cal is staring at me. He's one of those no-nonsense shrinks that takes the job very seriously, parties hard whenever he's not working, always raising one flavor or another of hell I guess you could say.

It's been three days since Teri wrote the message that started me on this strange little quest, and god alone knows what has been going on out in her little stretch of the roundings. By now she's reached Tragedy Valley, leading a party there, to develop a little way-stop that will serve ecospectors on their way to Telemachuston. She has used some of her money to loan her aunt a grubstake, so that she will establish a teeper there in Tragedy Valley (and her Aunt Callie gets to escape from the parents, which I rather suspect is more the point of the whole thing). Then no doubt a road will be thumped in to serve the teeper, and in time the rail line will have a spur there, and some day Tragedy Lake will be a well-known vacation spot, and the Falls of the Dancer will be something people go to for their honeymoons, and there will be some stupid story floating around about something bad that happened to a dancer (probably that she fell, tragically), which will gradually get so embellished that the folklorists will keep claiming there has to be some grain of truth in it somewhere, and people will also go there on vacation to do folklore research and try to establish who the dancer that fell was, and when.

But meanwhile—three days ago, Teri was still just

south of the railhead and walking over the pathway where she'll want a road thumped, and she took a minute to message me. She sent it via the back channel, using all kinds of little tricks to make the data trace tougher; any roundita always has an angle or six.

All we have to do now is decide what to tell Teri, get her in here, and get to work.

"Every time we take the memory, and we don't get what we went in after, it takes months for the problem to show up," Cal says. "And we *always* take more than we need to. We have to do that."

"But think what this one includes!"

"It includes a lot of things she'd want to lose if she could."

"That's the problem," I tell Cal. "She can't. They're important things in her life that she needs to know about. And knowing about it from the tape is not the same as knowing it from your own vivid memory! Think about what she's lost and the sacrifices she's made already, and the possibility that all she has is a good case of the creeps. Think about what we have to do if it's really the worst. Think about how much more she'll lose. Put all that together and it's not such an easy decision, is it?"

Cal sighs and shrugs and says that none of these decisions is ever easy, every one of them is something that any sensible person would lose sleep over, and he can't let me off the hook just for that. It's the first time I'm aware that he's not just here as my friend, either administratively to help me out with a difficult case, or personally to make sure I'm all right while I deal with it. "Am I being investigated?" I ask, though I already know the answer.

"All of us always are." He bends and pulls open the drawer where I keep my bottle. "You know this isn't held against you. Or against me. So I'm going to pour us two glasses, and you and I are going to sit and talk like old friends, and you're going to tell me the truth, exactly as you know it."

I take a deep breath and check my own thoughts, and so far as I can tell, he's right. I don't feel any intention forming to lie to him or to hold anything back. That relieves me quite a bit.

"I think you're right," I say. "I am going to tell you the truth exactly as I know it."

"That's what you would say, though, no matter what, isn't it? All right, start back when you got the message she recorded for you, three days ago, and make sure you tell me not just about the contact you actually made afterward, but about all the ones you thought of making or intended to make." Discreetly, he switches on his recorder, with a neat little move that only a practiced eye is apt to detect. It's a twin of mine, which now lies across the room, mute and ineffective.

⚙ **The morning after** the final night of the Gather—it was officially September 2, 2095—they turned the streetlights on early for people who were leaving. Dad'n'me'as up first thing cause we hadda be on time, but like Dad said we hadda be on time with our patient hats on cause with a buncha kids to get together an early start was not gonna happen, but if we didn't try to make it early, we'd never start at all. So we knocked down the tajj, packed up quick, and got over to Vestria's where we'd meet the party.

Vestria's was an egg-and-pancake place on Chowhouse Row, pricey enough to have its own enclosure and heater, and more comfy than good but comfy's what we wanted that morning. The food booths and the teepers usually stay open right on through the packup and the haul-out, cause all the ecospectors're trying to get everything all together and redded up for the next few months and they like to be able to get food without having to clean up after; leaving day is usually the biggest day there is for a food booth (and it's always biggest for a teeper).

I had the eggs in stewed tomatoes and the buckwheat

pancakes, both posreal good like always, and Dad had that weird thing called a scramble sandwich—pancakes with a thin layer of fluffy sweetened eggs between—that was school food when he'as a kid. I guess a lot of older people like that. Suppose it might be evidence of hereditary madness, Doc, or do you like it too?

The coffee was good and strong too and Dad'n'me sat chatting, idly rechecking the map, waiting till time to go stand out by the door and meet our party. We'as already in exosuits, but with helmets off and only the cooling running, just sitting and enjoying being together. It felt skoshy different, I thought, than times like this time had felt before. I wasn't wailing over a boy, whining about going to school, or trying to wheedle some last treat out of Dad . . . well, posreal, looked like I was behaving like a grown-up. Maybe the people that set up that FA knew more'n it looked like they did.

Dad went to use the restroom—he didn't grow up in an exosuit like I did and he used to say that he could never get over the feeling that he'as going in his pants, so he liked to go indoors while he could—is that okay, Doc, to have that on the recording?—anyway, so I knew he'd be in there a while, and I'as just enjoying a skosh more coffee when Perry slid into the seat across from me.

I could've said "What are you doing here?", which would've been a real good question, or I could've just told him to go to hell, which would've been a real good answer, but posreal no words came at all. The black hair and big blue eyes and the deep tan of his mask against the cream of his skin, well, it got me just like always. That square jaw and high cheekbones and the big rawboned shoulders

... he was still in his family food booth smock and you could see plenty of his body ... well, that boy still had some weird limward magic on me, Doc, and that's all there was to it. Turd though he was, he was one posreal beautiful turd.

So I took a deep breath, let it all go, and just stared at him.

"Mind if I sit down for a minute?"

"You already did."

"Uh, yeah, uh, listen. I just wanted to wish you good luck and everything and say it wasn't anything personal."

"Perry, there were all kinds of reasons I was crazy about you these past couple years, but posreal, your brains'as never one of'em. You dumped your fiancée and married another girl. It had fucking well better be personal, cause if it was all just business then you're not only a bigger bastard than even I would've thought, but you just blew the biggest deal of your life, too. Now, look, if you wondered if I'as okay, I'm not yet, no thanks to you, but I'm gonna be, also no thanks to you. And anything you try to do now won't help. And if you're afraid I might say bad things about you, too late. Posreal, too late."

"I just wanted to—um—"

"Don't think too hard. You'll hurt yourself. In fact, since you're not real good at thinking, and it's kinda painful to watch you try, go do it somewhere else. Or go home to Ruth and ask her to do it for you."

He left.

I figured he'd be telling his friends I'as a bad sport. And if he'as ever dumb enough to come see me again, he'as gonna be right, if I could help it.

"Heard your voice while I'as in the bathroom," Dad said.

"Posreal nothing," I said.

"I'm glad."

We were out there five minutes before the rendezvous time, just in time to see them turn off the street lights as the sunlight flared across the canopy far above. Of course no one was early. Families with kids never are, and it's worse when they're dropping'em off. Bound to be a few stragglers just due to kids being kids.

First one showed up only two minutes late; there was a logic to it, cause they showed up in reverse age order, which makes sense when you think about getting kids out of a house, especially when you hafta make sure they all have everything in their carry pack that they're gonna need for the next few months. So the first was the oldest, and it was Prigach, who was just a year younger'n me. He was a good looking guy, too. If those two facts were the only facts about him, I could've liked him. But beside those two there was the way he was pushy and rude and aggressive, and he was in the clique at my CSL school that me and my friends all called Those Guys We Can't Stand.

Course he was a real prince if you compared him to his mother, and she'd come along so the comparing was way too easy. The first thing Mama wanted was to have Prigach be the First for the traverse, instead of me.

"Sorry," Dad said, real reasonable but real firm, "I'm the Cap, I pick my First, and Teri's it. She's been my First twice before and I know and trust her better than anybody else in the party. I gotta have one I can trust that shares my habits, and she's the best for it."

So, if you can believe it, she brought up that Prigach was a boy.

Big mistake. Course. Dad had told me many times that he thought women were generally better than men out in the roundings, cause men get their egos involved and will stick with a bad idea a long time just cause it's theirs. So I knew her argument wasn't gonna get her any place. Dad just kept saying that I was his choice, and the Cap's word is law on an overland traverse, especially when everyone else is kids. "If Prigach needs to have a First on an overland traverse on his resumé, then maybe he should talk to the other party that's leaving later today, but I do believe they've got three people with their FA, whereas we just have two, so I'm not sure he can even get Second there. Whereas if Teri says she likes Prigach for Second then he has it."

Prigach's mother didn't like anything at all about all that, but since she was obviously not gonna move Dad even skoshy—you could tell that from his tone—then she eventually shut up.

"Let me consult my First," Dad said.

I shrugged. I hadn't wanted to be in this at all, but Dad had always been very clear about how things were supposed to work: feel whatever you wanted about the members of your party, but judge and speak based on what you *think*, not on what you feel. "Prigach will be a good Second, posreal. He's smart and he's good at any skill we're likely to need," I said. "Give him the job."

"You're Second, Prigach."

Mama left. You wouldn't think you could stomp like

that inside a big tent with a sand floor, but she sure managed.

Prigach still hadn't talked, which meant he was scoring more points with me than he usually did, and also made me feel kinda sorry for him since that hadda be pretty embarrassing. Once Mama was all the way out of sight, Prigach said, "You don't have to have me as Second. If you just said that to get my mother to stop being a pain, then it's a null contract as far as I'm concerned and you should pick the Second that you and Teri want. I don-wanna force myself on you."

Dad raised an eyebrow at me. Well, this one wasn't hard to decide. Contract's a contract, and all. "I want you for Second," I said. "I wouldn't've said so if I didn't."

As little as I liked Prigach, I hadda admit it made me feel good when his eyes glowed at that. At least I'd have a loyal Second. And maybe as he got older his human DNA would start to come out, or something.

There was just time for the pause to go real limward awkward, but not enough for anyone to think of anything to say to ease the tension, when Bianca came bounding up, helmet under one arm, carry pack under the other, and only one strap on her lisport pack on. She looked like a cloud of spare parts orbiting a skinny twelve-year-old. "Am I late?"

"You're the fourth person to get here out of seven, so you're exactly average," Prigach said.

I pointed out that "You're here and we haven't left. Want a hand with your suit checkout?"

"I oughta be able to do it myself, but hell, yeah." Her

face twisted into a sour frown. "I'm posreal not good at this."

Prigach and I ran the check on her and, course, everything was just fine—a roundita does not get to be twelve years old if she actually has any problems doing her own checkout. Bianca was just a very proficient attention seeker, and always so bouncy and glad to be alive that any sensible person would want to wring her neck: the kind that teachers, who are *never* sensible people, just love. Do you like kids like that, Doc? I suppose you probably never see'em anyway, hunh? You only see angry maladjusted people like me? Aw. That's nice of you to say that.

As soon as we had reassured Bianca that she had remembered her compressor and her oxygenator and hadn't arrived barefoot, she immediately started babbling to Prigach about all the guys that were part of his clique and how interesting they were. It was nice to still have my helmet off, because if I suddenly needed to puke it would be less trouble.

I couldn't help liking the way Prigach covertly raised an eyebrow at me. Maybe he was a better choice for my Second than I had realized . . . or so desperate for a rescue that he was willing to act like a person to get one. I just needed to think of the right thing to say to get my Second out of this—and I couldn't think of a thing.

Bianca went on talking about how exciting everything was, how much she was looking forward to next year, and all the people Prigach and her might both know plus all the ones that it was a shame he didn't know plus all the ones he was lucky not to know plus some others in no definite category. I remembered that I was like that for a few months before I got together with Perry, and wondered why Dad hadn't strangled me.

All the same I didn't say anything and I tried posreal hard not to be a killjoy. It's not like the world ever has an excess of fun and excitement or anything. I was actually pretty well tolerant of the little ninny. What a difference it made to get out of Completely Stupid Loser school and away from my sullen jerk ex-fiancé!

I had just about thought of a way to take pity on Prigach and wade in to his rescue, when Alik Lopakhin showed up, leaping along like a crazy rabbit; I'd encountered him a few times before (he was some species of distant cousin on my mother's side. Alik was a perfectly easy kid to get along with as long as you remembered that he was ten years old and limward precocious, made big allowances for that, and then tied him to a chair and gagged him. I figured he'd be pretty close to human in twenty-five or thirty Mars years, maybe.

He arrived bouncing so hard that his feet went up to nearly my face level. His awkward crash landing missed me by not much and Bianca by less, and he actually fell forward and hadda catch himself on his hands. "Did you pack your lisport with extra air?" Prigach said, using a cliched joke that most people hear for the last time before they're seven.

Bianca laughed anyway. If for any reason we ever had to depend on her sense of shame to save our lives, we were all dead, posreal.

"Aw," Alik said, "I was just afraid I was late."

"You are," I said. "But other people are later. And just a reminder, you're still inside the pavilion, no rooing."

"Yeah-sorry-I-forgot," he said. It came out as one word, cause that kid screwed up so often that he needed his apologies to be pretty much a reflex. Which course meant that he never meant any of 'em. "Hey, though, hey, I bet I'm too late to call dibs on Second."

"Naw, too early," I said, hoping the little wiener wouldn't get off on too bad of a footing with Prigach. "By about five Mars years, Your Runtliness."

Prigach grinned. "Foot of the line! Aside from my vastly greater age and experience, Teri immediately perceived all my good qualities—"

"What, both of 'em? Teri had already been a Second a couple times before she was my age." Trust that evil kid to say exactly the wrong thing in any possible situation.

But Prigach handled it fine. "Yeah, but she didn't get it cause of her age, buddy. It had something to do with the fact that she's better in the roundings than just about any of us, including me."

"Oh, go sand your handle," Alik said.

Dad, who had been sitting quietly, I think just watching how I connected with the other kids, cleared his throat and said he didn't think that was appropriate language.

"Yeah-sorry-I-forgot," Alik said, automatically as ever. "What's it mean? My older brother said it to my father and Pops got really mad."

Trying not to laugh, I looked at Prigach. Big mistake. He wasn't even trying.

"What's it mean?" Alik demanded, again, and even Dad started to laugh. "Is it one of those things like that?"

"Like what?" Prigach asked, limward innocent.

"From the way you're blushing," I told Alik, "yeah, exactly like that."

That got us all laughing madly, and Alik looked like he wanted to be mad but was afraid of looking even more ridiculous.

That's when our last two turned up, stumbling along a little awkwardly in their exosuits after a week of being out of them. Bivvy and Erin were sisters, ages seven and five respectively. We'd taken Bivvy to school twice before but this was Erin's first trip. No doubt it hadn't been easy to get her ready.

Neither of'em said hello as they arrived. Bivvy was never much of a talker, anyway. Erin began, without preface, "My sister braided my hair this morning and she did it all wrong and it hurts."

I knew how bad that can hurt—I remember how nice it was when Mummy gave in for my sixth birthday and let me depilate like a big girl—so I took Erin into Vestria's and put her up on a stool, and undid and redid her braids. She sucked her thumb the whole time. I guess she just needed to get in that last good slurp before going into the helmet.

After I made sure that what I had done was comfortable for her, I checked out her exosuit. I made sure her thumb was disinfected and dried before it went into her glove—I dinwanna think about what it'd get like if we weren't careful about that.

Erin said, "You're my friend."

"That's nice, sweetheart, it's always good to have friends."

"You're my friend so you're not Bivvy's friend."

I could see where this was going and tried to head it off. "Erin, I'm friends with *all* nice little girls."

"Bivvy's not nice."

I not only suspected that this might be true, I thought it maybe had something to do with something that ran in the family, but I managed not to say so. "Just the same, I'm friends to both of you, and you are not gonna change that."

"Contract." Erin was obviously bored with the subject already.

I touched her hair once more. "Now, does this feel good?"

"Yeah, now."

"Can you go all day with it this way under your helmet? You know you won't get to take your helmet off till night. Will you be okay?"

"Yeah, it's good, it's just like my mom does. Bivvy just did it wrong cause she's mean. Once we're outside, can we roo?"

"We expect you to."

"Contract! Let's go. I learned how to roo one-footed this year, like a big girl."

With the crisis averted, it only took a few minutes for Prigach and me to do the last rechecks while Dad gave a short, suitably stern lecture. We went out the pavilion airlock only about an hour and a half past the originally scheduled departure time, which was forty-five minutes earlier than Dad'n'me'd expected.

It was a nice day for fall. The sky was red-pink, and the aureole around the sun was almost purple. That meant plenty of dust in the upper atmosphere, which meant a warm night—not that we'd feel it in our suits or through the tajj, but you always hafta watch your energy budget, and a warm night saves you plenty.

❧❧ **We made good** time. Erin was skoshy too young to always stay focused on the job of rooing, but she still wasn't much of a problem cause she had decided that I was her friend, and so she wanted to stay near me. Dad just gave me point and let things work out.

Moving kids through the roundings isn't so much difficult as it's time consuming, and if you're not naturally patient I guess it would be a trip to hell. The big problem is that most kids play with their communicators all the time, talking with each other over private channels, switching around to see who else on the planet wants to talk about bugs or paint or the best kind of rocks for throwing, that kind of thing, and out in the roundings one valley, dune, or sebkhet looks far too much like another, so you can lose a kid pretty quick, and some evil force in the universe dictates that kids who get hurt or stuck do it right when they're out of touch. And you don't think about it, usually, but rooing requires limward concentration, and so you're not always looking right at the kid, or listening perfectly to everything they say. Stuff can happen.

So the usual way to do it is to try and keep the kids trapped between the older people; we were going in a triangle, with me at point, Dad at left rear, and Prigach at right rear, holding the legs of the triangle at about 150 meters. After a while it was clear that Erin would be sticking close to me but she was gonna travel three times as far as anyone else, skipping and bouncing over to anything she thought was interesting. After a while, I called Dad. "Cap, I wanna vary procedure."

"What you got in mind, First?"

"It's harder for me to watch Erin behind me'n it'd be in front, and she's not getting posreal far away—she seems to wanna run up for a hug every three minutes or so. I'd like to let her play out in front of me, say not more'n fifteen meters at a time?"

"Sure, if you think it'll work, I trust your judgement, First."

Prigach cut in, teasing, "Course we're the only party with a five-year-old lead, First."

"That's okay, Second, keep it up, and we'll also be the only one with a dead right rear."

You could hear the smile in Dad's voice, but if you knew him like I did, you knew it was the last smile before something happened. "Is this where I hafta impose some radio discipline on the general freq?"

"Sorry, Cap," Prigach and I said, in unison.

It really was easier with Erin out front; everything was smoother and I didn't hafta call for my rears to slow down nearly so often. We made it through a patch of badly eroded fretted channel country—really more'n halfway to badlands—in a lot less time than I'd've figured.

Afterwards, as we rooed up a big, low ridge, Prigach commed me. "Got time to talk on private channel?"

"For right now, yeah."

"Just wanted to apologize for the way my mom acted. I knew you were gonna be the First and I didn't want her doing all that. She just won't listen, a lot of times."

"It's okay. It wasn't like it was anything personal. And no one should be held responsible for what their parents do. Trust me. The first time Dad farts in the tajj, or cracks one of his really awful jokes, you'll see why I feel that way. Or more likely smell it."

Prigach laughed at my feeble joke. I decided he was getting more all right all the time. "So no hard feelings?" he asked.

"None at all."

We went back to general freq. It's not a good idea, in rough country, a long way from help, to stay on a private channel. In a sudden emergency it's too easy to forget you're on it, and try and call for help or shout a warning to someone who can't hear you.

We rooed on westward all morning. The railhead to Red Sands City, just a terminal at the end of the line, was five days away at the pace we could go with kids and with full carry packs, allowing maybe a half day of windage too. The funny thing to me was that when we did get there, it would be just a bit over two hours from the station to the city, and yet we'd be traveling much farther by rail than we were by foot.

At least the path Dad'n'me had laid out through this part of Mollyland, once we knew it was gonna be with a five-year-old and a seven-year-old, wasn't too messy. We had patches of badlands, some erg, some decayed crater, and some fretted channel to cross here and there, but nothing that would be terribly long or far to get through or around. There was no more'n three or four hours of bad country at a stretch, and plenty of easy-enough in between. For big parts of our trip we'd only need to do an APS check every hour or so.

Prigach was sure a different guy this year, I thought idly. Course people change. But . . . course. He was coming up on his first FA test. Trying to be mature. Funny how much more attractive that could make a person. I wondered what it had done to me.

We had descended the ridge and crossed a couple of ancient sandbars, and the dust deposits that leaned up against them. Keeping Erin from plunging into a hole or pulling a rockpile down on herself kept me busy. But after that we had a long easy roo, following a ridgeline gently upwards, so I called Prigach. "Got time for private channel?"

"Sure."

"Hey, are you going for FA soon?"

"Yeah, how'd you guess?"

"You're being such a nice guy."

He laughed. "Gee, thanks, Teri. And you just got FA, didn't you?"

"Yeah."

"So what's your excuse for being unusually nice?"

I laughed. "I don't know. I think they make you wait

for FA so long that when you finally get it, behaving like a grown-up has turned into a set habit. It's really a dirty trick."

"I should've guessed. Sounds just like them."

We went back to general freq again. The morning wore on; not a bad one but a tiring one. I kept Erin out of a couple more disasters, and Prigach fended off a couple of attempts by Bianca to get him into long conversations (he used me a couple of times, pretending he needed to confer with his First), and by Alik to obtain an explanation of handle-sanding.

For about the last forty minutes before lunch, I had more company. Besides watching Erin, I was being trailed by Bivvy. What we had here was two sisters close enough in age so that whatever one got, the other wanted. I don't mind little kids, I kinda like'em, posreal I do, and I can be reasonably gracious to them. After all, nobody got to fill out a form that said they wanted to arrive in the world as a little kid, and most of'em would be real happy to be something else.

I had lunch with both of'em leaning against my back— I made it clear that if they bickered, or even squirmed, they could both sit elsewhere—and that seemed to work pretty well. Besides, they wanted to be next to each other, anyway. Despite all the bickering, they were pretty close, and I had noticed after a while that on the rare occasions when Bivvy spoke, it was usually to tell me that Erin was tired, and when she said so, she was always right, and we needed to take a break. Erin often talked for both of them too, knowing when Bivvy was homesick and needed a hug or a friend.

Just a skosh after the lunch break, Bivvy and Erin were singing a song together. Everyone else had sensibly switched to another freq, but someone hadda listen in case either of'em got into trouble. It was one of those little kid songs that goes on forever and ever and ever. When they finally wound down, I reminded them to switch to general freq, and they did; then there was a strange noise in my phones, sort of a rhythmic, strangled wheezing. "Who's making that sound?" Dad demanded. "Is anything wrong?"

"I think Bivvy's homesick," Erin said, with a mixture of pride and malicious glee. "I *never* get homesick. I think Bivvy got homesick cause that's one of the songs that Mom taught us. I never get homesick cause I'm a big girl."

"Taking over point, First," Prigach said, and rooed by me, going like a maniac. He scooped up Bivvy, hoisted her onto his shoulders, and went whooping and bouncing up the side of the crater rim in front of us. She was squealing and giggling and having fun in half a breath.

Definitely I was glad to have Prigach along. If he ever wanted me to do a favor for him—say, for example, kill his mother—he had only to say the word. "Dropping back to right rear, Second," I said. "Where'd you leave Bianca? Buddy check, Bianca."

"With Cap."

"She's with me," Dad said, at the same time.

"Good, Cap. Buddy check, Alik?"

"Also with Cap," Alik said. "He's gonna show us how to run up a crater wall, so we're going a skosh wide south."

So my old man was still a big kid; things were normal, all right. I rolled my eyes and smiled. One of the best things about helmets is that no one can see your facial expressions; lack of practice is one reason why rounditachi are such lousy liars, and therefore so crappy at human relations, aren't we, Doc?

About half a kim past the crater wall, Erin said, "Do I get a ride too?"

What the hell. Really the two little girls had been great all day. I grabbed her and slung her up on my shoulders, and did some boulder bouncing up the slope in front of us. I rapidly acquired a whole new respect for Prigach's muscles—Bivvy was considerably heavier than Erin, and Erin was *work*. After we topped the rise, we had a kim on mostly level ground; as we neared the next ridge, Prigach said, "Okay, Bivvy, ride's over, I need you to help me walk point."

"Okay," she said.

"Good idea, Second," I said. "I need Erin to help me with the right rear."

"Okay, keep her back there with you, then. If she gets tired or loses focus, I'll send Bivvy back."

It probably helped that Prigach was the oldest in a big family; he seemed to have the touch with these sisters. Erin slipped down from my shoulders without being asked; if Bivvy was needed to help Prigach, Erin was certainly not gonna be less needed back here—especially not if there was the possibility of Bivvy being called in to handle it.

"I'm not tired at all," Erin said. "I can roo as far as we need to."

That big ridge, and the little pocket erg on the other side of it, were our last real obstacles for the day. Zilty later we were following a winding dry gulley with a nice hard-packed bottom, as the sun crept down toward the horizon in front of us. Everyone was pretty well quiet, now, except for the occasional position and APS checks. I'd see Prigach up ahead with Bivvy, now and then, and Dad and the two middle kids off to my left. Sometimes there'd be whooping in my phones as they ran up slopes together (to judge by the ratio of "yeah!" to "oops!" Bianca was already good at it, and Alik was getting there).

Not a bad group on the whole. Nobody new to the roundings—kids in their first couple years are such a pain, so it was nice that they'd all grown up out here, and knew what they hadda behave about and what'as negotiable.

When we reached the campsite, about half an hour ahead of schedule, it turned out that Bivvy and Erin were truly raised in the roundings; they didn't expect or need the tajj. "That's for *babies*," Erin said, scornfully, and Bivvy nodded. "We don't need the tajj, Cap, unless somebody else does."

"Well," Dad said, "not having to have it will sure save time, tonight and in the morning, and there's plenty of suitrations. Let's spread out all the power sheets we have and make sure everyone gets a good top-off charge and their tanks filled; then I'll dish out some suitrations, and we can stretch out for the night. Anybody'at wants to, you can read or watch something, or com chat, but stay in my sight, and I want signals off in four hours—Teri can tell you, I check."

"He does," I agreed. "Okay, you all heard the Cap, get out your collectors and spread'em out."

Everybody yessirred like they were supposed to—not even any backtalk from Alik, which was a posreal miracle.

By sundown, we were all sitting up along the low ridgeline of the dune, facing west, to see if we got the rainbow flash. You get that a lot if the horizon is straight, like it is in Mollyland, or up on Tharsis sometimes. Just after the sun sets there's a burst of color, running up the spectrum. Something about the atmosphere on Mars—like I said, I'm not a physicist.

We did get the rainbow flash, and it was something to talk about, one of the best I've ever seen. We all agreed that it definitely ended fully blue, and Alik, me, and Bivvy all thought it had started orange. (Erin agreed with us too but she distinctly changed her vote after she knew who had voted how.)

After letting us argue for a bit, Dad pulled up his helmet camera record from his personal werp, and ran the spectrograph on it. The very beginning of the flash was at 590 nim, which is so evenly between yellow and orange that we all got to be right, but it sorta spoiled the argument from an entertainment standpoint. Then we all went back down the slope, so we'd be facing east for sunrise, and stretched out on the firm, comfortable sand to watch, read, talk, or sleep.

Prigach and me plugged together with a fiberlink for a while, cause he was kinda curious about the program I was gonna be doing at RSCU, and we chatted just long enough for me to decide that he had definitely improved limward since last year and I was pretty well willing to promote him to human. But after we'd found out we agreed about food, sitters, sports, and movies, but not about music and only partly about books, there was surprisingly little to talk about, and it was close to signals-out time anyway—where had two and a half hours gone? Prigach must be a more interesting guy than he seemed to be—so we unhooked our fiberlinks and stretched out to go to sleep.

I got Haydn's Fire Symphony on a channel and set it to fade slowly as I half-listened, mostly just watching the stately dance of the moons, satellites, and chondreors as they crisscrossed the busy, blazing night sky. I'm not sure whether it's a real memory or not, Doc—is there any way to tell?—I didn't think so—but I think the last sight I recall that night was the Moon hanging below the Earth in the west, both shining brilliantly, a bright silver double spot.

·

👀 **So many alarms** on my exosuit were going off that I couldn't sort'em all out. I sat bolt upright in the dark, ripping the accesses open, punching the resets in the order I'd been taught until it was completely a habit: Start on the lisport. First the reset button for the oxygenator. Then reset the compressor. Reset exhaust, then the heater. Sensor pack: pulse, blood pressure, respiration, blood sugar, EK. Move to helmet, do communications gear. Back to lisport, water purifier. Waste recycler. Nanommunics package. Back to helmet. Screens and options . . .

My fingers danced and skittered over the buttons on my lisport pack and around the neck of my helmet, moving as fast as they had in any drill. As I finished two alarms were ringing again, so they had re-tripped; one was ululating and one was wailing. I didn't quite remember which ones they were so I ran through all the resets again until I got them; the ululator was the backup heater, and the wailing was the compressor output cooling unit. What the hell was that doing on, in the Martian night, with the temperature ninety degrees below freezing? Somehow it had turned itself on, started to malfunction, and screamed for help. I reset it and the lights flared yellow and green as it walked its way back to standby.

The whole thing couldn't have taken more'n a minute but it seemed as if I had been inside that awful cloud of noise forever.

I gasped, more from fear than from the minute or so when my fresh air had been cut off, and looked around. The southern horizon was ablaze with vast translucent sheets of gold and green, swiftly curling into long ropes of deep blue, then flashing, going black, returning as a great waving curtain of red. *It has to be an aurora, but— there are no auroras on Mars. The magnetic field doesn't trap enough charged particles to do that, they told us that in school!* Some tiny part of my mind was outraged that school had proven to be wrong and useless once again.

My hands were still dotting and prodding over the open panels on my lisport pack and the exposed inner collar of my helmet, triggering automatic repairs and checkouts. In my ear, the machine voice said, "You are temporarily functional, but many functions are classified as irregular or are not at nominal or both. This life support pack needs immediate maintenance by qualified technical personnel. Do not delay."

"Acknowledged," I said, as I finished doing everything I knew how to do. Surprisingly calm, I flicked to the emergency override suit-to-suit, general-hailing frequency, and said, "Dad, there's something *big* wrong with my exosuit." But in my phones there was only the powerful roar of static, and that was strange too cause static was normally almost absent with digital FM; to have so much audible static would hafta mean that there was an incredible amount of screaming white noise on every single channel.

I tried satcell and heard nothing at all.

In the dim light, just starlight and Deimos, I could see two silhouettes up and jumping around—Bianca and Alik. Their hands were stabbing at their lisport packs and I realized that whatever had hit me had hit them too. As I started to run to them I saw lights begin to flash green as systems came back on line. Then I realized that if it was hitting all of our suits, whatever it was, then other members of the party could be in trouble. I switched on my headlamp and looked around; the glaring blue-white circle on the ground erased all the dim hills and stars, so that I saw only where I looked. Mostly there was just the red-iron sand of the dune.

At the edge of the circle of light I saw a foot, and turned slightly. Prigach lay in my light, sprawled and not moving, at a strange angle; one strap of his lisport pack had burst and it lay crosswise on him, as if someone had just dropped it on his still body. I ran to him.

Something moved in the shadows; I turned and my helmet light shone on Erin, who was up and running wildly. I started after her, but Alik tackled her, and on the general frequency override, there was a squall of static, and I heard him say, "I'll take care of her! Bivvy's in trouble."

I turned around and saw Bianca bending over Bivvy and working frantically at the younger girl's lisport. I knelt by Prigach and slammed the grand reset on his lisport pack; all the lights flickered red for an instant and then went out. I flipped it again and nothing happened at all. Fumbling, muttering, I got my emergency jump from my battery pack into the bypass for his lisport, and tried to power him up that way; the display on my helmet said that nothing at all was coming from his lisport. I tried jumpering into every emergency plug on the guy's suit there was, and there was nothing.

I hooked to his telemetry and he was flatlined; no heartbeat, no EK, no bloodflow, nothing. I put my head down and braced my helmet against his to try for any sign of life; I heard no breathing but my own, and my hand, pressed down hard under his lisport, detected no heartbeat. His body wasn't cooler than normal yet. He could only have been dead a few minutes.

Through the wailing static on the suit-to-suit, I heard Alik say, "Teri, come quick—the Cap—"

I stood and swung my head around madly, found Dad in my helmet light. Alik was bent over him, pushing on his chest, exactly the way they teach you in first aid class.

I ran to him, put my head down on Dad's helmet; Alik
kept pounding on him, tossing me his fiberlink. I plugged
in.

"His whole lisport is black, Teri, and I can't get it to
reset or even to power up off mine. I thought I heard him
breathing in there but there can't be much air left in the
suit."

I made myself breathe one deep breath and hold it,
just like Dad had taught me, and then put my helmet down
onto Dad's helmet again. I could hear the gasp and sigh
from Alik pushing his chest. I linked in for telemetry, and
Dad was like Prigach, zero, nothing, nobody home. Alik
kept working and I worked my way through all the sock-
ets over and over as fast as I could but Dad was gone.

I realized that aside from Dad's sigh-and-gasp sound,
I could hear quiet blubbering and keening; for an instant
I thought it was me, then realized it was Alik, still working
as hard as he could on Dad's chest. "He's gone," I said,
and then, "he's dead, Alik. It's been too long now. We
won't be able to revive him. You can stop."

Alik pushed once more, hard, grunting with effort, and
then sat back. "What happened?" he asked.

Bianca's voice came in through the static. "Guys, help
me, something else is wrong with Bivvy."

We ran downslope. Bianca was trying to hold Bivvy
down; the small girl was thrashing around, not as if she
were fighting or trying to get away, but in something that
looked like a seizure. I plugged into her lisport telemetry
and found nothing working reliably; Bianca said "Her
communications were out but I was talking to her by

helmet-to-helmet, and I got all her lisport back on line, but now she's started doing this—"

The tiny girl's body arched backward harder and farther than I would have thought possible, and stayed that way. Her fists beat the ground randomly beside her, and then her arms flung out wide to the sides. Her telemetry showed everything red and stopped except for her pulse, which fluttered weakly. I started CPR through the suit, but then the pulse flickered out as well, and her body went limp. Fifteen minutes later, as the sun bounced over the horizon—swollen and red and spotted like an evil sore—we decided we hadda give up.

👀 **So many of** the deaths of the rounditachi were never properly autopsied, and the onset of the Sunburst was so abrupt and violent, and the bodies so numerous, that we'll probably never understand all the ways that people died from it. Teri and her party didn't know it, but they had missed what was in some ways the worst; the whole sun side of Mars had taken a terrible radiation dose, and many of the rounditachi that survived there died in the next few weeks of radiation sickness. All in all, Mars lost about 100,000 people, but more than half of those it lost were rounditachi—a whole culture wiped out, and much of the progress of terraforming set back by decades.

The best guess about the mysterious deaths in areas where radiation sickness was not severe rests on the odd observation that such deaths were concentrated in the polar areas, and that auroras were seen at both poles. Mars has a magnetic field, albeit a weak one, and thanks to the Sunburst, there were so many particles in the thin atmosphere that enough concentrated at the poles to make auroras. So one thought is that charged particles in the upper atmosphere may have swirled and flowed in ways that induced currents on the ground beneath. This was undoubtedly the cause of failure for many instruments, machines, and telemetry links, and also accounts for the failure of the communications and APS satellites. The speculation is that given that the life support packs have eight probes inserted directly into the bloodstream, people who happened to be lying in the wrong position, or were under exactly the wrong current-inducing event, or were sleeping on the wrong soil—*or angered the gods,* I always add silently— may have suffered substantial induced currents through the heart, brain, or both, and thus either died quickly or suffered seizures. In the absence of any better theory, that's what I think happened to Teri's party; they were just about in the worst place one could be without actually taking a blast of radiation, near the sunrise line and far to the south. The guess would be that Prigach Veriogaskis died instantly of an induced heart attack, Bivilina

Krabach of the delayed effects of severe shocks to the brain, and Telemachus Murray probably of some severe shock to some vital organ (my guess is that Alik and Teri were hearing what they wanted to hear; probably Telemachus died at the same time as Prigach).

I tap away at the old-fashioned keyboard and write my annotation to the report:

What fascinates me is that although Teri thinks about all this often and worries about exactly what caused the situation, the cause seems to have little or nothing to do with what happened afterwards. It was the loss of the father she idolized, and not the manner of the loss, that mattered in this case. It left her isolated and alone during the first great responsibility of her adult life, depressed and miserable at a time when she needed all of her energy and a deep commitment to important values, and most importantly, in charge when she wasn't yet ready.

I consider that opinion and decide to strike it later. Not right now, I need a paragraph there to fulfill the requirements of my report for Cal, but later for sure. She was as ready as anyone could be. Doing what needed to be done would have been emotionally difficult and demanding no matter what, and we have no evidence that her father would not also have failed at the moment of crisis. She was weakened, surely, alone without support and terribly unhappy, after a dreadful shock following what had been a month of intense stress. But as to whether she should not have been in charge . . . I don't feel that I can say.

Perhaps I don't want them to take her first regular party command away from her. Completing it seems very important to her. And if I procrastinate answering her for just a few more hours, she'll have finished and delivered her party safely to Tragedy Valley; I'm sure that would matter to her, anyway.

"That's my point," Cal says.

I turn and am startled to see him there.

"You've written the same paragraph about Teri's loss of her father four times. Scroll up the screen and see. And this is the third time that you've forgotten that I'm in the room, and have been for several hours. Come on, what's that say to you?"

❧❧ **Sometimes it's hard** to understand when the thing that is supposed to happen happens. Dad had always stressed that being First meant being a heartbeat away from being Cap, and that the day always comes, if you're any good, when "You're the Captain, Captain." So I looked around at all of us, sitting there as still as our dead. Bianca knelt beside Erin, who was cradling Bivvy's head in her lap and sitting very still. Alik stood motionless, arms hanging at his side, shoulders rising and falling; the static was fading from the suit-to-suit and I could occasionally make out his sobbing through it.

I would have thought I would want to curl up and die, but I really had just two thoughts; one was my Dad's voice saying "You're the Captain, Captain," and the other was that I hoped that when I hadda pick a new First, Bianca and Alik wouldn't be too terribly jealous of each other, cause I really didn't have the energy to be the referee.

"All right," I said, "I gotta call for help." I clicked from satcell to satcell to satcell channel, and it was all as dead as could be. I tried the big longer-wave emergency channels, and each was full of shrieks of white noise, punctuated by dozens or hundreds of distant garbled mayday calls. I put in a mayday call for us, as best I could, on each channel—just named the party, gave our expedition number, and told them we had three dead and four severely damaged exosuits—and hoped someone would be recording distress calls and would get around to us, but it sounded as if the whole planet was in some kinda godawful trouble—which it turned out was just what it was, should I say that, Doc? it's not like the record needs it from me—and in twenty minutes of listening I heard only distress calls, never anyone answering one.

NOTE FROM RECORDER: We know now, of course, that Central Receiving at Marinersburg was fried out and didn't get back on line for days, and everyone at the backup Central Receiving, on Phobos, was dead or dying. RESUME TRANSCRIPTION.

I couldn't give them our last position cause that was recorded on my virtual werp, which talked to my suit displays via satcell, and satcell was posreal not working at all. (At the time I didn't have any way to know that every comsat around Mars was dead and tumbling.)

Then I had Alik and Bianca and even Erin try their satcells, on the off chance that it was just mine that was dead, and it was no good at all; still nothing came in or went out.

It was now an hour past sunrise—where did the time go? Does that happen, Doc, I mean, when you're really upset, does time just go crashing by? Oh, yeah, I see. Yeah, it stands to reason.

The sun looked weird; course we know now that the Sunburst had stripped off a big chunk of photosphere and all that school stuff they say about it, but on that day, about all we knew was that the sun looked weird. It was blotchy and mottled from where all that hot plasma was flowing across it and all that cooled-off gas was falling back in and so on, like the most amazing awful case of sunspots that had ever happened, and with the filters on our faceplates full on so we could look directly at it, the streaks and bands were strongly visible.

"What's wrong with it?" I asked Alik, since he was good at school stuff.

"Wish I knew. Something big happened. That has to be why we had an aurora, even without Mars having much of a magnetic field, and that's what all that static is. I imagine it'll clear up faster here than it will around Earth or Jupiter—particles won't trap as much in our weak magnetic field so it'll dissipate pretty fast—but all the same, something big happened, that's for sure. Did you have anything about solar astronomy in CSL school, Bianca?"

"Not a thing. When did you?"

"I hadda do a report once, is all." Alik sounded a bit defensive; I guess precocious boys are sometimes kinda embarrassed about how much they know, especially if it's mostly useless.

"So is there anything we should do?" I asked.

"Get inside if we can, I think," Alik said. "Just get stuff between us and the sun, anyway. Maybe pitch the tajj between big rocks or something so it only gets skoshy direct exposure to the sun each day?"

It was something to do, so we did it. We spread the full set of collector sheets out. At least the tajj would be warm and have plenty of water, and there was plenty of food in the packs. By the time the sun was halfway up to the zenith, we had the full tajj up and power flowing in— although of our seventy collector sheets, eleven had turned out dead.

In CSL class, they always yell at you if you try to do DBI, Debug By Iteration, where you take a program, idea, or machine that isn't working and try to get it to work by just trying it over and over again. It's pretty dumb—practically a perfect fit to that old definition of crazy, doing the same thing over and over and hoping that it will come out different. Is that really a definition of crazy, Doc? Hunh. Interesting.

That was what we were doing, anyway, so I guess we were all crazy. We kept turning on every piece of equipment we could to see if it worked, and then if it did, we'd try it a couple more times just to be sure, and if it didn't we'd try it several more times in the hopes that it would. We did it in no order, all of us just wandering amid the stuff from our carry packs and the tajj sections, just as if the activity meant something.

Finally I realized what we were doing, and I said, "Friends."

"Yeah, uh, Cap?" Alik asked.

"Um. It's more'n halfway through the day. We need to eat lunch. Or breakfast. Since none of us has eaten. And we need to face up to at least three other things. One, we've got all kinds of stuff not working and we need to make a definite list, and stop trying all of it over and over. Two, nobody's coming to help, what little we can hear is all long-range radio and that's a mess, so once we know what we have here, we hafta figure out how to use it to rescue ourselves—cause we are not getting rescued. And three—" I wanted to throw up when I thought of this— "We have so much broken equipment that we're gonna hafta fizzy, um, the um, bodies."

Alik said, "Do we hafta?"

Bianca sighed. "Cap's right, and even if she's not, she's the Captain. We hafta."

Never heard of a fizzy, Doc? They're no fun. When we did a fizzy for Mummy, Dad and I cried the whole time.

Fizzy, F-S-S-I-I, Field Strip, Salvage, Inventory, and Inter. Or, putting it real simple, you take everything off a body, careful so you don't break any equipment, inventory it, repack it with your gear—actually at that moment it *is* your gear—and then you put the body someplace where it will mummify and then decay, and get into the biosphere. Rubbies, you know. You hafta do it so that it can decay without getting all over the place while any part of it is still recognizable, which is too upsetting for the dead person's family, so you hafta make sure water can get to it but wind can't, and since there are gonna be big scavengers on Mars soon, and a body on Mars tends to freeze-dry, you want to make sure nothing big can get in there to break it up and eat it.

There's all the probes and catheters to pull out, and there's a way to do it that they explain real good in the manual. We did Prigach first cause none of us had been as close to him, and I will always be limward grateful to Alik for having done the worst of the disconnecting. We left Prigach's transponder in case it might, somehow, recover and turn on, or someone was able to revive it on remote, so his family would have a better chance of recovering the body, and we put a cairn on top of him.

Then there was Bivvy; I did the unhooking on her. She looked so tiny, naked on the bare rock as we gently stacked the big stones on her. Erin kept asking if she would be cold, and Bianca and me just kept re-explaining, hoping she'd get it and be able to cope when she did. It's not so easy at that age to get the idea of death.

That left Dad. I don't suppose there's much I can say. We did it slow; we were all tired anyway, and Dad had always had a gift with kids so all the children had loved and trusted him, and anyway I wanted to memorize every single thing about him. When we had finished his cairn I sat there beside it and watched the sun go down, and let Bianca take care of getting the last load of Dad's stuff into the tajj. There was no rainbow flash tonight, or maybe I was down too low and the horizon wasn't smooth enough. The sun still looked slimy and evil and infected.

As dark rushed across the sky, I looked up to see a chondreor come in at a high angle and then burst in the mid-atmosphere; it hadn't been directed, and it had hit like a plain old meteor, without aerobraking or direction. The satellites were still up there, but I saw no engine flares and no maneuvering; they drifted dead, and the lower ones would be falling, the upper ones wandering into useless orbits. *If we can't fix this,* I thought, *in just a few years it will be as if we were never here.*

I knelt by the cairn and whispered "goodbye, Dad, I've got stuff to do. You know I'll do my best." I couldn't think of any more to say to him. We had no religion, few rounditachi do, and so all I could work up was a vague hope that if there was any kinda life after this one we got, and he was there now, that he was with Mummy; he'd missed her so bad these last few years.

Phobos rose, where the sun had set, and its light made a moving shadow that crept slowly, visibly in toward the cairn, like a blanket pulled gently over you when your mother tucks you in.

I was cold and tired, and Captain. I had kids to look after. I went inside. "First of all," I said, "we're all gonna hook up our exosuits for full checkout and repair, since the tajj system for that seems to be fine, and we're gonna get things back to nominal as much as we can. So everyone strip, now, and hook up."

We did. Then we reconstituted some food, and ate something warm and bland. I set up beds for all four of us and we sacked out; Erin was the smartest of us, she insisted that we drag the beds together and lock them so we could all hug if we needed to, and now that I didn't hafta be Captain, I let myself just let go and cry with everyone else, until finally we fell asleep.

⊶ **Next morning we** got up late and draggy, as you might have expected. I decided that more food and some antidepressants were the first priority. After that we tried the radios; there was far less static today, but it was still messy, and no one seemed to answer our hails. We tried answering other parties that we could hear calling for help, just to have someone to talk to, but they seemed to be mostly far away in the Northern Hemisphere, a lot of them around Tharsis, and it looked like our transmitters couldn't reach them. It didn't seem good that we were hearing other rounditachi and small remote settlements, but nothing from the cities.

The inventory revealed that between scavenged parts, we had enough to put together four mostly working exosuits; we just hadda decide who got which minor problems, all of'em things that a qualified shop would hafta look at and all of'em in the redundancies; course, that mattered more'n usual, since the primaries weren't nearly as reliable as they had been. We had about three weeks of food. Energy and water were open-ended.

The single best find of the morning was Dad's werp. For all the fun I'd made of it, it worked, and the virtual werps that all of us depended on were useless without satcell. It at least let us find out exactly where we were according to the last APS fix, and we broadcast that but there was still no one who acknowledged our messages.

The sun looked better today, I thought; the dark smears seemed smaller, the brightish spots less contrasty. Not that I was exactly an expert on misbehaving stars or that I could've fixed it even if I had been.

We tossed the morning's waste, and it seemed appropriate for all of us to kneel by the three cairns for a minute or so before we went inside to get out of our exosuits, give the autorepair systems another shot at them, and try and figure out what to do.

Erin sat quietly next to me, thumb in her mouth, head leaning on my shoulder. Bianca and Alik sat staring down at the floor. "Well," I said, "First question: do we think we're gonna be rescued if we just stay put?"

"Maybe, maybe not," Bianca said. "If you figure this was some kinda solar event that no one has ever seen before, and it destroyed a lot of electronics, things might be worse in the cities than they are in the roundings, and you gotta figure probably the trains aren't running and posreal the rockets can't navigate. And if you look at the map of Mars, and figure the event hit just before sunrise our time—" she pointed at the screen—"there're a lot more big cities in daylight than in night, and if whatever it was came from the sun . . ."

"I see what you mean. All right, that was kinda what I was thinking too. Maybe somebody's recording radio messages as they come in and they'll get around to us, but most of the people calling for help this morning were the same ones that were on the air last night, and it didn't sound like anyone had gotten an answer yet. So I don't think we can just sit tight and wait to be rescued, cause the food might not last that long."

"You got something in mind?" Alik asked.

"I wish I did," I admitted. "The other side of this thing is that we don't have APS, and over the distance and with the rail line angling the way it does, we don't dare just dead-reckon—we could end up walking for days parallel to the rail line, with just a tiny navigational error, and not knowing which side of it we were on. Real easy to get lost, stay lost, and wind up dead. Due west we'd run into fretted channel and get lost, due north would take at least fifteen days before we hit anything, and any kinda mixed course or heading northwest puts us up against mounting errors so that I have no idea where the hell we'd end up. With only the sun and the moons to guide by, we'd never be able to count on getting where we intended, in time."

"This is kinda stupid," Alik said, "but what if we *could* navigate? What if there was a way to just head where we needed to head?"

I thought for a moment. "Then I think what I'd do is this; I'd leave you two in charge of Erin, leave almost all the food behind with you, strip my pack down to just the essentials, roo my way over to the rail line as fast as I could, and then try to call a train and get to the city for help. If the trains are dead, the rail line at least would mean I wouldn't get lost, and I could still make Red Sands City well before you ran out of food back here, and get help headed your way. But to navigate, we'd hafta have APS, and if we had APS, we'd have satcell and we could com for help. Interesting question, Alik, but I don't see that it gets us anyplace."

"Well, maybe, maybe not," he said. He had been sitting at Dad's werp, scanning through files, looking for anything that might be of use. I'd started out doing that but when I discovered how much of it was baby pictures of me, and pictures of Mummy, I'd started to go to pieces, and Bianca had been smart enough to tell Alik to take over. "There's an astronomy program on this thing. Just a planetarium program, but it has universal output. And there are eleven encyclopedias, and four of them have articles about celestial navigation."

"You mean steering by the stars? Like the old ships?"

"Yeah."

"Will that work on Mars?"

He shrugged. "The stars are far away; there's no difference between their positions from Earth and their positions from Mars, that you can measure, except for the very closest ones, and we can figure a compensation for those if we hafta use them. The astronomy program can give you a view of the night sky from any point on Mars for any date and time. The werp can do all the calculating. The question is, do the encyclopedia articles teach us enough so we'll know what to calculate?"

That question took up the rest of the day. Did you ever try to learn a really complicated subject from a manual? Course if you were a roundito, Doc, I'd say you must've hadda, cause pretty much that's what you gotta do with every new piece of software and every new piece of field equipment. Not to say anything nice about CSL school—I never have before—but if there was one thing that was any good about it, it was the "How to Learn Something" classes where they'd make you pick up a topic just for the practice. It was just unfortunate that none of us'd ever hadda learn celestial navigation before, but given'at all we needed to do was get the werp to figure out what star we should be walking toward—or as we realized after a while, what stars, you can get real lost just aiming for one—and come up with a way to refigure our guide stars regularly, it just wasn't that complicated. There were all sorts of things we probably wouldn't need to know.

At first we were stymied by the horizon problem, cause the clearest article in any of the encyclopedias showed us an instrument that was supposed to be sighted on the horizon and on the sun or a star. We had all kinds of gadgets with bubble levels but a level doesn't point to the horizon, and the difference between level and horizon, what they call the dip, is twice as big on Mars; that meant refiguring all kinds of things from the formulae they gave us. Then we ran up against the problem that we didn't have any way of sighting an exact angle measure. "You know," I said, "I'd give a lot for one of those sextant gadgets right now, or even for one of those old telescope transits—"

"Wrong approach," Alik said, suddenly whacking his forehead. "Wrong. Wrong."

"What?"

If lives hadn't been depending on him, watching a stocky ten year old jump up and pace back and forth, thinking as hard as he could, might almost have been funny. "I don't know," he said, "but you know those find-the-hidden-assumption-and-that's-the-solution problems they like to give us?"

"Yeah. Yuck. I hate'em."

"Me too, but that's what this looks like to me."

He sat there and pondered, chin on his hand, like a bad copy of that famous statue, and then said, "So, the werp has a camera, right?"

"Right."

"And a built-in level for the camera, right?"

"Right."

"So if we take a picture of the stars, and compare it with what the picture would look like if we were already where we were going, it can come up with a correction, right?"

"Sure, any digital picture can be corrected, but I don't see how it does you any good to have a corrected picture—"

"What if we use the correction as our input? If we take a picture pointing the camera west, since we're east of where we want to be, won't it come up with a number that describes the way that all the stars are too low? Or numbers that describe it, a set of numbers, I guess, since the ones further south will be low by different numbers than the ones further north, right? So then . . . can we calculate from that?"

"Maybe you can," I said. "Me, I'm not any good at trig, and that's a trig problem, and even if I managed to get it figured out, I'd never trust my answer, cause I'm no good at it." Honestly, Doc, it was enough to make me wish I'd studied once in a while, or something.

But Alik wasn't listening. He was staring up at the light coming in from the dome on the top of the tajj, looking like a dwarf angel getting a revelation from an uncooperative god. "Hah! Hah. It's sloppy, it's so sloppy, but it will work."

"What do you have in mind?"

"We just keep calling up star maps, iteratively, for the time it is, till we find one that matches our picture; then we read off the location from that. Plain old rolling ball algorithm."

Now, even I know how to do those and like I said I'm no good at math; a rolling ball algorithm means you build a model of all the possible answers, good and bad, and treat errors like heights, so you're looking for the lowest error/lowest height. When a ball rolls down into a depression or a valley, it doesn't roll as far back up the far side as it rolled down the near side, cause of friction and all that. So you simulate it; you describe the error as a height and you roll a ball with friction—ah, hell, Doc, probably you had the math in school and I bet you didn't like it any more'n I did. I mean you seem like a nice guy so it stands to reason.

Anyway, once Alik had that figured out, he had a program to do it set up in all of ten minutes, and now we just needed to wait till night to try it out. While we waited, we ate again and kept dinking around with the exosuits. Between spare and salvaged parts and a lot of swapping, we could put together two fully functional lisport and com sets with their full redundancies, and two "partials," limited-redundancy exosuits. "Limited redundancy" was the words the manufacturers' lawyers used for "if anything goes wrong your heirs are shit out of luck."

On our partials, mostly the air and breathing systems were all right, with full redundancy, but the sticky place was the heaters; we had six fully working and one that farted constantly and had to be reset all the time. If you're gonna sleep outside, you really need to have a main and a backup, so there was no way the group as a whole could move.

"Looks like we're back to your idea," Bianca said. "Or a version of it. How about two people go for help, as fast as they can, and one stays back with Erin? That conserves food and resources."

"Who would go?" Alik said.

"Me, cause I'm the most experienced and the best at the roundings," I said. "And you cause you wrote this celestial navigation program and understand how the thing works."

Bianca nodded. Erin put up a small fuss when she realized that I would be going and she would be staying, but all three of us appealed to her interest in being a big girl, and that seemed to take care of it.

We ate another meal and napped till dark.

It's so hard to believe that Cal, who after all is a smart sensitive guy I've known for many years, who helped train me—Cal doesn't understand it at all. "But when you take away the sad memories," I say, "you take away so much of what makes a person themselves. Can't you leave somebody with..." I find myself staring into space.

"What's today?"

"October 5, 2095?"

"It's June of 2097, almost July. What happened in the last couple of years?"

"Let—" I begin, and he jabs a needle into my arm. Is that any way for a friend to treat a friend? I want to hit him, but I'm too sleepy. And all I wanted to explain to him is that so much it's our sorrows that make us who we are, and if you take those away, you take us away with them... or something. That maybe it's not good to wake up in a body that was willed to you by someone else who just left you a long recording... that needle hurt going into my arm. I'm going to punch Cal the next time he does that. But right now I'm too sleepy.

✦✦ **Since we were** still hoping that someone would answer our com call and we wouldn't hafta make the trip, we rested through the next day instead of going right away. We did all the repairs we could, made sure every tank and battery was charged up to full, and mostly just slept, especially Alik and me. We figured that we would get our first guide stars marked out as it got dark, and go then. That would give us the maximum possible time on the first night, while we were still fresh.

I have trouble sleeping in the daytime, I've never been good at changing sleep cycles, I was stressed limward, and I was posreal scared for maybe the first time in my life. So by the time the sun was going down, I hadn't had anything like the rest I should. Alik had been moving around restlessly every time I'd been awake to notice, so I doubt he was doing any better. Short sleep or not, though, it was time to get doing something.

With the sun about to cross the horizon and that curtain-fast sunset ready to fall, we all exchanged last hugs. I made sure I got a good one from Bianca and Erin both— whatever had happened, we had no way of knowing whether it was the only time in history, once in a thousand years, or about to happen again any minute, and the next time, if there was one, might shut down all our systems and leave us dying. Furthermore, I was leaving the girls with substandard equipment, and some of that wasn't backed up. This could limward easy be the last time we saw each other alive.

"All right," I said to Bianca, "I'm gonna act all Full-Adulty for just a zilty here."

"You're forgiven."

"Well, good, then. Last minute reviews for everybody. Bianca, what do you do if you have a good reason to think that help isn't coming?" (We had settled on describing it that way cause we'd hafta trust her judgement about what was a good reason, no matter how you looked at it.)

"Well," she said, "I take the list of star sightings you worked out in advance, put it in my helmet player. We pack for a nine-day trip if we still have enough stuff, to allow for time to get lost. Then we follow the star sightings till we hit the railroad, which oughta be four days. We follow the railroad north. It's farther than the way you're going but it makes sure we don't miss the rail line."

"Good. Erin, what do you do if anything happens so that Bianca can't take care of you?"

She sighed, obviously exasperated at the silliness of re-peating something obvious so many times. (I realized that I had now become one of those stupid grown-ups who had always frustrated me.) But she didn't argue; she just said, in a slightly pedantic tone, "Pack all the suitrations I can carry easy, the smallest tajj room, and at least ten solar collector panels. Walk north one hour, then west one hour, then north again one hour, over and over. Pitch the tajj every night and sleep inside it with my exosuit on, I can have my helmet open if I want. Keep going till I find the railroad, then follow it north. Every time I change direction, call for help on suit-to-suit and try the satcell."

"Good! Really good! Alik?"

"If anything happens to you, I record your position, keep going on our same plan, and go get help. I send them after Bianca and Erin first, then worry about rescuing you. And I quote, 'I'm the lowest priority and that's a Cap's order, Alik.' Right?"

"Perfect. Okay, then, let's go."

Alik didn't start off, though he was gonna lead for the first part, and the two girls didn't move to go back into the tajj. A long few seconds passed. "What's wrong?" I asked, like a moron.

Bianca sighed impatiently. "Didn't we say *everybody* was gonna review, Cap?"

"Okay, if anything happens to Alik, I continue to the train or to RSC, get help, and rescue Alik and you guys—depending on who's in what kind of shape and what's easier. All right?"

"Perfect," Erin assured me.

I laughed and hugged her, so we had to do one more quick round of hugs before setting out. The two of them went in and Alik and I got down to business. We crayoned our faceplates, marking a front arrow and circling three stars that had to be kept in their respective circles; it was sloppy and primitive and worked. For the next couple of hours, if we kept all three stars in their places, and headed for the point of the arrow, we'd be on course or near enough.

The dark had shot across the sky before we'd started our good-byes, and it was black night now, darker than I had ever seen in my lifetime, for most chondreors were somewhere back of their fail-safe points, and therefore were in orbits that would not bring them in, and the comsats were dead, no longer firing rockets to maneuver through the busy sky around Mars, and since they had always relied on dynamic maneuvering, many had been switched off while on trajectories that took them out of the sky: down into the atmosphere, out on an escape, or far away in a high ellipse. I found out later that in the first fifty hours after Sunburst, more'n three quarters of the satellites came in and burned up or tumbled outward and were lost.

Deimos was already low in the sky, and not much more'n a sliver anyway—you could barely see that it was anything other than a bright star; Phobos wouldn't rise for another two hours. I turned to take a last look back. The tajj's airy silver dome glinted in Deimos's light, sitting like a resting bug on the now-dark mass behind the white airlock door. The tajj looked as dark and heavy as the three low heaps of rock in front of it; I thought again that the next human beings must be at least a hundred kim away, across country that was still marked only with occasional footprints, and though my heater was working just fine, Doc, I gotta tell you, it chilled me right down to the bone and I don't think I really warmed up again for all the long roo that came after.

We were carrying suitrations for four days, so if we had to roo all the way to Red Sands City we'd do the last day hungry. Besides that we had the werp and as little else as we could manage.

Doc, if we had problems, I don't think anyone, anywhere, could ever tell us we didn't try hard enough. (For one thing if somebody did I'd hold him down while Alik kicked him.) At first it was easy enough going. Phobos came up about the time we shot the stars again and got our new guide stars marked in; according to the werp we'd been less than a hundred meters off course, but the ground had all been mostly just rocky plain, easy enough to travel even in the dark. We made great time and it was easy to come down mostly on brightly lit patches.

Just after that second sighting, we came over the low crumbly ridge where millions of years of dust had piled up against the place where an ancient lava flow had buried the still more ancient crater rim; there was a deep belt of the squishy stuff, leading down to a little three-meter cliff that we could pretty much just bounce down. It wasn't a bad spot, actually, all by itself, but looking out beyond it we could see that it marked the beginnings of our first stretch of fretted channel country.

It was about the worst way to hit fretted channels. We had to go crosswise, not down the channels; we didn't have APS so we couldn't just keep walking channel to channel and looking for gateways, so we'd hafta go over some of the high spots, at least to get bearings regularly. And the country itself hadn't yet encountered many outflows, let alone rain, from the terraforming, so there had been little water to sweep out the channel bottoms and knock down the more fragile parts of the spires and cliffs. Beyond us, reaching far over the horizon, a tangle of gullies and ridges, spires and holes, broken rock and dust drifts, dared us to see if we could keep a course. In the light of rising Phobos, it looked like wall after wall after wall, each with its jaggy sharp top, like a medieval fortress, or a twentieth-century border, or a concentration camp fence.

We were forty-five minutes ahead of schedule, but we had been planning to be as far ahead as possible anyway, knowing this was coming. Rooing fretted channel country is limward bad news even in daylight, and we figured no matter what we'd need more time than we'd have.

We took a quick accuracy-check sighting; everything seemed to be fine. The first channel was fairly wide and shallow and merely miserable. It was all loose big-grain soil, formed into solid-seeming clumps that broke off under our hands and feet all the time. Boulders twice as tall as me lay everywhere with all sizes of rocks, gravel drifts, and dust dunes between; it looked like a place where God never got around to cleaning up after creation. We climbed and descended, sliding and bumping, falling down times without number, narrowly missing overturning rocks on ourselves, all of it to reach a six-meter vertical wall that broke off as soon as we touched it with a spike.

We ended up following the wall a good five hundred meters north before we found a collapsed part where we could scramble up a spill of scree that was merely danger-ous rather than impossible. That put us on top of an ir-regular mesa, almost a kim across, and we rooed that in just minutes before we found ourselves at the edge of the next channel. This one was deeper and steeper, and a star fix showed that we were more'n a kim off course. "We'd hafta set new guide stars," Alik said.

"You say that like there's a choice."

"Well. Suppose we just concentrate on getting to the other side of this country, and then take a fix and work from there. Just head generally west, cause that's the way we hafta go, and south, cause the country is less wide in that direction, and figure that'll get us to someplace we can start making good time again. That's what I was thinking."

I dropped an arm around his slim shoulders. "I knew I brought you for a reason."

"Here I thought it was my looks."

I laughed, though it wasn't particularly funny. Alik needed to feel liked, and besides, I did like him. "Well, if we're just gonna try to get through, we still need to maintain some kinda course. And the bottom of that channel is posreal torn up, and looks treacherous as a teeper's credit. Here's what I think." I clicked on my laser pointer and picked out a distinctive spire of tuff on the mesa on the other side, whirling it around on the formation. "See that tall thing? I hereby name it 'Hat Man.' So that's what we head for. Now what are easy-to-identify places we can aim for on the way?"

I walked the laser pointer down a broken spot in the cliff that looked like it formed a climbable chimney; at the base of that was the "Elephant's Egg," a rock that gave us another landmark. Back from that were the "Weird Sisters," a bunch of rocks shaped like old-time nuns, and back from that was the "Blue Patch," an area of hard dark clay. Using the pointer, we worked our way all the way back to the "Big Duck Rock" just below us, then walked the spot of the laser pointer through the route twice more, memorizing every landmark from "Big Duck Rock" to

"Hat Man." After fifteen minutes of route-drawing, we had agreed on a course and we both felt ready to start.

It was scary in the dark. Feet and hands slipped often; we needed the helmet lights to see but they blotted out the reassuring stars. We lost a couple of landmarks entirely, finally just picking out the next one by dumb luck, but we got to the chimney well enough, and there we were lucky—it was firm and narrow and we went right up it. We crossed that mesa—by now Phobos was nearing the zenith—and started the process over again. Though there were only six kim to cover, and on level ground in daylight that's about forty minutes, it took us close to three hours, most of it spent groping and bumbling our way forward by headlamp, for all the world like old-time miners.

When we climbed up from the last channel and saw level ground stretching as far as the horizon, we both just wanted to roo, but the first thing we needed to do was take a fix and set new guide stars. As far as we could guess, to get through about six kim of fretted channel country, we had covered about nine kim in all. We were now about an hour behind.

"On the original plan, we'd never have crossed that country," I said, juicing up my oxygen a skosh cause my heart was pounding. "We were slated to cross it at a narrow spot with a thumped road, about forty kim southwest of here. We could never have done this with the whole party, not any way anyone would figure was safe. As it is we cut at least a day out of the trip—even though we're behind pretty bad."

"Not as bad as I was afraid we'd be," Alik pointed

out. "It was tiring and frustrating but not as time consuming as it felt like."

"*Nothing* could be as time consuming and frustrating as that felt like."

We had almost two hours then of near-level plain, and with the extra light of Phobos, now past its zenith and descending, it was easy to keep the three stars in their crayoned circles and just keep following the arrow. We rooed like racers the whole way, gulping water and little bites of suitrations on the fly. I gotta say, Doc, it was almost fun. We moved along pretty good and made back some time.

We got real lucky next, cause a stretch of badlands turned out to be pretty well scoured out—just a few mesas to skirt around, nothing that added much time—and then there was a long run up the side of a ridge, another one of those buried crater walls you find all over Mollyland, cause of all the stuff that got blown into it, raining down to make it dense with craters, right after the big one that made Hellas Basin, and then the big lava flows later on. Normally they're not bad at all—they're steep enough to have been scoured by the wind, and to have lost most of their loose stuff, but they're also very eroded so there's plenty to grab onto and the slopes aren't that steep—but this one ran north-south. Deimos, though it was brightening toward the full it would be in the morning, was far down in the sky to the west, almost setting now. Being in front of us, it gave no light to the slope we were climbing, and anyway, tiny and dim as it always was, it wasn't much better'n a bright star. Phobos was almost full, but already setting in the east, outracing the planet's rotation as always, bright enough but throwing very long dark shadows in front of us and making the surface of the slope a confusing patchwork of dark spots that we had to work through carefully. After a skoshy while, I turned on my headlamp and said, "Alik, we better just get up the slope and then take a sight."

"I was just about to say that, myself." He switched on his headlamp and we bounced up the slope, rooing fast and easy, now that we didn't hafta try to make difficult sights on stars high up above our heads, and cope with deep shadows on a badly lit slope.

We reached the top just in time to see Deimos silhouette a distant crater wall; the peak bit into the irregular, lumpy moon like a giant's tooth into a huge potato. The slope in front of us dimmed slightly, but it made little difference. "Well," I said, "if we want to roo down that slope tonight, we'll hafta keep going till we're reasonably far from the shadow of this ridge, so we don't lose the morning sun for recharging; if we stay up here we can just spread our collectors out and sack out. What do you feel like?"

"How long till daylight?"

"Fifty-one minutes."

"Sounds like time enough to get all the way down and put three kim into crossing that plain. I'm good enough for it if you are. Let me shoot a fix." He held up the werp, leveled it, and ran his calculations. "This is great. We're about two kim closer to goal than I thought we'd be."

Something about that cheered both of us up; we gulped warm water from our recyclers, watched the dim glow from Deimos die on the horizon for a minute or two (it moved less than a fifth as fast as the sun, so Deimos risings and settings were gradual), took a last glance at Phobos as it rocketed on down the sky behind us, and rooed down the slope. On this windward side, the surface had been swept smoother, and despite having to switch headlamps on and off all the time, we stayed on course and moved fast. When the sun finally came up, we had put the ridge over the horizon behind us.

Our final fix showed us that we hadn't made nearly the distance we had thought during that last hour, still "it was progress we don't hafta make tomorrow," Alik said, through bites of his suitration. The bright morning sun showed us a wide, rolling plain; there was still plenty of rugged country ahead, but at the moment it all lay over the close Martian horizon. We had already spread out the collector sheets and everything was powering up and re-charging very nicely; heat, power, water, and air reserves should be back to nominal well before the sun went down. "I'm gonna switch on everything and give myself extra padding and extra warmth, if you don't mind."

"I was gonna use the power massager on the back pads myself. Might as well, Alik; power is the one thing we have plenty of."

I triggered the face wipe to get rid of the crumbs of suitration, set the back pads to full inflate, added extra heat and massage, and stretched out on the ground. I was asleep after one single sigh.

I had set my alarm to turn off the opaque on my faceplate at twenty minutes till sundown, and fallen asleep facing west. So my eyes opened on the same Martian plane, but the sun was now on the other side. I sat up, surprised at first at how stiff I was, and then that I wasn't any stiffer. I rooed around behind the rocks, deposited some rubbies in my account—I wondered if the Development Corporation was still in existence, and if not, how anyone was gonna live—and came back to find Alik just darting off to another spot behind the rocks. When he got back, we ate suitrations, not feeling much need to talk, just sitting back to back for company.

"Do we hafta wait to take our fixes?"

"Yeah, I'm afraid so," he said. "I should have done that last night." He sounded sad.

I snorted. "Damn. My partner isn't perfect. Think I'll stretch out on the ground and just starve to death out of pure shame. We still have the collectors to fold and we oughta review the ground to be covered today; by the time we get all that done you'll have more'n enough stars to shoot your fix. Just redd the werp up so we're good to go as soon as it's really dark."

He shrugged. "I guess I do wish I was skoshy closer to perfect."

"Don't we all."

"Is that Full Adultly wisdom?"

"That's all they gave me. I just got the starter set."

We got to work. By the time the sun was down, we were good to go. Phobos would be rising a little earlier tonight, just after sunset, and that would help, but we wouldn't have Deimos for another couple of nights, and rising as close as it did to the setting sun, Phobos would barely be a sliver in the sky for its first hour or so. Fortunately the first long stretch was just across more of these bare plains, and we oughta be able to do it comfortably.

Though my legs and back ached as we started off, my spirits were coming up a skosh—at least we were getting something accomplished. My good mood lasted until we came bounding down a downslope into a patchwork of dirt that I had been hoping would just be what the oldtimers call "yolis"—I guess short for "aeolian dust deposits," which is what they made us call them in school cause it was supposed to Teach Us Something or Other. Those are just places where the dust was sorted by the wind into streaks according to density, and you get all these little light and dark patches that look like something from orbit but are really only a few millimeters deep. That was what I was hoping for, right till we got there and saw a low billowing cloud of fog, hugging the ground just a couple of meters high.

What we found was a freebie sebkhet; if any ecospector would've released the rubbies for this, it would've been
a posreal scorehole, we'd all have heard about it (probably
till we were good and sick of the subject!), and it would've
been on the map. But here it was—just a skoshy surprise.

The trouble with trying to cross a sebkhet comes in
two flavors. A sebkhet is a big, wide area that will someday
be a lake, once enough water flows in to back up. Typi-
cally there's some openings in it down into dry aquifers,
and some deep gravel beds, and things like that that will
drink water for decades before they back up and start to
block the water. So every biggish flood you get recharges
the sebkhet, but mostly it drains or evaporates, so it's usually just swampy.

The first problem that can give you is that although
exosuits are waterproof, the heaters aren't really designed
to deal with conductive heat loss, which is very fast, and
that water is limward cold when it's at its warmest. Plus
exosuits tend to stick to mud, so you can get jammed into
the stuff posreal quick too. The second problem is that if
it's frozen, it's slick and dangerous and hard to find footing, and you hafta walk, not roo, and it takes forever.

A few experiments showed us that this sebkhet was
about half frozen, so we were gonna have both problems.
We fought and struggled through that stuff, banging ourselves on ice and getting stuck in freezing goo, for a lot of
hours, Doc, and if adversity improves your character,
me'n'Alik're saints. It was four hours to make seven kim,
and practically all of that we made on a few big sandbars and
islands where we could roo a little; every time we had to
head back into the goo or onto the ice—or break through

the ice to get stuck in the goo—it was the same old story. Twice I went in over my head but in an exosuit, that's no deal; there's a secondary air tank that gives you half an hour's breathing, so you just inflate the air pads, kick out of the mud, and head back up.

By the time we were out, though, parts of the suits were so cold you'd've thought you were dipping your feet in icewater, and other parts were overheated in response, and all kinds of muscles were tired and in a nasty mood to cramp.

We shot a fix and we were on course, but it was time to change guide stars; it was limward easier to work with stars near the horizon and the ones we were using were creeping up in the sky. By now Phobos was much higher, and was waxing rapidly as it went; the glow on the billowing fog of the sebkhet was almost pretty.

"We're doing posreal good, all the same," Alik said. "It looks like a plain old cinder field all the way from here to almost the railhead."

Amazingly, it was, and that helped for other reasons, too. We had gobbled double rations and taken big drinks of water, set for extra warm. After a while the heating-cooling units on the exosuit began to even things out, and my rewarming body made me much more comfortable. And after another hour I could let myself feel a growing confidence; we'd hoped to finish the trip tonight, but we didn't hafta, and anyway by going through badly mapped and explored areas we'd cut so much distance out that we would still be getting there in half the time that the regular way would've taken. It wasn't perfect, but so far all the gambles we'd taken had paid off.

The cinder field was pitch black, and though Phobos lit it brightly for our first hour, after that most of it was black as the sky. Every once in a while we'd come down on a chunk of pumice or some other black rock, tumble, and hafta catch ourselves, but it wasn't bad all the same. Having some caution for the few rocks there were slowed us a little, but still we rooed along at almost top speed until Alik said, "Okay, my dead reckoning says, let's take a fix. We might be close."

"This is great, Alik. It's still almost three hours to dawn and—"

"Hunh." He was staring at the werp. After a moment, he said "Hunh" again.

"What?"

"Something weird. Posreal weird. This thing is saying we should've passed the railhead half a kim ago, but we would've had to go right through it, and I didn't see it, did you?"

"Naw, I'm sure we didn't just miss it. We would've seen it even if all its lights're out." I thought for a zilty. "Let me try working the gadget. Maybe different hands get slightly different readings."

"I'm sure I did it right."

"So am I. But it's possible that if we each do it right we'll come up with different answers. Machines are weird and this one's weirder than most cause of all the stuff you're making it do."

"Okay." He didn't sound happy but he handed me the werp.

I did it limward careful, of course—didn't want to embarrass myself in front of him—and when I got the answer, I stared. "Well, we *do* get different answers. I just got that we should be north and west of the station, by a bit over a kim." I showed him.

"Sheee . . . all right, let me try again." The position he found was a full kim off his previous one.

After enough experiments, we determined that all the points were falling within a three kim circle, which doesn't sound so bad until you realize that's more'n six square kim to search. A few more experiments showed that the height you held it at had an effect of a couple of hundred meters, and that you could wobble it through an angle of maybe a half degree before the internal level noticed.

"When we ran our tests at camp," I said, "We set it up on a rock, and we never moved it. That's what happened. We never checked it on the fly. And that built in altimeter is probably only good to ten meter or so accuracy—it was always intended to depend on APS. So basically we're as close as it can get us."

"So, I've just stranded us here." He sounded miserable.

I put an arm around him. "You've gotten us amazingly close, so far. We just hafta find our way for the last kim or two. And we have more'n a day to look. And we can't be that far off. The country we were expecting has pretty much shown up right on schedule, hasn't it? So we're off but not far off—the problem now is just finding the exact spot."

"I guess."

We set it up on a low rock, shot a few more points, and took an average; that seemed to give us a figure of point seven kim to the southwest. We set guide stars and rooed that distance—what, Doc? Oh, well, you know, of course I didn't get mad. He was ten. And his solution was the best we could do, which was good but not great. How accurate it could be was limited by the level, which wasn't perfectly accurate, and the sensitivity to height and the fairly crappy altimeter, and by the resolution of the camera itself. And then too, if I get the math guys right, we had screwed up anyway cause we were averaging results instead of data—I guess that makes a big difference, though it wasn't clear to me just how, cause nothing expressed in math is ever gonna be clear to me. Even then I knew what mattered, right then, wasn't the navigation but taking care of the navigator. I mean, it stands to reason.

Alik had done a great job but he couldn't let himself just have done a great job, he hadda've done the most brilliant job that was ever done, if you see what I mean. And I could tell that that was what was eating him, so I spent some time calming him down. I knew we were probably within two kim of the railhead, with about two days of food on hand—I knew we'd find it. He just wanted it to be perfect and was having a bitty skosh of a tantrum when it wasn't, which is pretty much what any bright person without social skills does, you know? Anyway, Doc, thanks for asking, cause since what happened happened, I think it's posreal important for Alik to have every record specify: the trouble wasn't his fault.

So we rooed to the new position and there was still no station any place we could see. We took fifteen measurements at the new place, and we were now off by half a kim, and headed back north. "At least the error seems to be going down," Alik said.

A few minutes later we were again at an empty point

on the featureless plain; we shot another set of measurements and averaged them, and the werp arrived at the conclusion that we were now off by half a kim south—that we had been at the train station before. "Time to sack out," I said. "This is definitely something to wait for daylight for, and I'm exhausted."

"So'm I, but I didn't want to admit it."

Battery charges were still good—we'd had a full charge the day before and that's good for up to two weeks—so we just stretched out, spread the collectors, plugged in for when the sun came up, and went to sleep. For one of the first times in my life, I slept right through it when the sun hit my faceplate, even though I hadn't opaqued it.

When I did wake up, it was close to noon, and I sat straight up, not quite sure where I was or what was going on. I sat up, looked around, and saw the train station about halfway to the horizon—maybe a kim and a half. I woke up Alik and pointed.

Alik let out a whoop, and we rooed our way over to it. "Let this thing be working!" he said. "I would so like to ride the rest of the way!"

"Me, too, limward."

The station was about as simple as a structure can get; a long low building with windows, adjoining a maglev track, and with all the facilities you'd normally need inside. The outside screen was blank, and nothing seemed to be working just immediately, but after we scouted around for a bit, we found a manual override on the airlock, and went in that way. There was an emergency reset procedure outlined on a wall poster—mostly just push this button, wait for that, push this button, wait for that, the usual kind of thing—and we worked our way through it. Lights came on, screens powered up, and fans began to hum. About a quarter of everything stayed dead, so it figured, since it was the most inconvenient one, that the com link to RSC would be one of them. On the other hand, the TRAIN RE-QUESTS AND SCHEDULES screen was glowing a pleasant green with the words FULL FUNCTIONAL.

"I think we can officially declare ourselves geniuses if we like," I said. "Let's get a train headed this way."

The screens said that there was a southbound train only 120 kim away, and we told the system that we wanted to board it; it accepted our identifications, and gave us an estimate of forty minutes. We took off our helmets to en-joy the inside air; after all, when you board a train, it's through an airlock anyway.

"I know they have food on the trains," Alik said, "but I'd like to at least eat something I can eat with my helmet off, right now."

"Go ahead, I'll join you."

So we gulped soup and chattered excitedly about what we'd do. "First of all, we get a party sent out for Bianca and Erin. It will be good to see them again, and besides Erin needs to get away from that cairn—it can't be healthy for a little kid like her, especially since she was so close to her sister. Then you and I get a real good meal and some nice person tells us what's going on. Then we have big meals and long showers—"

"Contract. I wish we could get hold of RSC and get the rescue underway sooner, though—hey. Hey hey hey."

"What?"

Alik looked so proud of himself. Yeah, Doc, I know

he had a crush on me, and he liked impressing me, and he did impress me pretty often. I figure when I'm a hundred and five, and he's a hundred, maybe, if he's gotten a little more mature . . . naw, just kidding. He never will.

Anyway, he did look proud of himself, and he did impress me. "Trains carry conductors and conductors have com rooms. Maybe the conductor on the train can talk to us, and to RSC. Sort of a relay. Worth a try?"

"Definitely worth a try."

He popped up, went to the console, and then said "Shit," emphatically.

"What's—"

"The train hasn't moved. It's still 120 kim away and the system still says it will be here in forty minutes." He started popping through info screens and said, "That information is updated as of about ten minutes before whatever it was happened. The train was in that position at that time. No actual contact with it since, and the power to most of the track sections between there and here is out. Let's see if we can turn it back on—emergency authorization and all that—" He started clicking his tongue and muttering the way he always did when a technical problem got interesting. Screen changed to screen faster than I could follow.

Doc, I don't think there's anything weird about it, and if you do, maybe you don't know us rounditachi as well as you think you do. Of course he thought there'd be an override someplace he could access. You'd *never* make that impossible out in the roundings. What if you got an accident and the only conscious member of a party was six years old or something? That could very well have happened to Dad'n'me's party, you know—what if we'd all been hurt but not dead and only Erin had been full functional? I don't know that she'd've done the right thing, but she was raised a roundita, and I can tell you she'd've tried, and did her best, and depending on just what'as wrong and what'as needed, she might've got it. So why would you lock her out of a system she might need to get at?

Hunh. Well, that's why I'll never be a sitter, Doc, even if they make me live in a city forever. Kids here never do have enough to do, you know. That's why they're better looking and dance better and they're more fun to just chat with than we are. But you don't let them do anything important and they all know that weeks go by when they aren't doing anything important—

Aw, come on, Doc. "Just growing up" is important, sure, I know, but growing up's not something you work at, it's something that happens while you work at something else that's important. And if you never work at anything important it never happens. That's why you worry about pranks and vandals. Since you don't let them do anything important—most of your sitter kids are what, twelve, before they have a community service job, and a lot of 'em don't even add a private sector job to that till they're out of school or seventeen—they have no importance to any adult around them except for all that love and family stuff they're always talking about at school, and nobody ever seems to notice that that's not something you can work at either. I mean, yeah, I suppose if your mother's too busy, she can't hug you as often, but how many mothers can ever get that busy?

Doc, we are practically at the twenty-second century right now. We aren't gonna be stupid enough to go back to what they did in the twentieth. That would be like bringing back the Roman emperor or slavery or high school or something. But look, no kidding, just in case anybody ever asks you, the reason you can't trust a sitter kid around anything dangerous is cause you never let them do anything important—cause to do anything important, they have to be trusted with something dangerous. You tell a kid that she's not allowed to be any value and sure, she'll start smashing things just to prove she's there. I guess if you told me that all I could do was go to school, have a social life, and work on my healthy normal development, the best you could hope for is that I'd get drunk all the time and not hurt anyone—and I don't think you'd get the best. I guess I'd break things and spoil stuff, just so I'd matter.

Anyway, so of course Alik, being a ten-year-old roundito, and not worrying that anyone would break something important just cause they could, was expecting to find that there'd be access to fix things that any literate person could get at. It never would've occurred to him that anybody would be trying to lock him out just cause he was young. He'd probably been responsible for his whole family's lives half a dozen times by then. And so when he found there were all those lockouts, he didn't think they were supposed to protect him or the train, he just thought more stuff was damaged or had gotten misset by whatever the thing from the sun was. So he hacked it and got it working on his command.

Would it've been better if we'd just sat there? We

didn't know it but without us, people were gonna die, Doc, and—yeah, so something bad happened. And I haven't forgotten what you're gonna hafta do to me or anything. But how many dead people would that be? Of course it's worth it. Doc, for a guy with all that school, sometimes I swear—well, if you were ever to turn eco-spector, and I hadda train you, I'd hafta watch you around the rocks. They might outwit you.

⚅ **Cal sits quietly** in the chair across from me. I'm crying. I'm ashamed. "Third time," I say.

"That's right, it is," he says.

"New job."

"Don't worry about that just yet. We have a few more questions to look at."

"I'll cooperate as much as I can."

"We're going to be asking both of you."

I shudder with fear; I don't want that. But I say "all right."

◖◗ **While Alik was** trying to figure out what was going on with the power system, and why he couldn't just start doing restores and resets on all the sections that were out, I got busy with the station's other equipment. They had emergency long range radio, and that took no time at all to get on line—they didn't think I might be too irresponsible to work it, I guess. So I got on the air and discovered that there was a slightly different mix of stations calling, again mostly from the Northern Hemisphere, but it was all the same—we're here, we're in trouble, is anyone there? And the only two-way contacts I could overhear were between parties out in the roundings, just talking to each other to keep their spirits up.

Then I heard a calm young voice saying "This is Bianca Nakaomi. I'm stranded in a tajj, in eastern Mollyland, at about fifty-three south, sixty-seven east, with one other survivor, Erin Krabach, age five. Two members of the party—"

"Come in, Bianca, this is Teri."

"Teri!" I heard a whoop in the background from Erin. "Did you get through?"

"Kinda. We're at the station. Alik's okay too. Things are a mess here. We're trying to get help moving toward you but so far we're not in touch with anyone. How are supplies?"

"Food for thirteen more days, and I've got the synthesizer making protein and sugar goo, so we won't starve, but we might wish we had. Erin's homesick and lonely and bored. Our other backup heater finally died completely so now if we try to move we'll hafta use the tajj, but if there's a reason to we can try to walk out."

"I don't think there'll be a reason to," I said. "I have a lot of faith in Alik, and I think he'll get us a working train or a working com into RSC real soon."

It was a relief to just talk with someone familiar. We chatted about the trip and about what Erin and Bianca had been doing in camp: mostly a lot of maintenance, some fussy repair work, and then killing time with entertainment. It sounded like life in prison, and I guess I was just as glad that I had plenty to do.

Then a voice broke in. "Trying to contact Teri at the station, whatever that is."

"Hang on, Bianca . . . This is Teri Murray. I'm at the southern railhead, seven hundred kim southeast of Red Sands City. We seem to have a dead train stuck on the tracks about a hundred twenty kim away. No contact with any authorities since the accident several days ago—"

"Teri, this is Wandasue Enriquez, and we're a large party, sixty-eight alive, camped at thirty-four north, eighty-five east. We have what looks like about forty cases of radiation poisoning, rations for about twenty days. If you do get into contact with any city, we need help right away."

"Got it," I said. "Have you been able to hear the rest of the party I'm talking to?"

"Nothing distinct enough to make out."

I relayed the information about Bianca and Erin to Wandasue. In a few minutes, nine more parties called in; looked like I had the best radio on the planet at the moment, so I carefully took down everyone's information and made sure we had it in the station's computers, Dad's werp, and our suit memories. The short summary was that everyone was in trouble, and no one had gotten an answer to a distress call. If anyone had been in daylight at the time of whatever it was, they were always coping with much more severe electronics damage and generally with radiation poisoning, mostly below lethality but plenty of people were sick and couldn't be in exosuits cause of skin peeling and bleeding.

I took all the information down and promised to relay it if I found anyone to relay it to. Then, having been on the radio for about three hours, I went off the air, stretched, and went to reconstitute a bowl of soup for myself. "Do you need anything?" I asked Alik. He'd been muttering in the corner for all this time.

"I need a bunch of software engineers to report to me for a good beating," he said. "There's an amazing number of safeties and blocks here and I've already hadda beat my way through three different passwords. It looks like this stuff was only supposed to be used by engineers from the maglev company; how the hell do they expect a system to work if people can't fix it when it breaks? But I think I'm finally in, and I'm trying to do remote restarts on everything. I just hafta break into this one set of files to get the script."

"The script?"

"That's what they call it. According to the manual, things hafta be restored and powered up in a particular order or it's dangerous. Of course they don't tell you what the dangers are so you can make an intelligent choice. And instead of just giving you the order and telling you to make sure to do it, they lock it up in something called 'the script,' for some reason or other. Probably the same reason that the railroad won't run without a bunch of engineers coming out to visit it. Like I said, I don't know how they expected anything to work if they weren't gonna let anyone fix it." He looked at the screen again. "Hah. Well, that's the script. It looks like it was originally executable code, so I guess there was just a button you hit to run the script, but I never found the automatic, so I guess I'll start in manually, as soon as I get it figured out."

"Soup or something?" I offered again.

"Yeah—I should eat."

I got Alik a bowl of soup and a sandwich and watched it disappear into him as he sat and tapped and clicked. I did a radio check in as it got late, and found two more stranded parties. One of them had a physics whiz in the party who had this idea that Mars might temporarily have an extensive ionosphere from what had happened, and that was why long-range radio was working better for distant stations than for close ones, but I couldn't follow his argument very well and anyway it didn't really have anything to do with anything that mattered just then.

Anyway, it did kind of explain why we were getting so much signal from Tharsis, which was thousands of kilometers away.

I had put another bowl of soup into Alik—he was so engrossed that probably I could have fed him paper clips and string and he'd've been just as happy—before Alik said, "Okay, I think we finally got something here. At least it looks like I understand everything the script was supposed to do. Let me start trying."

He clicked and grunted and the screen danced with messages; "Do you know what all those mean?" I asked him.

"Maybe half. I think I know what all the important warning messages would be." He kept going.

On one screen was the only thing I understood—a map of maglev track between the station and Red Sands City. Sections were starting to go green; after a while, a few flashed to green and back to red. Alik was muttering more. A few minutes later, he said, "Well, here's what we have. Six bad sections right behind the train, and the train control box reports massive malfunctions. I'm guessing it crashed on the track—probably the power and the emergency power and every other piece of emergency equipment went out, and all of a sudden it just settled three centimeters and was scraping along at three hundred kim, leaving wreckage behind it. Then there's two bad sections of track between us and it, so even if we had a train here, we couldn't even get as far as the wrecked train. So we're stuck here. I did manage to get power back on to the internal compartments of the train, cause I needed to talk to its computers, but—"

"Can anyone hear me?" a voice said.

We turned toward the sound. A froyk was staring out of the screen; not at us, cause the camera was off, but Alik clicked it on, and the froyk said, "I'm Roger Clevenger, leader for a traverse party, Band Eleven of the Austral Nation, and we've got a bad situation here. We've been without power for four days and out of food for one. I'm hoping you're someone who can help."

"I'm Teri Murray," I said.

"The girl on the radio. Our transmitter didn't seem to reach you. So you're at the station south of us." He seemed to sink slightly in his chair, as if just a skosh more defeated. His big eyes were sunken and the fur on his face was matted. Probably he'd had no way to groom himself. "I was hoping for help, but I guess you were too."

"We're kind of all stuck together," I said, trying to sound sympathetic. He did look sad. "Nobody seems to be getting any rescue anywhere. I guess we don't even really know if the cities are still there."

"Yeah . . ." He looked down. "I've got forty-six survivors in Band Eleven, and . . . well, you know about our metabolisms?"

I felt something cold at the base of my spine. "Did getting the power back on for the train help?"

"A little bit. But reconstituted unmodified-human food only goes so far; it's like we're missing vitamins. So the kids are happier because they're eating—we've got all the reconstitutors running—but we're having to ration Marsform food. And when they don't get enough of that . . . well, they'll keep getting sicker. They've been pretty bad the last day. And the calorie requirement is 7500 a day for a child and 12,000 for an adult—we basically have bird metabolisms—so it goes a lot faster still." He sighed. "So thanks for getting the power on—it'll keep us going for another day—I don't mean to seem ungrateful—but—"

"How many kids?" I asked, knowing that froyk bands are mostly kids.

"Thirty-four under the age of ten. We were doing their first major overland trip, out to the Prome and back . . . we were going to visit some of the reserved land—"

"Hang on. Were you gonna pick up rations here, at the station?"

Alik jumped to the keyboard and started pounding; he'd seen where I was going with this.

So had Roger. "Yes—yes we were!"

Alik whooped. "We've got two thousand standard child rations and one thousand standard adult, here in storage, for Marsforms. How many a day—"

"Five is normal. That's at least ten days' worth. We can *walk* back to RSC if we can get those rations." Roger's face fell; I'm ashamed to say I couldn't help thinking of a big dog in a children's show. "But right now I don't know if I have anyone left who can walk even to the station. With the adjustable metabolism, we were all running very high just to stay alive while the power was off, and most of our solar collectors were zapped dead. I hadda eat two ration packs to get up enough energy to feed everyone else—that's why I didn't call you right away. I don't know if I could walk to you, and I think I'm in the best shape of anyone right now—"

"Then I'll come to you," I said, amazed to find myself saying it. "Sounds like you need about a hundred kid rations and forty adult, say, so that you or someone can get into good enough shape to come back here and pick up the rest? If I get there in five hours from now, can you hold out till then?"

Roger nodded vigorously. "If you're willing to do it, don't delay—I was expecting the first deaths today, and now with the power on we still don't have more than a day and a half before I start to lose the youngest children. But if you get here in five hours I think everyone will make it."

"Then I'm on my way," I said. "I'll call you when I leave."

I turned and grabbed up the expansion modules for my carry pack; 140 rations is a lot even when it's regular-human reconstitutables, about twice a normal load, and froyk rations are bigger and heavier.

Alik said, "I'll keep working on things and I'll check in twice a day on radio. You won't need the werp, so I'll keep it, and if I hafta I'll go get Bianca and Erin and bring'em here."

"Perfect," I said. I had found the right storage unit and was starting to count out rations.

"Uh, Cap?"

"Yeah."

"It's dark out now. Stick close to the maglev track and be careful. You won't have a partner for this one."

I glanced up, saw his face, and gave him a hug. "For a guy who's ten years old, you're a worrier."

"Aw . . . it's just I'm gonna be lonely, till Roger and his people get here."

"What about me?" I said. "I'll be coming back with them—"

"Why?" Alik looked puzzled. "Why not just go straight on, after you get the rations delivered? Take a few suitrations and figure you can make it to RSC—that way at least we'll finally have contact with one city and be able to see what's going on, you know?"

"Good point. And I would bet that Roger and company will all end up here eventually, so you won't be lonely for long."

Alik nodded; I looked at him a skosh closer. "What else is the matter?" I asked.

"Aw, I'm a big baby."

"Let me be the judge of that. I say you're a great partner."

"Posreal? That's nice. Limward nice." He sighed. "Really the big problem is something that shouldn't be a problem at all, and I am just being a baby. I just kept hoping that my folks's expedition would call in."

I hugged that kid for all I was worth; it hadn't occurred to me till then that though I'd lost Dad, I didn't have to worry about him or Mummy, and that Alik and Bianca and Erin'd all been coping with worry about their families as well. Besides, I was grown, FA and everything, and much as I'd miss Dad, I didn't really depend on him anymore . . . sometimes the thing that lets you go on with life is knowing how many people have it worse.

That reminded me that though a Marsform can do a hell of a lot more'n I can on the surface, I can't die of starvation in five days flat. So I got back to packing.

With three days' suitrations plus the 140 ration packs,

I was loaded down pretty good by the time I started, and I'd hadda pack carryons up top so that I was really top-heavy. (Of course on Earth I'd never have been able to lift that load at all.) The big problem was that though Martian gravity makes things lighter, it doesn't make them less massive—they still have the same momentum. So you're able to pick up a mass that can whip you around more, and your lighter weight means less friction with the ground, and the whole result is that when you're rooing with a heavy pack, like everyone always says, a few million years of evolution are there to trip you up.

I figured that with the rail line there to guide me, especially since they run them through firm flat ground as much as they can, I ought to be able to roo twenty-five kim an hour—after all, I could do thirty-three when I was racing, and I'd done thirty many times out in the round-ings with a full pack.

But this was way, way beyond a full pack, and at every landing it tried to fling me to my face, and at every takeoff it tried to flip me over backwards. With the auxiliary bags on, I was tied to something big and rigid, and couldn't move my back enough to shift my balance properly. After a bare few kim I was double bouncing like a little kid, catching myself and then re-jumping, which meant I was losing the momentum that makes rooing effective; every so often I would fall into a disgusted fast walk, only to find that as I accelerated the pack, it would begin to push me forward when my heel touched, tiring my ankles and calves and always threatening to throw me headlong. Soon I had oxygen enrichment cranked way up, and painkillers feeding into my blood, and three hours into the trip, I was still less than a third of the way there. I would have to make the time back somehow.

You can't let all those kids die, Teri, Dad's voice seemed to say in my head—"they'll be fine if you're on the job, Cap," had been Alik's last words to me before I'd closed my helmet and stepped into the airlock. Everyone had limward faith in me.

Except maybe me, and after I got this load of food to those kids, I was gonna hafta sit down and give myself a real good pep talk about my need for more self-confidence.

Though the track kept me from getting lost, it was always a barrier too, because I couldn't safely move on its too-narrow concrete surfaces, or in the open ditch between the rails, and its embankments were too slippery and at too steep an angle for me to move comfortably on; my feet didn't stick enough and my pack yanked me away from the surface too much. So after a while I was just working parallel to the track, rooing as much as I could, double bouncing when I hadda regain balance, dropping into a walk when my legs hurt too much or I needed to catch my wind. The hours crawled by and the track beside me went on seemingly forever, as I followed it through low passes and over cuts in crater walls, now and again walking its rails as it passed through tunnels and over channels.

Phobos rose, a big sliver on the western horizon as it backlit the distant scarps and wrinkle ridges, shrinking and waxing as it climbed to the zenith, till it was almost full as a small bright light overhead. At least the shadows were shorter and I could see more of what I landed on.

I was getting posreal bad tired, and I'd fallen once in the last hour, just from touching down leaning a little too far forward, a bitty skosh off my rhythm. The pack's momentum had nailed me facedown cause a pebble under my toe had rolled, but it wouldn't've if I'd been a skosh more coherent.

I promised myself that in ten more minutes I would stop and have a long drink of water and a double suitration, and give myself another anti-pain boost and a wake-up shot. I just plain needed to take that hour or so to get fully recovered or I'd be no good to anyone. Ten more minutes and I'd take that hour—at that hill up ahead, I decided.

The open space around the track narrowed; I was about to pass over a high causeway, maybe four meters above the hummocky valley floor around it, with steep sides. The narrow clean double stripe of concrete, shining under Phobos, was the only level surface there was. I dinwanna bound around in the broken rock down in the valley, but I dinwanna hafta walk to my rest point. I concentrated as hard as I could and tried to roo along the rail.

I did all right, but my feet were starting to hurt real bad, and I was so tired. Though I tried to concentrate, my brain was drifting, and the concrete rails were only about fifty centimeters across. The pack was getting loose, somehow, too, and I could feel it yanking me, twisting my balance. I'd hafta fix everything at the rest point. Maybe I'd take a nap, too. Maybe from there I could call on the radio and make sure they knew I was late but still coming.

The overloaded pack was so heavy and awkward, and worse now that it was moving around. The balls of my feet twisted, scraped, and ground as I flung myself down the narrow rail. I cranked oxygen to the max and still couldn't seem to get enough.

The land all around, covered with black dust, was so dark that it was like I rooed forever from star to star, across the empty sky, on that narrow bridge of the concrete rail—like me, and the rail, and the stars, were what there was in the universe. I looked up to see Phobos and the Magellanic Clouds, and back down to the rail. I seemed to be running straight into the Great Square of Pegasus on the northern horizon, and it looked no farther away than my intended rest spot.

I was just starting to wonder whether maybe I ought to just sit down and take care of myself, and not try to get all the way to the place I had picked out for a rest—which seemed farther away than ever—when my toe clipped the inside edge of the rail. I flew forward, about to land in a big skid on my face, throwing my hands out to try and keep my faceplate from taking a scraping, trying to tuck my feet under to prevent falling.

One foot planted and caught, and my ankle gave with a sharp stabbing pain. I lunged forward trying to take the weight off it, not thinking, and stepped right off the rail into empty space, flipping forward in a tight, uncontrolled, whirling somersault. I had a glimpse of the stars rushing past me, and then the steep gravel slope of the embankment slammed into my back, and my broken ankle jammed for an instant against the slope, sending me into tucked-up agony that only rolled me faster. I hurtled on down to the bottom, rolling like a lumpy bowling ball, and smacked my back against a wall of rock.

I never saw the big boulder that I had shaken loose. It

dropped almost a meter before it came down on my legs, and it seemed to me like by the time it hit me I was starting to think about moving. Does that kind of slowdown in your memory mean you really would have had time to get out of there, Doc, or is it just your brain coping with the experience by making it your fault, instead of just something that happened to you? Most of us—well, most rounditachi, anyway—are limward more scared of getting hurt by something that didn't involve being stupid or careless or unalert. "He should've been more careful," said at a funeral, means "it won't happen to me, cause I am."

"Just one of those things—ran out of luck—" now *there's* a posreal scary idea.

I heaved twice, hard, and confirmed that I was too thoroughly pinned to move. I tried chinning the release to at least get some water, but none came; the reservoir in my lisport pack had been crushed, and by starlight I could see that the water I could have stopped for at any time, or even just drunk as I rooed, was now boiling off in the thin air and coating the side of the boulder with frost. I hadn't packed suitrations anywhere convenient cause I hadn't planned to eat on the first leg of the trip; they contained enough water to make me comfortable, but they might as well be on another planet now, for I could reach none of the releases on my pack.

My legs were hurting worse and worse. I wet my lips, clicked over to suit-to-suit distress, and called for help. I got nothing; down on a crater floor, as I was, this was hardly surprising. There probably wasn't any other human being in this crater; for people to hear my suit-to-suit, they would've hadda been flying overhead.

I tried satcell and it was just as dead as it had been ever since the emergency, but I tried calling every com number I could think of anyway, along with all the emergency channels I could remember.

I was starting to realize that aside from being in terrible pain, and dreadfully thirsty, and so on, that I was also probably only a few hours from dying. Still, your brain resists knowing that, you know what I mean, Doc? It stands to reason. When it comes to the last shutdown, knowing you're gonna doesn't do you any good, and fighting on in a state of delusion might.

So instead, I started worrying about my feet, under that boulder. It was far too big to get it off my legs. I could tell that at least my right leg was broken. It hurt incredibly, and chances were that with that heavy rock lying there, half as big as a small tajj room, neither blood nor suit heat'd circulate down to my feet.

That's what I mean about not thinking about death, Doc. Given how bad it was, and that the most likely thing that would happen was that I would die of blood loss, or of lisport failure followed by exposure, probably within a couple hours, I kept thinking about my feet, how afraid I was that I'd lose them, they'd freeze-dry if I had a leak in my boots, and I couldn't tell if I did but it didn't seem unlikely. They'd hafta amputate . . . I was more afraid of that than of dying.

I lay there, exhausted, at the end of all resources, and figured that though help wasn't gonna come, at least I could call for it, and after all I might be wrong. I flipped from channel to channel to channel, sending out distress calls on all of them, doing my best to sound calm and collected as I reported where I was, how bad my injuries were, that lives were depending on me, and so on. When I got tired of going through all the suit-to-suit channels, I'd try satcell again for a while.

Then, as I was making a satcell call to the Red Sands City Wilderness Rescue—and about to get back the same silence I'd been getting ever since the Sunburst—a pleasant female voice, like a trained actor playing a good mother, said, "Teri."

"Hunh?"

"I'm answering your distress call, Teri. Are you still coherent?"

"Yeah . . . yeah. Who are you?"

"Please repeat your location and status."

I did. "Is satcell coming back on? There are people I need to call." Then I remembered that I didn't need to call Dad, and bad as things were, I managed to feel worse.

"Some of satcell is coming back on. Are you in a lot of pain?"

"Yes, and I can't reach my painkillers. And my water tank ruptured and I'm very thirsty."

"Is there anyone else you're worried about? Were you on your way to anyone or anywhere?"

Doc, I have felt so limward stupid about that. That question was a giveaway that I wasn't dealing with any search-and-rescue outfit. But hurting like I was, it went right by me. "Uh, yeah . . ."

"Please give locations and com codes if you know them."

So I rattled off all the information for Alik, for Erin and Bianca, and for Roger and Band Eleven, and then realized that, in the exosuit's memory, I had the information for all those people I'd talked to on radio back at the station, so I gave those too. "Excellent job," the voice said. "We've got help on the way now, to you, and we'll have it soon for everyone else. Are you in much pain right now? Do you think you're in danger of severe injury?"

I felt like laughing, it was such a stupid question. "I think I'm about to lose my feet," I said, and explained that my legs were pinned and crushed under a boulder. "I'm guessing I might have a few hours to live but if help doesn't get here soon I'll probably be on artificial limbs for the rest of my life."

"Just relax," the voice said. "Help will be there soon. Tell me about yourself. Are you in school?"

There wasn't anything else to do, and the voice seemed so interested and sympathetic. Whenever I needed to I could just whine and cry about how much it hurt, and the voice stayed right with me, comforting me and reassuring me. I told it about all the bad things that had happened lately, the big ones and the trivial ones, and it seemed to listen and to always say something that was more and more comforting. Finally it said, "Teri, would you like to feel a lot better?"

"Of course. I sure as hell couldn't feel any worse."

"Then there's something you need to say to me. If you say it, I can help you."

"What is it?"

" 'Let override, let overwrite.' "

"*No!*" Too late, I knew what I was talking to. Infiltration probes come in from Earth all the time; this was a little probe, a skosh bigger than a soccer ball, somewhere far overhead, carrying a copy of Resuna and equipment to tap into communications. Planetary Defense should have shot it to pieces as soon as it switched on, long before we—

I realized that Planetary Defense was almost certainly down, like everything else.

"Teri, I've already called in all the emergency notes, but I'm not getting any responses. If you're going to keep your feet—maybe even if you're going to live—you need help to come soon, and I can organize that for you, but you have to help me too. You have to say 'let override, let overwrite.' I can bring you help if you'll just say that."

"Go away," I said, and clicked to hang up that call. But I couldn't leave my suit communications all the way off—the distress transponder was running no matter what, and anyway I hadda be able to hear any rescue call that I might get—and a moment later the same voice was in my phones.

"Teri."

"Go away."

"You know they can extract Resuna these days. You can cheat me—they'll help you. Get the rescue and once you're rescued, they'll detect me and take me out of your memory. You don't want to lose your feet. Think how proud your Dad used to be about how well you could roo and get around the roundings. Don't you want to be able to do that again?"

"They make artificial legs. I know rounditachi that have them," I said. "Go away. I don't want you to take my mind."

"I've got a rescue on the way to you, Teri."

"I thought you said they weren't answering."

"It's not from the cities. I have two rescuers I can send. I can override Roger's pain and starvation and make him come and get the boulder off you and carry you back—"

"That will kill him! No!"

"—or I can bring Alik with supplies and a jack and get you taken care of that way. You'll still be hurt but you won't lose your feet. You know how kind your Dad always was to Alik, and you remember how much Alik valued that; it would make Alik feel so good to be your rescuer—"

"It will still be dark for hours and this route is really dangerous—"

"It was dangerous for you with an overloaded pack, but Alik is a good rooer, you know that, and the equipment isn't that heavy. He can get to you quickly with it, just rooing down one of the rails—"

"He's too small and it's too dark and dangerous. I'd rather lose my feet than have him hurt or killed—"

"Think how sad Erin will be when she sees you without your feet," it said, "and think how unhappy Alik will be. I've already talked to him. He's willing to come and rescue you—"

"You have not talked to him. He wouldn't say that thing you want me to say." I felt a little quake in the back of my mind; apparently even thinking about saying it called the words close enough to the surface. What that meant, Doc, if I learned this right in school, was that I already had Resuna, the kernel of it, I mean, in my head then, and it would only take those four words running clearly through my speech centers to trip off the full generation—speak those four words, or think them with enough concentration, and a brand-new powerful copy of Resuna would grow into my mind, from the kernel. After that, the phrase "let override, let overwrite" would forever be available to put Resuna in charge of me, whether I spoke it or someone else did.

"What thing is it that Alik wouldn't say?" the voice purred.

"Stop that, I'm not gonna think it—"

"Not yet. But you will. It must be very cold and dark and frightening where you are."

I couldn't help it, Doc, I tried to look around, and all I could see was the dark shadow of the boulder on the side of the embankment, and then, way up in the sky, the constellation Phoenix glittering in the bit of sky between the boulder edge and the top of the embankment. And Resuna was right; I was cold and in pain. Uselessly, I clicked my pain killer buttons again.

"Wouldn't it be nice to see Alik and a jack? And just think how much he'd like being able to do this for you. He loves to impress you, and your Dad was such an influence on him—you're both 'the Cap' to Alik, and you've heard the respect in his voice—"

"Stop it."

"If you won't let me send Alik I might have to send Roger, and he's the leader of a big band, all those kids depend on him—"

"Don't send anyone."

"Doesn't it get lonely lying there all by yourself, especially wondering if I really did call for help? I did, by the way, Teri, I recorded messages all through the system, but you know as the system's coming up, nobody's picking up messages just yet—"

I hung up again, and tried clicking through com codes to see if any other satcell came up. It was definitely coming back on line, though whether it was real satcell or mimicry by Resuna probes was impossible to tell. Twice the com signal went through but all I got was the 'temporarily unavailable' message; once I tried calling Danielle, but instead of her, Resuna answered the com. "Teri, you need the help. They can take me out of you but you need something to control pain and your metabolic processes till help can get there, and I can send the help."

Alik's voice cut in. "Teri, listen to what Resuna says. Your Dad wouldn't want you to die or to lose your feet."

"Alik! Did you let it—"

"I *had* to, Teri, it wouldn't tell me where you were or help me go for you if I didn't. It'll be all right, you'll see. They'll take Resuna out of me in a day or so. Now I'm gonna come and get you. You don't hafta say the phrase if you don't want to, I'm on the way—"

"Alik, no, it's way too dangerous and way too far and—"

"I'm already on my way, Teri, just going through the airlock now. Talk to me on the satcell while I do this, okay? It's kind of scary and I'm lonely, and I wish I was already there and with you. I wish I had your dad to help me, too."

Now, Resuna can control feelings, or just set them aside, and so it could have made this easy for him, but I knew it didn't want to. He was lonely and scared, and so was I. So I know it was stupid, Doc, but I kept talking to him. Even knowing that Resuna had obviously already bullied its way into him. And he bounded down that track with perfect concentration while talking comfortably to me, and meanwhile I started to get warmer and feel better—which might have been hypothermia or tiredness, or just not being so alone.

Alik'n'me talked about school, and people we both knew, and what a nice person Bianca was and the fact that she didn't actually notice him, and whether or not there would be any ecospecting in the future, and on and on, and he bounced along that white rail in the darkness, and I lay there as the Phoenix crawled out of my field of view. And sometime along the way, Resuna coached him into saying whatever the right thing was to me, and I said "Let override, let overwrite."

Our minds linked through that high, incoming probe, and I could see through Alik's eyes, and he through mine. My pain, my fear, and my thirst all went away. After a while, Roger joined us in Resuna, and then Bianca, and we were all linked together via satcell. It was all so much better and easier to live with.

By the time Alik scuttled down the embankment, the power jacks already out of his pack and ready to go, I was pretty near cheerful. I could feel all kinds of other things far away, behind my mind, like dim shapes seen through a curtain—fear, maybe, I think there was some fear. But that was all, Doc. If life and everything was just about people being happy, you couldn't keep Resuna out for one second, trust me, it stands to reason.

"Gotta get you out of here," Alik said. "I'm so glad you're still conscious. I was worried."

I felt his concern and support; maybe, way back, I felt the terrified ten-year-old boy, who had just been grabbed and made a hero of, but mostly I just felt Alik's reassuring presence in my mind, through Resuna.

He sank four power jacks. I felt the gritty grinding through my thighbones, as the jacks vibrated their way into a solid position under the boulder. When they were all placed, Alik looked them over carefully, then checked with me, before we agreed that it would work. Then he switched them on, and dragged me back, and there I was, two crushed legs, but free.

Resuna shut off the pain, though something leaked like a bad smell around the edge of my mind, as Alik yanked my legs straight and sprayed them with instant cast material. Then, with my pain and his exhaustion covered, we divided up the load of rations, and started the awkward hike up the track to where Roger and Band Eleven waited—wide awake, and in no pain, cheerful as they make people, and grinding the bones in my lower legs to pieces with every step. Until Resuna got my emotional balances right, I thought that was kinda funny, and Alik was having a bitty skosh of trouble with giggling about his blistered feet.

🎲 **I had been** awake for two days straight and hadn't thought a cop thought or a shrink thought in all that time; I'd been an unskilled rescue worker, and a nurse, and that was about all. It happened that my apartment was fairly deep in the rock, and I'd been at home asleep when the Sunburst happened, so I hadn't gotten any radiation to speak of, and therefore it was my job to take care of people who had—once the fires were out. And there were plenty of fires; induced currents in millions of conductors, not just wires and circuits, but plumbing and fences and the structural steel of buildings, had seen to that. Less than an hour after Sunburst, the mayor had made the hard decision, sounded the pressure alarms for twenty minutes, and then vented RSC to the outside air, extinguishing many fires and making the rest much easier to fight, but also killing a couple of hundred people who hadn't been near a working alarm, or hadn't been able to get to an exosuit or a pressure shelter, or had ignored the horns, assuming they were one more malfunction in a city full of them. And we had been fortunate, here, as one of the few

Martian cities that had been sheltered from the radiation *and* daylight during the first hours of the emergency.

Com links of all kinds were mostly out, still, even five days after; they had gone through satellites, Mars had never had a period of stringing cable yet, and with the APS satellites dead, they couldn't accurately launch replacements; anyway, many of the replacements themselves were damaged or dead, and all needed to be checked out. So we knew there were people in trouble out in the roundings, but there weren't more than seventy thousand of them, and there were almost three million in the cities, and forty-five to one is the kind of ratio that's compelling when you're about to lose everything.

So when a runner came and got me and dragged me to an office, the part of me that wasn't too tired to think at all was guessing that either I was going to be put on regular physician duties, though I hadn't done those in a decade, or perhaps sent out to some field hospital or maybe rotated to another, more desperately needy city, if they finally had a rail line working. I hadn't expected two guys in the rust-and-black uniforms of Planetary Defense, or Cal, to be sitting there waiting for me.

"It's very bad news," he said. "A big wave of probes from Earth came in while almost all of Planetary Defense was down."

"I'd've thought warcraft would be radiation shielded and EMP proof."

"They are," the taller man, with gray hair, said. I noticed he wore no insignia, and neither did the other. "But the communication system isn't, and the radar can't be, and though we can slug as hard as ever, right now we're nearly blind and deaf. But about three hours ago, one of the probes broke in on a satcell channel and gave us the locations of a lot of stranded traverse parties in bad trouble. Apparently it had been talking to all of them. It freely admitted that it had memed as many as it could. So we've got to go out there and dememe all of them, right now—in the middle of all this other stuff."

I thought about the many times I had faced Resuna as an opponent, and said, "I've never known it to reveal itself before."

The younger man shrugged. "Maybe One True is trying out a new tactic or strategy—it's intelligent and creative, after all. Or maybe this Resuna is being used to probe our defenses, just to see what we do if it's pleasant and cooperative. Anyway, it downloaded itself into at least four people down in northern Mollyland, all of them in bad situations. They've probably memed everyone around them, too."

Cal handed me a cup of coffee and I realized I must look exhausted.

"So you want us—" I began, blinking and stupid.

"We need someone—which means you two doctors—to figure out what One True is up to. A fast low orbital ship managed to grab the Resuna probe and keep it from self-destructing, so we'll have readouts from that, and we've got a lot of the brain-reading gear you're used to available—we kind of scrounged from all over. We've got an emergency high-powered hovercraft waiting, and believe me no one is happy with us for commandeering it in the middle of the emergency. So grab a bag and your exosuit—we can issue you either if you don't have them or they got lost or destroyed—and we'll meet at Portal Seven in one hour."

It was about noon as the hovercraft roared out, headed south beside the tracks. A big military emergency one like that makes at least 300 kim, so we were at the stalled train in less than two hours; it was still broad daylight as the airlock on the wrecked train opened to our override keys.

We walked into sort of a party. There were Marsforms everywhere, mostly little kids, running around and playing and yelling. In the middle of the group sat a very tired looking older Marsform, fur matted and dull, but smiling and cheerful, and laughing and joking with him there was a younger unmodified boy, the helmet off his exosuit, who had his feet curled under him in a strange way, and a pretty teenage girl, her head freshly depilated, with big sad violet eyes, who sat giggling and joking with them, ignoring the spreading deep red stains on the sloppy casts that covered both her legs.

I introduced myself, and the cops with us began carefully processing everyone into the locked cells in the hovercraft. The girl went on a stretcher; as she passed me she stuck out her hand, and I clasped it for a moment, walking beside her. "I'm Teri Murray," she said. Horribly, she giggled. "Do you think you can do anything for my legs, Doc?"

"I'm a shrink," I said. "That will be other people's job."

"So as soon as you take Resuna out of me, it's gonna hurt like hell, isn't it?" she asked.

"We'll give you other pain blocks."

"That didn't answer the question."

"The answer is yes."

"Oh. Well, I guess we'll be talking a lot?"

"We will."

By now they were carrying her up the ramp into the hovercraft, and she turned and said, "Well, good, cause sometimes I get lonely, and I love to hear myself talk."

◗◖ **We knew we** would have to take a big block of her memory; Resuna had been very active, binding itself onto her pain and loss, her love for her father, her dreams and hopes, and everything else it could find. So we had her start her story many days back, and talk about it in plenty of detail, because once we put you through that, watching the recordings is the only memory you're going to have; to erase deeply enough to get all of Resuna, we take big blocks of time, and everything that was in them, out of the memory.

So after Resuna was suppressed and scattered in Teri, we left the pieces there for a while, and she made the recordings while I talked to her, and between us we tried to make sure that she would have everything it was important for her to remember. We talked about putting a front end on it that would tell her that her father was dead, and about the broken engagement, and so forth, but finally she decided to just tell it her way, in more or less straight chronological order.

The day we did the erasure, I held her hand right through it; she was scared, and being a roundita, didn't want anyone to know it. "Hey, does it hurt? I never asked, Doc. I never knew anyone who had it done."

"I've had it twice, Teri. Getting infected with Resuna is practically an occupational hazard."

"Did it hurt?"

"I can't remember," I said.

She grinned. "Well, then at least it works, eh? Okay, let's get me strapped in and clean out my brains."

I don't think she thought of this before the procedure started—I hope she didn't—but the reason for all the straps is that the procedure gives you quite a seizure. I was telling her the strict truth—I didn't remember it hurting *me*. But I'd seen it done many times, and I knew more than enough from the way people flopped and screamed. I didn't want to see that happen to her, but she was afraid, and so I stood by the table, letting her squeeze my hand and staring at me with horror and shock—and I hope not betrayal—until I could see that she no longer recognized me.

After they brought her out of sedation, and showed her the recordings, and let her recover, she came to see me for the exit sessions. "Who am I?" she asked me.

"Officially you're Terpsichore Melpomene Murray, daughter of the late Telemachus Ajax Murray and the late Leslie Patricia Tharsisito Murray. With the exception of a few recent weeks, you have all of Teri's memories, and certainly all of her DNA."

"Am I the same girl, Doc?"

"You aren't the one you would have been, if that's what you mean. You remember hearing about things rather than experiencing them. That makes a difference, Teri. I won't lie to you and pretend it doesn't. You're missing some of the biggest events in your life and all you have for them is diary entries. You're still a fine person and you will still make something of yourself in the world, but you are not who you would have been."

"Was it worth it to take Resuna out?"

The question startles me; no one has ever asked it before. As far as I know, I never did. I stammer that information out and ask her why she asked.

"Well, here's the thing. Resuna actually called in a report on the situation, and got us some help. It didn't hafta. It could've kept those froyks running back and forth to the station and kept everyone alive. It could've infiltrated. Some of the probes coming in probably did. So I was wondering . . . what if Resuna only wanted to be friends? Or at least what if the copy I had only wanted to be friends? What if it was just lonely too? And if they can be individual, is it still okay to shoot every one of them that shows up? And to get rid of it, I lost a big, big part of myself—it was a part that hurt, but it was mine. What if that's the way it was?"

I sigh. "That's one of the questions they're looking at, Teri. But here's another one—that Resuna you talked to was the only one that did that. We know they're getting more individual, that One True seems to want to be made up of more specialized units. Maybe what you got was a defective one. Because of the hundred or so others that came in, they all found people on satcell or suit-to-suit, out in the roundings, and did their best to lock them in and copy-download into their brains. And how did it happen that they all arrived on a direct shot, no setting-up orbit, right after the Sunburst? Officially no one knows what caused explosions that size in the outer solar atmosphere . . . they talk about things like antimatter asteroids, or a Neptune-sized body that no one saw somehow, or a cloud of antineutrons, and so on . . . but the timing of the biggest wave of Resuna packages we've ever seen is kind of suspicious. You might be looking at something One True did deliberately—so that the One True that gave you Resuna, and saved you from dying alone and miserable, is the same One True that set off the Sunburst and killed your Dad. He was just sort of a little side cost of getting Resuna planted on Mars, perhaps."

She looks at me, sadly, painfully. "There's no testimony about that on the recording, is there?"

"None at all."

"So I'm never gonna know, am I? Whether the Resuna that was in my brain knew about the Sunburst in advance, whether it was part of a plan . . . not anything, right?"

"That's right. So you take your choice, Teri. Either you were lonely and desperate, and one more-human-than-most Resuna heard your cry and rescued you . . . or it was all part of the same brutal trick that One True played on us, trying to grab another planet for itself . . . or it was all a series of terrible coincidences. You aren't going to know, I'm not going to know, and nobody in Mars government, from the maintenance office guys that are still cleaning up the mess in the cities, to the Chief of Planetary Defense, is ever going to know. We make our bets, and we get on with our lives. That's all there is. As a good friend of mine said once, you eat what they put in front of you. Even if it's a big dish of uncertainty."

She looked out the window for a long time, and said, "But what if that particular Resuna just wanted to be friends, and maybe it wasn't very good at it? I mean, it stands to reason, that if One True, or some Resunas, or both, were finally trying to talk to us, they wouldn't be any good at it at first."

❧❧ **I show Cal** the recordings and explain to him that I think we can just cut out a couple of weeks. "Even if we could just stop the recordings there," I say to Cal, "basically it would be all right. She got a little unpleasant shock from the way that boy dumped her. She became closer to her Dad for a little while. And after that we could just drop a nice veil over what happened next. . . ."

Cal is one of those no-nonsense shrinks that takes the job very seriously, parties hard whenever he's not working, always raising one flavor or another of hell I guess you could say. "Look at the dates on the recordings," he says. "And then at your calendar."

They differ by almost a Marsyear. I stare at them; what happened in the last year?

"We have had a version of this conversation several times," he says. "You've been memed, and we interrogated your Resuna."

"And you learned?"

"That One True's purposes, to a copy of Resuna, are no more scrutable than the ways of God to man. It just thought it had tried to do the right thing. It liked everyone it could remember being a passenger on, and thought it was good for them. Now do you remember Teri's getting released—we took your advice, the first time, about not taking too much memory—"

Then I start to remember.

"You got a recorded message from Teri," he said. "Do you remember that?"

I do. It's been three days since she wrote the message that started me on this strange little quest, and god alone knows what has been going on out in her little stretch of the roundings. She's leading her first overland party as the starting Captain. By now she's reached Tragedy Valley, with her group of forty, to develop a way stop that will serve ecospectors on their way to Telemachuston. She has used some of her money to loan her cousin Callie Tharsisito a grubstake, to establish a teeper there in Tragedy Valley (and her cousin gets to escape from the parents, which I rather suspect is the point of the whole thing).

Then no doubt a road will be thumped in to serve the teeper, and in time the rail line will have a spur there, and some day Tragedy Lake will be a well-known vacation spot, and the Falls of the Dancer will be something people go to for their honeymoons, and there will be some kind of story floating around about something bad that happened to a dancer (probably that she fell, tragically), which will gradually get so embellished that the folklorists will keep claiming there has to be some grain of truth in it somewhere.

But meanwhile—three days ago, Teri was still just south of the railhead and walking over the pathway where she'll want a road thumped, and she took a minute to write to me. She sent it via the back channel, using all kinds of little tricks to make the data trace tougher; any roundita always has an angle or six. Still, she obviously didn't completely trust it, because she used "lolo" instead of writing out "let override, let overwrite."

I look at the message on my screen again, and click, and the date swims up:

Sunday, June 9, 2097

That was not three days ago; that was more than four weeks. I feel sick and confused, and horribly, I know exactly why. Then there's her header:

To: Doc
From: Me
Subject: Vertigo

And there she is on the screen, talking fast and not
happy.

> Doc, I'm calling you after everyone's gone to
> bed. It's bad out here and I don't know if I'm
> bad or it's bad, if you know what I mean.
>
> I keep having these thoughts, almost like a
> voice in my head, and what they say is:
>
> "Just think lolo real hard. Just say lolo out
> loud. You know you want to. You know it's what
> you want to do."
>
> And the bad thing is, Doc, I think I want to.
> It's so lonely being leader and Dad is not here
> to back me up and everyone is young couples who
> keep looking at me like "Why aren't you mar-
> ried?" and I have nothing to say to them. Posreal
> it's lonely. And once you've said lolo you're
> never lonely again.
>
> But I oughta be able to deal with all this, so
> easy. I oughta. It isn't like me to let ordinary
> responsibilities and problems like this, just
> the normal stuff any Cap gets, get to me this
> way.
>
> I am most scared by what I am most scared
> of . . . which isn't that I'll say it, or that I
> still have it, or anything.
>
> What scares me is this: What if I say lolo and
> nothing happens?
>
> What if you really did get Resuna all the way
> out of me?

There I will be, having said lolo, and still
myself.

Then I'll know I'm a sellout and a traitor
but I'll still hafta go on being me.

Last night, I dreamed my dad was washing my
back and calling me Teri-Mel and we were talking
about the broken engagement, and then we were
leaving in the morning one day out on the trail,
and I think it was after the Gather. Now, that
didn't exactly happen, but it kinda did, parts
of it, and I'm wondering if those are the fragments coming back, or if it's just me imagining
it from the stories you recorded before you
erased that part of my memory. And if it's the
fragments coming back, could Resuna still be
loose in me?

I keep thinking this, Doc: I donwanna infect
anyone with Resuna. I donwanna belong to it.
That's just me, being independent. You know I'm
a roundita, one hundred percent, and rounditachi are that way.

But I'm so tired of being alone and discouraged, and maybe all I need to do is think lolo
real hard.

So I have a plan. If I want to say lolo, so bad
that I hafta try, I'll wait till I'm out in the
roundings solo, about ten days from now, when
I'll be up in the Prome away from everybody, and
in the bottom of some crater to limit radio re-
ception, I'll lie down at night, turn off the

transmitters, break off the antenna so the transponder doesn't have the range, turn off my heater, and open a suit vent on slow leak. Then I'll say lolo. Figure if I've got a Resuna, it'll save me, and then I'm somebody else's problem; and if I don't, I'll pass out pretty fast, and they say it's really just like falling asleep, the pressure drop knocks you out and then your temperature starts to fall and you don't wake up till after you're dead. That's what they say. And if I'm a traitor and a coward and all, all by myself, I won't have to live with it.

But see, Doc, what if it's just vertigo? Some people can't look from a high place without wanting to throw'emselves off. Maybe I'm just scaring myself for no good reason.

And just maybe all those memories that I wish I still had are somewhere in Mars's One True, if it has one. If there are enough other Resunas out there, and I can meet the right one, maybe I could get it all back. I know it's mostly terrible stuff but Doc it ought to be part of me and it's not, so maybe the "me" I have now, the one sending this message, the one I keep trying to want to save, isn't even really me, if you see what I mean.

And, and, and.

I just keep thinking of more.

Maybe a covert Resuna is making me want to say lolo. Maybe I just don't want to be all by

myself with so much missing from my life. Maybe I
shouldn't have agreed to lead a party this soon
and I'm just stressed by grief and confusion and
loneliness.

Maybe it's just vertigo, you know?

So I think the words, softly, now and then,
and I keep my hand on my valve.

Message me back, right away, Doc. We gotta
talk.

Me, Teri-Mel

The first thoughts I had . . .

"Cal," I say, "I would have sworn she told me to take
a few days and to keep her secrets, and none of that is in
there."

"It never was. It was in you. It's a new Resuna, a more
sophisticated version—you might call it an upgrade."

"God, what a joke on me, I never install those."

"Self-installing is the word that comes to mind," Cal
says, and he looks like he's in terrible pain. "It really does
seem to be kinder and gentler, and more compassionate,
and it individuates faster—but those are all ways in which
it sinks its hooks deeper. You know the rules, third time
you're memed, you're out of a career as a shrink. Probably
when we revise the standards, we'll take it down to two,
since this new Resuna gets in so far and is so hard to pull
out."

"When was Teri's message? I thought it was three days
ago."

"We've had this conversation before. I'm taping this

so you can see what you were like, because, dear old buddy, when you wake up and have to start a new life, you're going to be lim ticked off at me, posdef."

"Is *my* slang going to fall back three generations too?"

Cal shrugs, and gives me a gentle smile that warms my heart, before he says, "I'm really going to miss you." He hands me a pill and a glass of water. I feel a scream of terror in my mind; something knows what that pill is, and is afraid of it. With delicious fury, I swallow the pill, gulping water to make sure it goes all the way down, and clamp my jaw; we are *not* going to bring that pill back up.

Cal looks at me as if I'm dying. "You took the pill on your own," he says. "Try to remember that later, not that you'll be able to. And we'll do a big wipe while you're still groggy from the pill. You're lucky that you've been talking for five straight days, copying recordings, putting things in order. You'll have a pretty good idea of who you were, even though the pill isn't selective."

I can't quite remember what pill Cal means. And why is he here?

I check the date on the calendar on my werp screen. June 29, 2097. Not three days ago. Two weeks ago. Was I in the office all that time? When did Cal come out? What did I record?

I realize something, know that I won't remember realizing it in just a short moment, and feel stabbed to the heart. Next time we meet, I won't be able to tell Teri anything of what she was like before. Since she was clearly memed for most of a Mars year of her life, between her two erasures, all of that and a long time before will have to go, and I was the living person who knew her best in that time—

I'm sitting with Cal and my memory is going. This has happened before. I hope I wasn't terribly boring while I made recordings for myself, because if I was, it will be a long few weeks during recovery.

There's a girl and I don't know why she matters. I'm no use to her now and won't be again. Like all of us, what's her name is in her own head. Is this this time, or is this some other time?

I feel myself in a white coat facing Cal and arguing: We could take out more memory. We could substantially turn her into an amnesiac and put a new personality in on top, and at that point we'd have saved the body of a girl, in which to try and build another one. But we didn't do that. We're saving as much Teri—that's her name, Teri, and I know her because?—damn, we're saving as much Teri as we can; it just happens that the part we're losing is the part that was my friend for some very lonely months.

The pill I must have taken, to judge by the water glass in my hand, must be fast acting, wide ranging, and not very discriminate. That would lead me to the answers to important questions, like—

"What did you decide to do about Teri?" I ask the blank-looking man facing me, whose name I can almost recall. "What did you decide? What did you decide?" I'm shouting now, louder and louder. "What did you **decide** to do about Teri?"

I know they will have read all of my correspondence,

monitored every call, done everything to make sure that I am me and my actions are my own . . . but they wouldn't have waited . . . they could never have afforded to wait.

The blank-looking man is a shrink, I think. He's here with three cops. The cops approach me slowly, deliberately, as if not wanting to provoke me into charging. I stand—I hate feeling weak and this is better—but there's nowhere to run and I don't have the size or speed to knock the cops on either side of the desk down.

The third cop holds his hand out, and I extend my arm. I watch as he peels back my sleeve and the needle goes in. It stings and I feel cold fire running up my arm.

The shrink is a colleague I vaguely remember. They must have flown him in. His name was there a minute ago and now it's not. He looks terribly sad. "We're sorry," he says, "but it's all too entangled. We're terribly sorry. You'll have to forget all about everything that happened, and about her."

"What happened? About who?" I ask. They don't answer, and the man looking at me, whose name I can't recall at all, looks as if he's going to cry. I wonder what's wrong. I sit down and watch and time passes.

I guess those men are workmen, and I must be moving, because they are taking everything from the shelves and the desk, books, papers, all the electronic stuff. One of them tosses a bottle of good whiskey into a trash can, and I feel a little miffed; he might have offered it to me. But everything in the room is going into boxes. No doubt when it's all in boxes they'll deal with me again.

They're being thorough. I sit and wait for instructions.

❦ **I remember this** guy Cal from before. I've been making recordings with him now for a few days, and it's time to get on with it. He says he can't let me visit Doc, and he seems to be really sorry. I tell him I'll have to write to Doc and tell him I've found another middle-aged shrink.

Cal laughs and says, no, he's an old one.

He asks me to make one last recording.

So the day it started, I should have been waking up in the roundings, Dad a few meters from me, a few weeks before my sixteenth birthday, with my FA to take soon, and planning to marry Perry. That was what I expected when I opened my eyes. My first thought was that this was some terrible nightmare and I was dreaming about being back at school. Then I saw a kindly looking older guy standing by my bed, with a face that looked like it really needed a good ironing, all jowls and loose flesh, and a nose and cheeks that said this guy had been a real good friend to the bottle, but it hadn't been to him.

He stuck out his hand and told me his name. "I'm

afraid I have some very bad news for you; some terrible things happened to you in the last few months, and you won't remember any of them, but we have recordings of you telling the story, in your own words, and explaining a great deal of it."

I tell the story, and I get into the straps like a good little girl being tucked in for the night, and they give me the pill and the needle.

❦❦ **So the day** it started, I should have been waking up in the roundings, Dad a few meters from me, a few weeks before my sixteenth birthday, with my FA to take soon, and planning to marry Perry. That was what I expected when I opened my eyes. My first thought was that this was some terrible nightmare and I was dreaming about being back at school. Then I saw a thin, vigorous old guy in a white coat standing by my bed.

He stuck out his hand. "Most people call me Doctor Cal, as they're going through this process. I'm afraid I have some very bad news for you; some terrible things happened to you in the last few months, and you won't remember any of them, but we have recordings of you telling the story, in your own words, and explaining a great deal of it. You made a couple of very good friends during the time you don't remember, and you'll be meeting them too. I want to introduce you to the first of them. . . ."

He motioned toward the bed beside mine; there was a man, unconscious, who looked younger than Doctor Cal, but in much worse shape. "This is the person you were talking to, and about, in many of your recordings. You'll be talking quite a bit this time around too, I'm very sure." I'm still bewildered, and I want to ask where Dad is, and if it's all these months later, where Perry is, and what's happened, but I'm already feeling terribly tired. Doctor Cal has a nice smile, but he looks sort of sad around the eyes, when he says, "Sleep now. You two are going to be great friends."

❧ **Ever since, just** once, I forgot to turn on my CO2 scrubber for the first ten minutes of a walk outside, and got just a tiny bit uncomfortable before I figured out what it was, Teri always checks out my lisport pack with terrifying thoroughness. Then she makes me check out hers to be on the safe side. I don't mind doing that, and I suppose the practice is valuable, but when she checks mine over I can never get over the feeling that a teenage girl is fussing over me as if she were my mother.

"More like your nurse," she says, "or maybe your zookeeper. Posreal, Doc, I ain't gonna lose a good friend—let alone a partner—just cause he's skoshy sloppy. You want to get away from me, you hafta work at it limward harder than that."

"Contract," I say, just as if I'd grown up in the roundings.

The fourth time we met, from her standpoint, and the third time from mine—once on a train, twice in a hospital, before—was so far the least eventful, and the most consequential.

I couldn't stay a shrink and she couldn't be anything but an ecospector. Every time a mind gets memed, it gets more vulnerable to future memings. Though she'd been memed while out in the roundings, the roundings were still a safer place for Teri than the city, for there were fewer people, there was less contact, and she would spend less time looking into computer screens. As for me . . . Resuna had had me so many times, and so deeply, that it was thought best to isolate me, not give it another shot if it could be helped. Time to retire me like an old snake dog that had been snakebit once too often—if that's how it worked on Earth. I wonder if we'll ever have hunting season here.

Silly question, of course. There's that old phrase about the most dangerous game, and that's what I spent most of my life hunting. What do I care for lesser sport, eh?

But once they realized I'd been memed for several days, and that it had all gotten tangled into my long-term memory, and that I was about to have my third deep erasure in five Marsyears, it was clear that hunting Resuna through the corridors of the brains of criminals, misfits, and plain old madmen, was over for me. Certainly I couldn't go back to my old profession.

But in my long months of relearning the records and finding out what had happened to me, the more I heard about it, the more Teri's profession had sounded like fun. Physical exercise, few conversations, stuff to do, lie down when you're exhausted, get up when you're rested, a whole planet to bring to life. I was the oldest and the least-well-prepared student in the first class of RSCU's new program in ecospecting, when that finally opened a Mars year late, but I knew how to learn a subject new to me, and I liked it from the beginning. I went from apparently hopeless to pretty good at it in just a Mars year and a half.

Teri came in in the class behind mine. She was rich and could have done anything; she had decided she'd enjoy trying to be the best ecospector in the history of the planet, since she was already one of the richest, both in her own right and as her father's heir. We recognized each other at once, of course, from the recordings; we knew we'd gotten along; so we sat and talked for one afternoon, and by the end of it we were fast friends.

Now, in my old occupation, I might have said that she was young and missed her father badly and after her catastrophic broken engagement (and perhaps after Prigach had died just when she was beginning to feel attracted), even if she was getting it all at second and third hand, in the internal story she constructed for herself, she was mildly afraid of any relationship that might lead to the whole love-sex-marriage business. In my old occupation I might even have thought that perhaps she needed some therapy, rather than to indulge her feelings by developing a close friendship with an older man. And I might have said I was a lonely, miserable man who was cut off from the only work for which he'd shown much talent, and furthermore when that sort of lonely man likes the company of a young woman that much, someone ought to keep an eye on him.

But in my new occupation, I can laugh at that, and any number of other things. One of these days Teri will undoubtedly want a romance again; she's a healthy young woman. And she certainly won't want one with me. One of these days, for that matter, I might want one myself; I've already started to notice that rounditas my age are far more interesting than any of my ex-wives ever were, and though a long time ago I thought I'd given up, maybe I haven't. One of these Gathers, maybe. Meanwhile I have a partner who's a good friend, and we laugh every day. Things happen, you know, silly and trivial things, and the world changes around you, and there you are to see them.

I wish I could feel and remember the things that are in the records; sometimes I identify with them so strongly that I almost seem to step through them and find myself there, again, in my office, with that bewildered girl who had gotten into such terrible trouble. But though I can't really ever remember, try as I might, what it was like to be a boozy old police shrink, more and more memory is growing in to replace that, and the spaces of my memory are filling up with Teri's laughter as we roo down a dune face, or my own shout of joy when a geyser takes the sunlight as it bursts out of a new-drilled well, or the soul-penetrating groan that comes when you straighten up after a whole afternoon of slow patient working through wet, torn-up badlands. I've given over whole weeks to putting trees in along a river that is flowing for the first time in a billion years, and every day we would look back to see only a couple hundred meters of progress, and then Teri would sigh, halfway to a laugh, just because it was good to be here, and I'd be chuckling myself.

So I let her fuss and tease about whether or not my exosuit is really ready, and then I check hers over thoroughly, but already my heart is out beyond the city walls, out where the last sight of a straight line or a right angle fades away and the night sky isn't smeared or spoiled by the glare of any artificial light, not even over the horizon. "Let's get going," I say. "I want to get all the way to that far campsite if we can, tonight."

Teri shrugs. "I'm sure we can make it if you really wanna, Doc. What's the hurry?"

"I'm a driven overachiever with too much norepinephrine and really rigid toilet training," I say, and she snorts at that.

She knows perfectly well that my real answer would be her answer: because it's as far into the roundings as we can get today. And out there, you wake up in the morning the second the sun hits your faceplate, and it bounces up like it's got places to go and things to do. Checkout completed, thumbs up, we send the air from the lock back into the city, pass under the rising door, and just *roo!*

acknowledgments

It is frequently said, in this position in the book, that the book would have been impossible without certain people. This particular book was so much of a struggle that it was pretty well impossible even *with* the fine people I'm about to mention. But it did get done, and I owe a deep debt of thanks to the usual suspects: Patrick Nielsen Hayden, my editor, for immense patience and forgiveness; Ashley Grayson, my agent, for constant assistance and support; and Jes Tate, my research assistant, for speed and persistence. I'm also indebted to Soren DeSelby, for the finest copy-edit I have seen in more than twenty books. Thanks to all of you, it was merely difficult.